The King's Knights

*Honorable knights who fight for their king...
and their maidens!*

Valiant and honorable, William and Theodore
are loyal to their king and their cause. Tight as
brothers, they'll let nothing—and no one—
distract them from their critical missions
in the name of the crown.

Until these elite warriors meet their
match and must fight a battle of wills with
the strong, unconventional women who
have captured their hearts!

Already available—William and Avva's story:
The Knight's Maiden in Disguise

Theodore and Medea in:
The Knight's Tempting Ally

Alewyn and Johanne in:
Secrets of Her Forbidden Knight

And now meet Benedictus and Adela in:
Bound to the Warrior Knight

Author Note

Thank you for picking up Benedictus and Adela's story. Theirs is the last in my King's Knights series, and it's been a real pleasure getting to know these two characters after so long.

Sir Benedictus has always come across as cold and severe, but as his story developed, I realized that rather than being stern, he is reserved and quiet. He's also deeply loyal and driven by a need to protect those who cannot protect themselves, whether that is his closest friends or the country as a whole. He marries Lady Adela for strategic gain, and it is not long before she gets under his skin. On first appearance Adela seems meek and mild, but that disguises a strong will. She challenges Benedictus, and gradually their marriage of convenience becomes something more...

I love hearing from my readers. If you'd like to get in touch, please visit my website, www.ellamatthews.co.uk.

ELLA MATTHEWS

—

Bound to the Warrior Knight

HARLEQUIN
HISTORICAL

HARLEQUIN®
HISTORICAL™

Recycling programs
for this product may
not exist in your area.

ISBN-13: 978-1-335-72381-9

Bound to the Warrior Knight

Copyright © 2023 by Ella Matthews

For questions and comments about the quality of this book,
please contact us at CustomerService@Harlequin.com.

Harlequin Enterprises ULC
22 Adelaide St. West, 41st Floor
Toronto, Ontario M5H 4E3, Canada
www.Harlequin.com

Printed in U.S.A.

Ella Matthews lives and works in beautiful South Wales. When not thinking about handsome heroes, she can be found walking along the coast with her husband and their two children (probably still thinking about heroes, but at least pretending to be interested in everyone else).

Books by Ella Matthews

Harlequin Historical

The King's Knights

The Knight's Maiden in Disguise
The Knight's Tempting Ally
Secrets of Her Forbidden Knight
Bound to the Warrior Knight

The House of Leofric

The Warrior Knight and the Widow
Under the Warrior's Protection
The Warrior's Innocent Captive

Visit the Author Profile page
at Harlequin.com.

To Gemma, Darren,
Gabriel, Dylan and Loki

Chapter One

England, August 1337

Adela's tight braid pulled at her hair, making her scalp itch. Her hands twitched, desperate to scratch the spot but she kept them linked in front of her, hardly daring to move even to breathe. The words of her marriage ceremony, the one binding her to the stranger opposite her, droned on to her left.

She kept her gaze fixed forward, centred on the man she was marrying. He was completely still, save for the rise and fall of his chest. If she hadn't seen him stride toward her earlier, she would have thought him a statue. He was tall, taller than she'd imagined whenever she'd thought about him over the years of their long betrothal, and broad. She would probably fit inside him twice, not that she would have the strength to split him open and find out if the width of his muscled arms was anything to go by.

The priest stopped talking and the room plunged into

silence. Adela pulled in a shuddery breath. This was it. She was married. Bound to Sir Benedictus for the rest of her life. Only death would part them now.

She glanced up at him then, daring herself to look at the stranger who now had complete control over her life. Dark eyes peered down at her from under a heavy brow; firm, unsmiling lips were pressed into a straight line. Her heart twisted painfully. She hadn't held out any hope for a loving union. She knew Sir Benedictus's reputation. All of England had heard of the man who sat at the right-hand side of the king. Ruthless, cold, and ambitious, her new husband was not a man to be crossed. But life with him had to be better than the life she had been living. That belief was the only thing that had sustained her through the past few desolately empty years.

Their gazes met and held. His eyes were dark and fathomlessly deep. She could not read any expression in them. A strange quiet stretched between them; a moment stopped in time. She could almost believe they had both turned to stone.

Then her father was slapping Sir Benedictus on the back, breaking the spell. 'We must celebrate this fortuitous union. Let us begin feasting.'

Adela didn't miss the look of distaste that crossed Sir Benedictus's face. It was gone before he turned to look at her father, the smooth, impenetrable mask back in place. 'I had hoped to be on the way back to Windsor before…'

'Nonsense. It is not every day my youngest daughter marries. I would be a poor father-in-law if I did not put on a celebratory feast in your honour. Come, you will enjoy it.' Benedictus grimaced and heat warmed Adela's skin at her father's presumption. 'I have selected the finest meats and wines just for you. My neighbours will be talking about this evening for years to come.'

Adela dropped her head as her skin burned. Her father was so blatant in his admiration of her new husband, or rather her husband's high-ranking position in the kingdom, and he didn't seem to care or perhaps notice that this made him look ridiculous. This feast was not for her or for Sir Benedictus; it was so that her father could show off his new eminent son-in-law to the barons whose land surrounded their own. It was quite the coup to land such an important man as a son-in-law even if her father had had to part with a large dowry to secure him. A fact that everyone knew and that everyone had speculated about endlessly since their betrothal many years ago. A betrothal that had shaped Adela's life even before she'd been properly aware of it.

It had taken so long for Sir Benedictus to commit to the binding ceremony that people began to believe he would not go through with it. Her father's self-satisfied smile showed just how pleased he was to prove the doubters wrong. Adela was certain he would conveniently forget Sir Benedictus was only marrying her for the dowry and remember only that the union raised their family's status.

'Very well, I will eat before I leave but I must head back to Windsor today,' said Sir Benedictus, his voice deep and husky. 'I have important matters I need to attend to.'

The two men headed off to the Great Hall together, leaving Adela without a backward glance as if she were no more important than a rug to them and not an expensive one at that. The chamber emptied of the few remaining witnesses, no one speaking to her as they filed out. It should upset her that she was ignored but it didn't. She was used to it. She had been betrothed to Sir Benedictus, the Monceaux heir, since she was ten years of age. Her role in life set, she had been forced to live a constrained life by her father, who believed she must be pious and devout to be worthy of her illustrious husband. So keen to impress the Monceaux family with the purity of his daughter, he had kept her largely isolated apart from long sermons on duty from him and heavy religious teachings from the family priest. Life had so far passed her by with little variation. Joy was something she had only seen from her chamber window. But she would not think about that now.

She shook her shoulders, releasing the muscles she'd held tense all morning. It was better she'd been left. She didn't know how to make small talk with people she barely knew, and now she wouldn't have to sit through the feast and watch her father preen and act the righteous man who feared God and loved his country. She knew better. She knew he cared only for himself and his own pleasure and having to pretend otherwise was hard work. She was finally getting away from him. That is, unless...

She hadn't missed the way her new husband had referred to *his* return to Windsor and not *their* journey to the king's stronghold. The king was in Antwerp, thumbing his nose at the French king and while he was gone, he had charged Sir Benedictus with the running of the country. As cunning and sharply intelligent as her new husband was rumoured to be, he would not have mistakenly left her out, which could mean only one thing; he had no intention of taking her with him when he left.

Adela plunged her fingers into her hair, loosening the strands of her tight braid and sighing with relief as the itching finally stopped.

Benedictus may not want a wife, may have taken years to turn the betrothal into a marriage, may only be finally marrying her because the king needed more money in the form of her dowry to pay for his pointless war, but she would be damned if he left Castle Valdu without her. Leaving her father's stronghold was the only thing that had kept her going over the long, long years of waiting for Sir Benedictus to marry her. She was going to have to muster all the courage she had to ensure that wait was over.

Benedictus's new wife, Lady Adela, hadn't attended the wedding feast and nobody had appeared to notice. Not her parents, who were too busy showing him off to care that their daughter was missing from her own celebration, and not any of the guests who were wolfing down the food in front of them as if they had never eaten before. The food was…nothing particularly special, but Benedictus supposed not everyone ate like the royal household every day.

Benedictus wondered if Lady Adela had found something to eat and then pushed aside the small pang of

sympathy for the birdlike creature who was so forget-
table no one was thinking of her on the most momentous day of her life.

He did not have time for pity. There was too much at
stake for him to be worrying about one small woman
even if she did have the most arresting eyes he'd ever
seen.

During the marriage ceremony he'd thought only of
the length of time the whole thing was taking. Every
moment that passed was a lifetime away from Windsor
where he was needed most. The king needed money for
his war with France and this marriage was the quickest
way to get hold of some. Benedictus's loyalty to King
Edward was absolute. Tying his life to a stranger was
not something he'd questioned. He had stood in front
of her, watching her as she had resolutely stared at his
chest. Her whole demeanour suggested she was meek
and mild and that had left him feeling cold. He hadn't
wanted to marry her, had put it off for as long as possible, and her whole being had suggested that was the
correct decision. If only he had been able to hold off
for longer.

That was until their eyes had met. Dark green and
framed with long lashes, the look she'd given him had
hit his heart like a lightning strike. There was nothing
docile about those eyes; they spoke of a fire banked for
now but ready to burst into flames. He'd been unable to
pull his gaze away as something strange had stirred in
the pit of his stomach. Her father had broken the spell by
being a pompous fool and Benedictus had been grateful.
He did not want to feel anything for his wife, not pity,

not compassion, and certainly not desire. Not anything, in fact, that would distract him from his life's work.

After what felt like weeks, so much ale had been consumed during the celebratory feast that Benedictus was able to slip away. The whole elaborate event wasn't about him anyway. The Valdu family was celebrating being linked to the Monceaux family, which was what they'd wanted for years and for which they'd paid handsomely. He could have warned them that the union would not necessarily benefit them, but they would find that out for themselves. He knew his parents only wanted the link with the Valdu family for the strategic place the Valdu's stronghold held within the kingdom. His parents would call on the connection when they needed it and not a moment before. Besides, Adela's father had legitimately only sired girls, and Benedictus had no doubt his parents were planning for a future when a child from Benedictus and Adela's union would be installed as leader of the Valdu estate. It would mean the Monceaux reach stretched across the whole of England. The union would mostly benefit Benedictus's family and not the Valdus, but they didn't need to know that now.

His parents might be annoyed with him that he had given the substantial dowry to the king, but they would acknowledge that Benedictus had made the right political decision and that would hopefully negate the words of their disapproval of him. Not that Benedictus cared what they thought. He had managed to block out their criticism of him years ago. They were never satisfied, no matter what he did. The great Monceaux name was their only consideration and he had long since learned to live with that.

He stepped out into the courtyard, inhaled deeply, grimacing as the foul smell of the latrines assailed him. Still, it was better than being cooped up in that Great Hall being shown off as if he were a tournament-winning stallion. His new father-in-law was a sanctimonious bore, but he lived far enough away that Benedictus would probably not see him often, if ever again.

Benedictus had no time to spare for a wife and no interest in making a marriage work. One look at his parents' stilted relationship was enough to tell him that such an institution was not for him. Better to be alone that swamped in competitive bitterness.

Besides, it was hard enough for him having to make conversation with people he knew but at least he could walk away when it became too strained. With a wife, she would always be there, in his private space, expecting him to talk, to put her at ease and to give her attention, and he did not have the time for such things.

He strode toward the stables. The stable master for the Valdus would no doubt be enjoying his baron's largesse in the Great Hall, but it would not matter. Benedictus was not above getting his hands dirty and the sooner he got away from Lady Adela's family, the better.

He stepped over the stable's threshold and ground to a halt. There, sat atop a chestnut mare, was his wife, her hands folded neatly over the reins of her horse, a small bag attached to her saddle.

'What are you doing?' Surprise made him sound harsher than he'd intended. He saw her flinch but didn't apologise; he did not want her to think he was soft-hearted. He could not afford to give in to the empathy she aroused at the sight of her sitting there alone waiting for him.

She cleared her throat; her voice was raspy, as if she had not spoken for some time. 'You said you wished to leave for Windsor as soon as possible. I did not want to delay you and so I got ready immediately.'

Normally, Benedictus would be impressed with such punctuality, but this was not a normal situation. 'Windsor is no place for a young woman.'

She grimaced. 'I am past my twentieth summer, Sir Benedictus. That makes me no longer young.'

His stomach tightened. She may think she wasn't young but there were ten years between them and a wealth of experience she would never know about. It was one of the reasons he'd not formalised their arrangement before now. Her innocence would make it awful for her to be tied to a man such as he. But it did not have to be; he did not have to tear her away from her family and everything she knew. 'You may stay here.'

She shook her head. 'You are my husband. My place is by your side.'

'It doesn't have to be.' He didn't want her with him and he didn't want her misguided sense of duty to get her to do something distasteful. 'I expected you to stay here with your family and have made no provision for you at court.' He wasn't so much of an insensitive brute that he didn't miss her stricken look at his words. He didn't want her to think he was rejecting her personally. She may be perfectly pleasant for all he knew; he just didn't have the time to find out. 'When the war with France is over and things are safer, you can join me then.' He might be dead by then and this young woman would be free to marry someone better suited to her. That man was not Benedictus.

She shook her head. 'I am coming with you this evening.'

'No.'

'Yes.' They glared at each for a moment, those green eyes sparkling. She looked away first, which didn't feel as much of a victory as it should have.

'You do not know what you are saying. You would not enjoy life at Windsor. It is ruthless and hard and nothing at all what you are used to.'

She turned back to him; her striking eyes narrowed. 'With all due respect, Sir Benedictus, you know nothing of my life. You are my husband and my life is with you now.'

'I forbid it.'

He winced at the look of pain that crossed her face. He was a cur to speak to her so. He despised men who ordered their wives about as if they had no feelings. He didn't want to be like them but she was leaving him with no choice. If she came with him, she would expect time from him and he had none to give.

Her next words gave no hint of upset he could see written on her face, and a shard of admiration lodged in his chest. People so rarely stood up to him but this slip of a woman was giving it a good go. 'You can leave now but I will only follow.'

He ignored the flicker of desire that flashed through

him at the show of her strength. It had been far too long since he had held a woman in his arms; that was all it was. It was nothing for him to be alarmed about. The moment this was over, he would forget about it. 'That would be foolish in the extreme. Do you know what dangers line the route to London? You would not make it to the first town.' He shuddered at the thought of some-one so inexperienced and vulnerable out there alone.

'Then my death will be on your conscience.'

His fists curled. 'I have no conscience.' That wasn't true. He wasn't entirely sure why he had said it. He just needed her to stay in her father's castle. He didn't have time to look after an innocent; not when the future of England depended on him and him alone.

'Well, then, I will have to keep up with you.' Ram-rod straight on her horse, she peered down at him with the force of a queen's gaze, so different from the mild bride; his body sparked in an alarming way.

They stared at each other and, as the moment stretched, he felt his resolve waver. He shouldn't do it. He should march her back to her parents and leave her here and yet, he found he couldn't. For some reason she was determined to come with him and for some reason he didn't have the conviction strong enough to stop her.

He stepped around her and strode toward his horse. 'You had better ride fast.'

She didn't respond. He paused to turn around to look at her. She was wearing a small smile, not triumphant, a genuinely happy one. His heart turned over uncomfort-ably. She was not traditionally beautiful; her face was too angular for that but the smile softened her features, making them very pleasing indeed. Yes, her presence was going to be a complication.

He saddled up Flame in record time and joined her at the stable door. 'I've no time to waste.'

'You'd better start, then.'

Despite himself, he found he was smiling for the first time in months. He kicked Flame into motion; it was time to ride.

Chapter Two

They rode quickly, faster than Adela had ever moved
before. Not used to sitting on a horse, every tiny part
of her body ached but she would not complain or ask
to go slower. Not when her new husband had made it
very clear he did not want her to come with him. Short
of him dragging her back to her parents, nothing would
have stopped her from leaving with him. For so long
she had pinned all her hopes on marriage setting her
free that it would have killed her to return to the life
she had led for so long. Strangely, Benedictus's words
had not hurt her; he'd been honest and in her opinion
that more than made up for his rejection. Dismissal she
was used to; honesty she was not.

Sir Benedictus and she hadn't spoken as the leagues
had passed them by. Now the summer sun had completely set over the horizon and there was no sign of
him slowing the pace of their journey.

Whenever Adela had imagined this journey, and
she'd thought about it a lot, she'd always thought she'd

be transfixed by the scenery, at sights she'd never seen before, and she was. It was just that somehow her gaze kept returning to her husband. He had pushed back his sleeves to his elbows and every now and then she got a glimpse of his muscled forearms as he rode ahead of her. The sight of them made her stomach squirm oddly and she couldn't for the life of her understand why. They were just arms after all.

They were now farther away from her home than she had ever been. She inhaled deeply and smiled as the fresh air filled her lungs. There was no stench of other people, only the subtle hint of heather as their horses brushed through it, disturbing the flowers and sending plumes of pollen into the night air.

It didn't matter to her that the surly man riding before her seemed determined to ignore her; this was the freest she'd ever been. With every stride of her horse's legs the shackles that had held her down for so long loosened. Soon, they would fly off into the wind completely and she would know, if not happiness, then at least contentedness.

She didn't notice they were slowing until Sir Benedictus spoke. 'We should stop.'

Even though every bone in her body was crying out for a rest, she would keep riding for as long as he wanted. She would be the most amenable wife in the whole kingdom; he would realise he had not made a mistake in bringing her with him and he would not force her to return to her parents. 'I can keep going if you would prefer.'

He grunted. 'The horses need to rest.'

She was glad his back was turned to her so that he could not see the heat spreading across her cheeks. Of course, he was thinking of the horses' comfort and not hers.

'I know of a river, not far from here,' he continued. 'We'll stop there and let the horses drink their fill. We can also catch some sleep. We will not reach Windsor today.'

The evening was warm and yet goose bumps crept across her skin. She had never slept outside before and hadn't prepared for the eventuality, either. Her saddle-bag contained only a few changes of clothes, two for the day and one for more formal occasions, as well as her favourite lavender soap and a brush for her hair. There was nothing to protect her from the elements or from animals that made the night their home.

Her resolution to be a biddable wife wavered for a moment before resolving itself once more. She swallowed down her protest to find a tavern for the night; she would not say a word, not let Sir Benedictus know how scared she was at the idea of sleeping without walls to keep her safe. She would be glad instead. Glad that, although there were no walls to protect her, there were also no walls to keep her in.

All too soon they came to the water, and Benedictus came to a complete stop. He leapt down from his stallion, the muscles in his arms flexing, and led the animal to the river's edge. Every move he made was confident and precise, so different from Adela, who until now, had tried to hide any movement she made lest she attract her father's unwelcome attention. Over the years she knew her steps had become mouselike and subservient and she hated it.

She slipped down from her saddle before leading Bramble over to the water, too. The horse drank gratefully and she rubbed her hand along her long neck, taking comfort from the animal's warmth.

Behind her she could hear Sir Benedictus moving around her, and presently the smell of woodsmoke reached her. 'I have some food left over from the feast earlier,' he called to her. 'Come and join me.'

A small fire burned, its flames sending black specks into the night air. Sir Benedictus had set it slightly away from where the horses were standing. She made her way over to it and lowered herself to the ground opposite him. He leaned around the flames and handed her a slice of beef pie. Her stomach roared as her fingers closed over the pastry. She had forgotten that she had eaten barely anything earlier. Too frightened by what the day held to have an appetite. She bit into the pie and groaned; nothing had ever tasted so good.

Neither of them spoke as they ate, the silence growing and stretching until the air vibrated with it. She had nothing to say to this hulking stranger and even if she had, she doubted she would be able to get the words out. She had always been quiet, but years of forced isolation had left her out of practise of making idle conversation. She had no idea how to start.

The sound of his throat clearing was like a rumble of thunder. 'You should rest. It will be another long day of riding tomorrow and I don't want to stop until we reach our destination.'

She nodded. His comments did not seem to need a response. He was obviously used to being obeyed and there was no reason for her to disagree. She was exhausted and yet she didn't move away from the fire; neither did he.

'You rode well today.'

The unexpected compliment took her by surprise. 'Thank you. It has been a long time since I have been on a horse. I am pleased I hadn't forgotten how to do it.'

He frowned. 'You must be aching badly, then, if you are out of practise.'

Every muscle was screaming in agony. 'No. I am fine.'

His dark gaze locked with hers and a jolt shot through her. 'I don't ask for much from this marriage,' he said. 'But I do request that you never lie to me. I will pay you the same courtesy. I will not be able to tell you much about my life, but I guarantee that what I do tell you will be the truth.'

Her cheeks flamed but she held his gaze. 'Very well,' she agreed. 'I will honour your request.' She turned her attention to the flickering flames in front of her. 'Everything is sore.'

'You will feel worse tomorrow.' She didn't know how to respond to that unsympathetic but practical statement and they lapsed into silence once more.

Another worry began to press on her, a worry she had resolutely ignored until this moment. Her mother had told her that the marriage would need to be consummated and that she was not to complain or resist when her husband approached her, but to lie back and submit to his will. If the act hurt, she was to ignore the pain for

the sake of a harmonious relationship. The only problem
was that Adela had no idea what her mother was talking
about. She'd braced herself to ask, but her mother had
stood and finished their conversation with, 'The more
frequently you submit to his needs, the quicker you will
get with child. Providing the next Monceaux heir will
be a source of great pride for our lineage.' And with that
final comment her mother had swept from the chamber.

The idea of submitting to something that hurt when
she was already in agony had the food in her mouth
turning to ash. She forced herself to swallow the pastry
even as her throat seemed to narrow impossibly. She
wiped the crumbs from her dress until there was not a
speck on the fabric.

She desperately wanted children, had longed for
them for so long. The idea that someday there would
be someone to love and take care of had often been the
only light in her drab and dreary life. If creating one
hurt, then so be it. She was ready.

She glanced across at Sir Benedictus. He was gazing
at the fire, giving no indication what needs he might
have from her, or even that he remembered she was still
there. Her eyelids felt heavy. She wanted to lie down
but she didn't know if that was what he wanted, so she
stayed upright. Gradually, she pulled her knees up to
her chest and rested her head on top of them. An owl
hooted somewhere nearby, bats flickered overhead, and
the horses shuffled on their feet but still Sir Benedictus said nothing.

She closed her eyes and gradually her world went
black.

She woke as strong hands touched her back. She froze, her whole body locking in fear. 'It's only me,' murmured Sir Benedictus.

Her muscles stayed locked in terror. It was his presence of which she was afraid. Even though she had prepared herself, now the moment was here, she did not want to be hurt.

'I didn't mean to wake you. You will be stiff as a plank of wood if you sleep like that all night.' He moved her gently until she was lying down. She started to shake. She bit her lip to stop herself from crying out. She had told herself that she would endure whatever it took to satisfy her husband. That it would be worth it in order to escape from the life she had been living before, but now the moment was upon her, she realised she was not as brave as she had hoped.

'You are cold,' said Sir Benedictus, mistaking her terror for shivers. 'Where is your cloak? I will fetch it for you.'

'I... I did not bring one.' In truth, she didn't have one, having barely left her bedchamber for many years.

'Did you bring a blanket or anything to keep you warm?'

'N-no.' Her teeth were chattering now. A reaction to the horror sweeping through her.

Through the blind panic, she could hear him muttering darkly. The words did not sound complimentary, but she could not concentrate to understand them.

'We will have to share my cloak.' A thick material settled over her. 'My body heat will warm you, too.'

She felt him lie down beside her, not so close that

their bodies were touching, but close enough that she could sense him from the tip of her head to the soles of her feet.

As the moments passed without any movement from him, her shaking subsided. His breathing settled into a steady rhythm. She wanted to turn to check whether he was asleep but she didn't dare move. If he slept then any movement could wake him and remind him that she had not done any satisfying of needs, whatever that might entail.

Gradually, over many heartbeats, her body relaxed once more and she slept again.

Benedictus listened to the soft snores coming from his wife. It had taken her an age to stop shivering and to finally nod off to sleep. He rolled onto his back and stared at the starlit sky, trying to will his body into submission. He hadn't expected *that* to happen. Hadn't thought that lying down next to his wife would cause desire to rage through his body, burning him from the inside out. His hands had shaken with longing to touch her; even lightly skimming his fingers to the soft skin of her neck would have satisfied him but he had kept his hands to himself, tucking them under his arms until he was sure he had control of his body's actions.

That Adela was terrified of him was obvious. She had seemed so brave in her father's stables. She'd defied him when so many men, far bigger and stronger than she, had given in to him. It was in such contrast to the meek woman he'd met during their wedding ceremony that he'd momentarily been fooled into thinking

she was fearless. She wasn't. Something must have propelled her into making such a drastic decision to leave
all that she had known to travel many leagues with a
stranger who frightened her.

It couldn't be that she found him attractive. He knew,
because he'd been told many a time, that his features
were stern and forbidding. He had done nothing to put
her at ease or to try and make her like him. Things at
her home must have been so bad that she would rather
travel with him than stay behind. The thought made him
want to return to Yanworth, the seat of the Valdu family, to drag out his father-in-law and demand to know
what the man had done to Adela that life with a gruff,
forbidding stranger was better than remaining in her
father's protection.

Benedictus let out a long breath. Even knowing all
this, knowing that she was here for reasons he couldn't
fathom but had nothing to do with him, his body still
wouldn't calm down. He rolled out from under the
cloak, hoping that the cold night air would help. It didn't.

He closed his eyes tightly. It had been so long since
he'd felt a woman's touch; so long he could barely remember it, had not mourned the lack of it in his life, had
barely even noticed. He'd thought desire was a thing of
the past for him, thought that he was too old, too busy
making sure the country didn't fall into enemy hands to
feel it. He'd been wrong and that knowledge was humiliating and inconvenient because his slip of a wife was so
frightened of him, she shook violently at his approach.

He sighed. A different man would slake his needs
and not care if the woman was hurt in the process. She

was his wife and by law he could take her whenever he wanted. He was not that man.

He would not take Adela against her will, or even if she allowed him when it was clear it was not what she wanted. If that meant she never was ready for him, then so be it. He rubbed his eyes; the following months were going to be worse than he had imagined.

Adela awoke the following morning cocooned in the cloak and, even though every muscle and bone ached, surprisingly rested. She sat up and looked around her. The fire had died during the night, but the morning was already warm so it made no difference to her temperature.

Without turning round, she knew that Sir Benedictus was no longer beside her. The silence was absolute. She pushed herself up to sitting and gazed around their campsite. He was nowhere to be seen. Her heart slammed against her chest. Surely, he hadn't left her here alone? He hadn't wanted her to come with him and now he had his dowry…but no. He'd told her he would always be truthful and she'd believed him. If he had wanted to leave her, he would have woken her and told her. She twisted round; Sir Benedictus's horse was next to hers and she let out a shaky breath. He couldn't be far away if his horse was still here.

She pushed back his cloak and made her way down to the stream. The water was icy cold, wiping away the remains of sleep as she splashed it over her face. That done, she picked up the cloak and brushed it down before folding it neatly and slipping it into one of Sir Benedictus's saddlebags.

'You're ready to go.'

Adela jumped and whirled round. Sir Benedictus was standing behind her, a strange look on his imposing features. She glanced down at his arms but his forearms were covered by his sleeves. She was strangely disappointed.

'Of course.'

He paused. 'Good.' She thought he might be about to say something else, but he didn't.

He strode toward her. She stumbled backward, her body urging her to run from the threat of a predator. He froze. She continued backward; her back bumped against Bramble. There was nowhere else for her to go. Her breath caught in her throat; her fingers slipped over Bramble's coat as she tried to hold on to her horse.

Sir Benedictus held up his hands. 'I am not going to hurt you. I promise. I will never hurt you.' He stayed where he was, his hands risen. His gaze locked with hers; his breathing steady. His expression was as unreadable as ever, but he kept himself completely still.

Slowly, her heart rate returned to normal. 'I'm sorry,' she said, wishing she could remove the last few moments from his memory. She had reacted ridiculously. If he was going to hurt her, he would have done so already. Besides, his reputation was for being a formidable opponent, an extraordinarily intelligent man but not a cruel or violent one. 'I am just not used to someone of your size. I will become accustomed to you, I am sure.'

He continued to stand there, studying her. She forced

herself to remain still under his intense gaze. He shifted on his feet and dropped his hands. 'You have nothing to apologise for. I have spent most of my life trying to look as formidable as possible. Men twice your size shy away from me. I should have explained my intentions before I moved. I was only going to help you onto your horse. May I?'

He waited until she nodded before stepping forward and placing two large hands around her waist. The press of his palms burned against her skin, even through the fabric of her dress. He threw her up onto the saddle as if she weighed nothing and then his touch was gone. Her skin tingled strangely where he had held her. She swept her fingers over the area but outwardly, the spot felt no different to normal.

'You need to eat more,' he said as he swung himself onto his horse. 'There is virtually nothing to you.' The tone of his voice did not suggest he was criticising her, but she did not know what to say in response. 'The kitchens at Windsor are good. You must tell them what your favourite food is and they will prepare it for you.'

She could not imagine such luxury. Nobody had ever asked her what she wanted to eat before. Meals were generally brought to her bedchamber with no thought as to what she would enjoy. She'd learned to force the food down otherwise she wouldn't eat. 'I do not want to be any trouble. Whatever they prepare for everyone else will be good enough for me.'

He snorted. 'You are my wife. I am running the country in the king's absence. Nothing will be too much of an inconvenience for you.'

He kicked his horse into motion. Adela followed suit, touching a hand to her neck as Bramble started to move. Her heart was beating uncomfortably fast. It was strange enough to become a wife but to be someone who must be pleased was so unbelievable as to be other-worldly. She could not conceive of a life where people would try to please her. Could not really fathom a life outside her father's stronghold. 'What will I do at Windsor?'

The silence that followed her question stretched on for so long that she began to wish she hadn't asked. He hadn't wanted her to come with him. Perhaps he was about to tell her that she should return home. She would not. Since leaving Castle Valdu she may have been uncomfortable, she may have been afraid, but every moment had been better than the stifling existence that had made up her life before her marriage.

'There are many things to do at court,' he said eventually. 'Most of your time will be spent socialising with other women. I am sure you will find plenty to amuse yourself.'

'Oh.' Should she tell him she did not have much experience at socialising? It was probably better not to. They were still not far enough away from her father's stronghold for him to realise what a bad bargain he had made.

She may well be as pure and innocent as her father had wanted her to be, but she had no doubt it made her a bit dull. She couldn't recall ever having made anyone laugh or even be interested in her enough to hold a protracted conversation. She had nothing to offer Sir

Benedictus other than her dowry, which he'd already received. Of course, there was her ability to produce an heir for the Monceaux family, but he'd not mentioned that at all.

She tugged at her neckline. Her clothes felt uncomfortably tight. She wanted him to have no complaint of her as a wife; wanted him to never think he should send her back to her parents. But she had no idea how to bring her most important role in this marriage. Her thoughts swirled around until she couldn't take it anymore; she had to know. 'What about...um...what about your needs?' Her whole face flamed. She wished she could stuff the words back into her mouth. Hearing herself out loud made her realise just how naive she was.

He turned slightly, a small frown creasing his forehead. 'What needs?'

She blinked. Surely, he *knew*. The alternative was impossible to believe. She had no idea how old he was but thought he must be over the age of thirty. Old enough and experienced enough to know exactly what went on between a man and a woman in order to create a baby.

But what if he didn't? If neither of them knew what to do, then how would she get with child?

Since she'd been aware of her betrothal, the thought of having children to love had been a salve to her. Yes, providing an heir for the Monceaux name was important but it was the thought of young people, who would love her unconditionally just because she was their mother, that she had held on to for so long. She knew that must be true because despite her mother's general lack of interest in her, Adela still loved the woman and would have done anything for a crumb of affection. Adela's children would never doubt that she adored them; they would never have to prove their worth by always being good and pure and they would *never* have to endure arbitrary punishments for imagined transgressions. They would know love.

She had pinned all her hopes on her husband being the one to provide her with these longed-for babies but if he didn't know what to do… It was a disaster she'd never contemplated. Perhaps Benedictus was making fun of her by being confused about her question. She risked a glance at his face. Those stern brows were as straight as ever. Teasing probably wasn't part of his personality.

She tightened her grip on her reins, searching for the words to explain herself. In the end she settled on being blunt; he struck her as the sort of person who would prefer it. 'I'm referring to your need for an heir.'

For a pulse, he merely stared at her, his dark eyes blank. As she watched, the skin on his face turned a bright, fiery red. The sight surprised her more than anything since their journey had started. He looked away; his gaze fixed resolutely on the horizon. Their horses raced on and neither of them spoke. His skin colour gradually returned to normal. She shifted in her saddle, her stomach squirming, unable to break a silence that was becoming unbearable.

They reached a bridge and slowed to cross it. 'I…' He rubbed his forehead but still didn't turn to look at her. 'It…' He shook his head. 'My need for an heir is not something you need to worry about now.'

'But…'

'We are strangers…' He let out a frustrated hiss. 'When we know each other better, we can think about producing an heir. You don't need to worry. I shan't…' His shook his head again, his skin turning pink again. She was glad he wasn't looking at her because her own skin was burning. 'I shan't bother you, if that's what you are worried about.'

So his needs and creating a baby *were* something for her to worry about. That was not reassuring. They crossed the bridge in a thud of hooves against the wooden slats. She would have to be happy that he would not force his needs on her until they knew each other better. Although if they continued with the same awkward conversations, then it would take some time before they knew each other at all. Instead of being upset that it would be some time before she had children, she should relax and concentrate on the knowledge that she would be spared the pain and inconvenience for the time being. She was adept at focusing on something positive even when the world around her barely allowed for such thoughts.

They stopped for a break when the sun was directly overhead. Sweat clung to her skin and she wiped it away with the corner of her sleeve. Benedictus handed her the final slice of pie, not eating himself this time. The pastry was slightly damp, but she ate it anyway. She was so hungry now; she would have eaten anything.

'It is not far.' It was the first thing he had said to her since their awkward conversation many leagues ago. 'We will reach Windsor by nightfall.'

She nodded.

'I wasn't expecting to bring you with me,' he continued. 'And so my chambers are not fit for a woman.'

'Chambers?'

'I have two for my personal use, although you will never need to be in one of them.'

Two chambers! She had not expected that. She'd known he was important but somehow the breadth of that importance had eluded her. 'Why will I not need to be in one of them?' Not that she cared, but now that they were making conversation, she wanted it to keep going. Their strained silences were becoming almost unbearable.

'I have an antechamber from where I run my operations. There will be no need for you to be in there. It's uncomfortable, deliberately so. I do not want my men getting so complacent they fall asleep.'

'That seems hard.' She clamped her mouth shut. She hadn't meant to criticise him; if she had said something similar to her father the punishment would have been prolonged and severe.

Sir Benedictus didn't appear to be cross by her comment, though; tilting his head to one side he seemed to consider what she had said. He took a swig from his water skin. 'I must be hard. If I show any sign of weakness, I will be taken advantage of at best and disposed of at worst. The country is in a time of great peril as we edge toward war with France. I will not allow anyone to doubt my ability to rule in the king's absence. If I appear harsh, that is a good thing.' He stood. 'Come, let us continue with our journey.'

This time she didn't shy away when he helped her
back on to her horse. Her skin still tingled oddly at his
firm touch, but being held was unfamiliar to her so perhaps that was what was causing the strange sensation.

She could have asked him about his other chamber, but he already had his back to her and she didn't
know quite how to start another conversation. Besides,
she already had much to mull over. Benedictus called
himself hard. He had not smiled once since she had
met him. But he had shared his cloak with her when
she was cold, reassured her when she was frightened
of him, and told her that he would not force himself on
her. Perhaps he was not as hard as he liked to believe.
At least, she had to hope so; had to hope that he was a
better man than her father and to believe that she hadn't
made a terrible mistake.

Despite darkness falling, Windsor was a hive of activity; nothing like her father's stronghold where work
ceased as soon as sundown occurred. Torches burned
as blacksmiths continued with their hammering, and
inside the stables men rubbed down horses, which appeared just to have arrived back from travels inconceiv-
able to her. Those horses were abandoned as soon as Sir
Benedictus was spotted. Before Adela really knew what
was happening, she was divested of her horse and her
saddlebag and was being propelled by her husband into
the castle, her feet barely able to keep up with the pace.

'My clothes...' she said, trying to turn around to
get them.

'They will be brought to my chambers.' He continued
to guide her inside and through some imposing thick

wooden doors. At first, she tried to remember the path
they were taking through the castle, but she soon lost
her bearings down the long winding corridors. 'This is
my antechamber,' Sir Benedictus said at last. He pushed
open the door. A large, dark-haired man was sitting behind a large desk. He stood as soon as he caught sight
of them.

'Anything to report?' barked Sir Benedictus.

'Yes, sir.' The man's gaze flicked to Adela. 'There is
much to report.'

Sir Benedictus nodded. 'Please will you show Lady
Adela to my bedchamber and then return for a briefing.'
Sir Benedictus began to walk toward the desk but the
other man stood rooted to the spot, his mouth agape.
'Lady Adela is my wife,' Sir Benedictus added. If anything, the man's mouth hung even lower at this explanation. 'Lady Adela, this is Sir Theodore. One of the
king's knights and one of my most trusted men. You
will be safe with him.'

Sir Theodore finally seemed to regain control of his
mouth. 'Very well, Ben, I will take *your* wife to *your*
bedchamber.' Ben. It was hard to reconcile the domi-
nant man who prowled around his antechamber with
that short nickname. It sounded almost friendly, which
her husband was not.

Sir Theodore moved toward her, his eyes twinkling
with amusement. 'Good evening, Lady Adela. It is a
pleasure to meet you.'

She cleared her throat. 'Likewise.'

'Shall we go? You must be tired after your journey.'

'That would be very kind of you, Sir Theodore.'

'My friends call me Theo.'

'She is not your friend, Sir Theodore,' growled Sir Benedictus, but Theo seemed undaunted by her husband's harsh tone. He winked at her and she bit the inside of her mouth to stop herself from laughing. She immediately liked this smiling-faced knight. And, for all his gruffness, Sir Benedictus must like him, too. He wouldn't allow him in his private antechamber if he didn't. Perhaps her time here would not be so daunting as all that.

Chapter Three

Benedictus massaged his neck. Three days travelling and a night catching up on everything he had missed in his absence had turned his bones to instruments of torture. He felt every one of his thirty-two years as he stretched his arms above his head. He'd managed to catch some sleep at his desk but not enough, and the hunched position had only made his aches worse.

There was a brisk knock on his door. Before he could call, 'Enter,' Theodore stepped into the room, his normal smile absent.

'Where have you been?' Theodore demanded without preamble.

Benedictus had known Theodore for many years. They'd trained together as boys and become knights around the same time. He was one of the few men who spoke to him as if they were friends, although it had been some time since Benedictus had laughed with him or spoken to him about anything personal.

'I have been working here since you last saw me, Theodore.'

Theo frowned. 'Theo,' he corrected. Why Theodore wanted his name shortened was a mystery to Benedictus. It seemed important to one of his most trusted knights and so he tried to remember although he almost always forgot. The forgetfulness seemed to enrage Theodore, which, for reasons Benedictus didn't want to dwell on, was one of the reasons he did it. Theodore looked even crosser with him than normal with his thick eyebrows cast down in a heavy frown. 'And what about attending to your wife?'

His new wife. Benedictus's heart thumped strangely at the thought of her. Adela would have been alone last night; sleeping in the large bed Benedictus had indulged himself with a few years ago because he had the wealth and very little on which to spend it. The truth was he hadn't trusted himself to join her. She was acclimatising herself to a completely new world. She did not want or need a husband who was so desperate to feel a woman's touch; he did not know if he could be gentle or patient with her. Even the thought of her in his bed had been tormenting enough. His heart might have stopped completely if he'd been forced to sleep by her side.

Had she been grateful for his absence? Part of him hoped it had been worth the effort of not going to her, that his absence had made her more relaxed in this strange place. But a small part of him, a part that was pathetically needy and not at all like him, hoped that she had wanted him there. Not because he wanted her to be miserable—he wasn't quite the unfeeling monster everyone thought he was—but he liked the thought of being needed for his company rather than what he could do for someone. And that was why his wife was more dangerous than anyone could ever know. He'd worked hard not to care about how other people regarded him and now he couldn't stop thinking about how Adela perceived him. It was ridiculous.

'How did you end up with a wife?' Benedictus jumped; he'd forgotten Theodore was still with him.

'We've been betrothed for many years.'

Theodore's eyes widened, which was understandable. Benedictus never discussed his private life with anyone, and his engagement to a young woman was something only he had discussed with his parents.

'How many years?'

'Ten.'

'What?' Theodore shook his head. 'And I thought no one could surprise me anymore but you have just…' Theodore shook his head again. 'Is that why you never…? No, I can see from your deep frown you're not going to answer that question. Why on earth have you not married her before now?'

'She's ten years younger than me.'

Theodore whistled. 'I see your point. She would have been a child when the betrothal was put in place.' Benedictus winced. The thought of having a child for a bride had always sent a wave of nausea through him. But it must have been far worse for her, growing up and knowing she was going to have to tie herself to a much older man, a man the whole country knew to be a heartless monster. A man who came from a line of such strong, unyielding men, whose family had been clawing their way to the top for centuries, not caring who they destroyed on their way.

He could have let her out of the decade-long agreement, let her marry someone nearer her age, if it hadn't been for this damned war and Edward's need for money. Benedictus swallowed. For some reason the image of her big green eyes gazing up at him popped into his head, their look so trusting and innocent, so in need of someone to keep her safe. If he'd not married her, she may have fallen prey to someone much worse; someone who would take that naivete and destroy her. Or someone who saw that spark in her and snuffed it out.

Benedictus rubbed his chest where a new ache had taken up; probably because he'd slept weirdly, slumped over his desk instead of stretched out on his mattress. It was definitely nothing to do with the thought of his wife with another man or the niggle of guilt at leaving Adela all alone trying to worm its way into his brain. He didn't do guilt or second-guess his motives. If he did, he'd lose control of his mind thinking of all the things he'd ever done and the things that he hadn't.

Theodore was still frowning at him. 'You should still spend time with your wife, Ben. She may have grown up, but she is still innocent and needs someone to support her. That person must be you.'

Benedictus rubbed his forehead. 'I told her that she should remain with her parents, but she would not listen. I know I am not an ideal husband. I cannot give Lady Adela the attention she undoubtedly deserves. I have a country to run and no time to be a doting husband.'

'That's not a good enough excuse, Ben.' Theodore's

jaw was tight, which was unusual because it was rare
to see him angry; Benedictus trusted him for his level-
headedness. For some reason, his fellow knight was really worked up about Benedictus's marriage. 'I know
your parents aren't the best...'

No. Theodore had crossed the line. 'My parents'
marriage is not up for discussion.'

Theodore tsked in annoyance. 'I wasn't going to discuss them. I'm merely pointing out that they have not
shown you how a good marriage can be.' His face softened. 'Medea makes me very happy.'

In his head, Benedictus counted slowly to ten. He
knew Theodore was nauseatingly content. He was always smiling all over the place and looking longingly at
his wife if they had to be apart for more than a few moments. It was preposterous in a grown man, especially
one who was a trained fighter and a superior knight,
like Theodore. That life was not for Benedictus. And,
it had nothing to do with the warlike landscape of his
parents' marriage. It was because he, Benedictus, was
not a loving person. He was practical and logical and
not the type of man who would ever gaze lovingly at
a woman, his wife or otherwise. That behaviour was
for fools.

Still, perhaps he should have gone to his private
bedchamber last night. He wasn't such a brute that he
couldn't control his actions. Sleeping on his mattress
would have been more comfortable than a doze at his
desk and he could have seen how Adela was faring. He
had thought about Adela, alone in his chamber, far more
frequently than he would have liked. He had even risen

to go to her more than once before reminding himself that the safety of the kingdom was his priority right now and he didn't have time to check on a young woman, one he had repeatedly warned not to come with him. The safety of the kingdom was what Theodore should be thinking of right now, too. 'My wife is not of your concern.'

'She is completely alone in a strange place, Ben.'

'Benedictus,' Benedictus corrected, his patience with that ludicrous nickname finally snapping.

'What?'

'You like your name shortened. I prefer mine longer.'

'Right.' Theodore rubbed his hand through his hair. 'And Lady Adela?'

'I suggested she remain at her father's stronghold. She wanted to come to Windsor. I did explain that I would not have time for her.' Had he? Perhaps he hadn't been explicit about that part of the reason he didn't think she should come with him. He *had* made it clear that she shouldn't come to Windsor. It wasn't his fault she had stubbornly refused to listen. Yes, he could have fought harder against her, marched her back to her father and requested she stay with him but for some reason he hadn't. The fact that she'd wanted to be with him had held far too much sway over his thought processes than it should have. He had been flattered, which was the vainest, most foolish thing in the world. He normally abhorred people trying to sweet-talk him into things he didn't want to do but somehow she had snuck past his normal guard. It was those damned green eyes that had swayed him, the way they had held far too much of his attention, touching a place inside him he had long thought dead. And then there was his belief that something bad must have happened to her, so bad it had made her long to leave, which had persuaded him to keep her with him when all his good sense had told him it was a bad idea.

He was a fool because, like everyone else, she wanted something he could give her. It was not like she wanted to be with *him* in particular. She had wanted to get away from the Valdu family and yes, he could understand that desire. He'd been desperate to get away from his parents the moment he'd realised that was a possibility, but that wasn't the point. He should have hardened his heart, something he was normally able to do without any soul-searching, and refused to bring her with him, but he hadn't and now they would both have to live with the consequences.

'England will not fall into the hands of the French if you spend the morning with your new wife.'

'You don't know that, Theod… Theo. You don't know all the information passing my desk every moment of every day. I must keep up with it or the kingdom could fall.'

Theodore snorted. 'It is not your sole responsibility, Benedictus. The king is the one in charge, not you. Edward is hardly worried, is he? The reports of him and Phillipa enjoying themselves in Antwerp do not suggest he is working himself to the bone.'

'I'd be careful if I were you, Theo. That sounds dangerously close to a treasonous statement.' Theodore only rolled his eyes, undoubtedly realising Benedictus's threat was merely a diversion tactic. Benedictus felt his skin warm; he was rarely so obvious. 'King

Edward left me in charge. I must succeed in keeping England safe and out of French hands. The Monceaux family never fail.'

Theodore stared at him for a long moment. Benedictus held himself still. He was the man who made people squirm, not the other way around.

'But a wife…you've only been married…' Theodore shook his head. 'It cannot be more than three days.'

'The marriage ceremony was two days ago. And I don't see what that has to do with my work here.'

Theodore stood. 'If you cannot see that what you are doing is wrong, then I cannot help you.'

How dare he! Theodore had overstepped the mark this time. 'I do not need help.'

'That remains to be seen.' Theodore rubbed his back as he made his way toward the door. 'You need to change those benches. They are worse than the rack to sit on.'

'They are not meant to be comfortable. I don't want people to relax. I want them to be alert when they are in here.'

Theodore turned back to face Benedictus, the look on his face a strange mix between pity and anger. 'Benedictus, the men who come in here are loyal to you. They are the best there is. I don't think it should be beyond you to give them a little comfort.'

Benedictus didn't say anything as Theodore let himself out of the room, closing the door quietly behind him. He picked up the report in front of him, but the words swam in front of his eyes. He rubbed his face; it didn't help. He pushed himself to his feet; perhaps a walk would do him good.

Chapter Four

Adela folded her hands on her lap and then unfolded them. She stood and paced to the window, gazing down at the courtyard below. People were scurrying about, full of purpose. Her stomach twisted. Here she was again, trapped in a chamber while the rest of the world lived. She was just as alone here as she had been at her father's stronghold. She had swapped one prison for another, although admittedly this one was far more comfortable.

The chamber door opened and closed with a thud.

Her heart pounded even as her body froze, her gaze fixed unseeingly on the view beneath her.

'Lady Adela, I trust you are well,' her husband's deep voice rumbled about the space.

She turned slowly. Sir Benedictus was standing just inside the doorway. The chamber seemed so much smaller with his hulking presence.

'Yes, I am well, thank you. And you?' She grimaced at the mundane pleasantries. She wanted to ask him what had been so important that it had kept him away from her on her first night here; to demand that he give her some attention, no matter how small and to ask him what exactly she should do with herself, but the words were stuck inside her.

Sir Benedictus cleared his throat. 'Good, I'm glad. And did you sleep well?' This was torturous. What little rapport they had had on their journey to Windsor had completely evaporated, leaving this desperate awkwardness in its wake.

'I did sleep well.' She hadn't. She had barely slept at all. She had waited and waited for her husband to come and when he hadn't, she'd been too bewildered to relax. She had managed to drift off as the night merged into the early dawn only to wake not long later by the sounds of castle life carrying on without her. Although she had promised him truthfulness, pride would not let her admit any of this.

His gaze roamed around the chamber, looking anywhere but at her. 'You should go to the Great Hall later. That is where everyone will be.'

Her heart skipped a beat. 'Will you?'

He paused. 'No. I have things to do. My men will be there to oversee things, however.' She wasn't disappointed. The ache around her chest had nothing to do with the knowledge he wouldn't be spending time with her this afternoon as well and was more to do with the anxiety of meeting people she didn't know when she had so little practise of doing so.

'What things do people do there?' She couldn't begin to imagine large groups of people mixing.

Sir Benedictus shrugged. 'Gossip, mingle, political manoeuvring. It's where the business of court is supposed to be done but where very little is ever achieved.'

'What will I do there?'

'There will be lots of women in attendance. You can make some acquaintances.'

Adela opened her mouth to point out that she had no idea how to go about doing such a thing but Sir Benedictus seemed to think their conversation had finished. He nodded once, muttered, 'Good,' turned and left as abruptly as he'd arrived, leaving her none the wiser as to how her marriage was going to work.

Adela rubbed her hands together as she hovered by the door to the Great Hall. The noise inside was deafening. The people inside would barely notice one small woman amongst their crowds and yet she couldn't bring herself to step over the threshold. Up in Benedictus's bedchamber, this venture had seemed like a good idea but now it seemed like a horrific ordeal.

The morning had passed with familiar slowness. She was so used to the boredom of inactivity that she had almost let it wash over her and swallow her up as it had done so many times in the past. Finally, Sir Benedictus had arrived and here she was blindly following exactly what he had told her to do with no idea how she was going to do it.

She'd thought to disobey him. It was too much to go to the Great Hall alone, but as the morning had dragged interminably on, she had resolved to begin her new life at Windsor without Sir Benedictus. She had promised herself that once she was married there would be no more sitting in a chamber as life passed her by. She'd summoned up her courage and walked from the bed-chamber to the Great Hall, following the rumble of chatter through the convoluted corridors. But now that she was here, now that she was truly thinking of doing something to end her loneliness, her feet wouldn't follow the commands from her head and would take her no farther.

She turned on her heel; Sir Benedictus's bedchamber was warm and peaceful. Nobody had hurt her there; nobody had even bothered her. She would return and come back to the Great Hall when her confidence returned. Another day or two would not hurt her.

'Lady Adela.' Adela stopped. Hardly anyone here knew her name, but the voice was too cheerful to be her husband. She turned to see Sir Theodore striding toward her.

'Sir Theodore. I trust you are well on this lovely day.' The politeness that had been drilled into her since a child outweighed her natural reticence and she managed the courteous greeting without too much trouble.

'Indeed I am. Are you heading into the Hall?' Theodore gestured toward the cavernous room just beyond them. 'Let me introduce you to my wife. She is very excited to meet you.'

'Oh?' Nobody had ever been excited to see Adela before.

'Yes. She cannot believe Ben has finally married.' So that was it; Adela was wanted because she was an object of curiosity. Her feelings must have shown on her face because Sir Theodore's smile fell. 'Of course, Medea is friendly and not at all a ridiculous oaf like me. She will be able to introduce you to everyone of importance.'

'Oh, I…' She was about to tell him that she was planning to return to Sir Benedictus's bedchamber so that she could keep out of the way, but Theodore gave her no time. He swept ahead of her and she had to scurry to catch up.

'I should tell you,' said Theodore as he cut through the crowds, 'that Ben has a good heart and underneath that gruff exterior is a decent, honourable man who will make a loyal, if not loving, husband.'

Adela didn't know how to respond to that, so she didn't. So long as Sir Benedictus wasn't an evil husband, she was sure they would rub along well enough together. It wasn't as if she was expecting to love her husband and to find happiness with him. She was pinning all her hopes for love onto the children she expected to have, although how that would happen if her husband didn't spend time with her, she didn't know.

Theodore arrived at the side of a woman with the wildest hair; the look they shared so intimate Adela had to turn away as something painful lodged in her chest.

'Lady Adela, please allow me to introduce you to my wife, Lady Medea.' Lady Medea beamed at her and Adela felt something inside her loosen at the open warmth in the woman's gaze.

'You must call me Medea and I'll call you Adela.' Medea shot a quick glance at her face. 'Unless, that is, you object.'

Adela shook her head. She'd never met anyone like

Medea, so openly friendly on immediate acquaintance. She instantly liked her more than anyone she had met before.

Medea grinned. 'Great. I think you and I are going to get on very well. You must tell me all about yourself but perhaps we shall save that until we are somewhere private. In the meantime, I will introduce you to some people. The sooner you get to know the lie of the land the better.'

Medea slipped her arm through Adela's and began to guide her around the room, Theodore slipping away at some point, so quietly Adela didn't know when it had happened. 'I'm going to have to make it known that you are Sir Benedictus's wife. There's no way around that, really. I'm afraid that, when I do, you'll be deluged with attention. Some will be genuine curiosity as to how you managed to unite yourself with such a powerful man. Most will see you as a way to talk to the big man. Very few of the people you meet today will be sincere in their regard.'

Adela didn't want to admit she wouldn't know a genuine person from an egg. She nodded instead and so began a bewildering tour of the Great Hall and the courtiers who roamed around it. By the time servants were rushing in, pulling long tables from the edges of the room, readying the place for the evening meal, Adela was exhausted. She'd never heard so many words spoken in an afternoon or perhaps ever. Without Medea she would have been lost and probably would be vowing never to leave Sir Benedictus's bedchamber again.

'From what I've learned this afternoon, I don't think

I can trust anyone,' she said as Medea tugged her to the far end of the Hall.

Medea laughed. 'Life at Windsor gets better. I was lost when I first came to court but now I find the political manoeuvring and posturing entertaining.'

'Really?' Adela couldn't imagine ever finding pleasure in the long conversations about France and what the king was up to in Antwerp. It had been so difficult to follow everyone's opinions and *everyone* had their own piece to say, seeming to believe she wanted to know it in great detail.

Medea had been right; once it was revealed Adela had married Sir Benedictus the attention on her had been intense. Now she really wanted to retire to the silence of Sir Benedictus's bedchamber and sleep but it seemed that was not an option because the evening meal was about to begin.

She knew, from her father's castle, that the more important members of the household sat on the benches toward the top of the Hall, while the lesser members sat toward the door. Medea placed her at the far end of the table, the closest to the top table. Delicacies, such that she'd never seen before, were placed in front of her but her appetite, always temperamental, had completely left her.

Many of the diners on all the long tables were turning their heads to look at her. An intense whisper had started up farther down the table and although she had no way of knowing for sure, it felt as if many of the hushed voices were talking about her.

Suddenly, the voices silenced.

'What's going on?' murmured Medea, looking up from where she was filling her trencher with food.

Adela didn't respond. She couldn't. All the air had been sucked from her lungs. Sir Benedictus stood framed by the large entranceway; seemingly unbothered by all the intense stares in his direction, he held his head high. His gaze flicked over the assembled men and women. Adela's heart kicked when his look settled on her and then he was striding toward her, his long confident gait eating up the floor as if it were no distance at all. If the chatter of the Hall started back up again, she didn't hear it.

Her heart began to race uncomfortably as he neared. Out in the wilderness, during their ride to Windsor, Benedictus had clearly been a large, powerful man, but here in the king's court he was a towering presence. If she hadn't known better, she would have assumed he was the King of England himself.

All too soon he was next to her. She had to tilt her head up, up, and up to look him in the face. She swallowed as his solemn gaze bore down on her. From the expression in his dark eyes, she could not tell if he was cross or pleased to see her. His formidable brow gave nothing away.

'Lady Adela, you must join me on the top table.' His voice was like a low rumble of thunder. Without waiting for an answer, he strode on.

She sat, watching him walk, hardly able to believe she had married such a man. What had she been thinking, forcing him to bring her here? If she wasn't careful, she would be crushed by him. Medea nudged her.

'You must go to him. You cannot snub Sir Benedictus in front of all these people. He would not be pleased.'

Adela pushed herself to her feet and stumbled after her husband. He was standing behind an ornately carved chair, watching her approach, his jaw firm and unsmiling. He indicated with a tilt of his head that she should take her place on the chair he was holding.

'I can't sit here,' she mumbled as her sleeve brushed his. 'This is the seat for the queen.'

'You are my wife. If I am standing in for the king, then my wife will sit beside me on the queen's chair.'

For a moment she debated running away from him. It was too much. She hadn't realised marrying Sir Benedictus would bring her so much scrutiny. She had underestimated just how important he was. She had gone from being invisible to something so completely different, it was as if she had travelled to another world. No wonder her father had been beside himself at the thought of uniting her family with his. It was almost as if the Valdus of Yanworth were now linked with a higher being by her marriage. If she had known all this, maybe she wouldn't have been so insistent in running away from her previous life, but she had and now she would have to deal with the consequences; she could not go back.

There was nothing to do now except do as he requested. She slipped onto the chair; Sir Benedictus pushed it in until she was close enough to the table before lowering himself onto the chair next to her.

As she settled into her seat, she realised that the hum

of conversation had resumed in the Great Hall but beside her Sir Benedictus was a silent statue.

A new trencher was placed in front of her, but she could only sit staring at it as thoughts tumbled about her brain.

'Can I help you to some food?' Sir Benedictus asked eventually.

She turned to him; his focus was on the tray of meat in front of him. His jaw was tight, as if he was in pain.

'Yes, please.'

'Is there anything you don't like?'

'I don't know.'

'You don't know…?' He seemed to wait for her to elaborate but when she didn't, he loaded her trencher with a little of everything before helping himself.

'Do people normally look up to the top table so much?' she asked when she finally found her voice.

'No. They are curious about you.'

'Oh.'

'Do not worry. Their interest will fade.'

She picked at a cut of meat and managed to swallow a few mouthfuls before Sir Benedictus spoke again. 'I meant to say earlier, the change you have made to our chamber…it is good.'

A small dart of pleasure shot through her. 'Thank you.'

'Did you embroider the tapestry yourself?'

'Yes.' My goodness, could she not think of a sentence to say that was longer than one word? He must think she was a simpleton.

'You are very talented.'

Warmth spread through her. Nobody had ever said anything so lovely to her. 'You are kind to say so but really the elaborate detail in that tapestry is because I've had so much time on my hands over the years.' There, she had managed to say a sentence, even if she had just made herself seem so impossibly dull. Sir Benedictus was running the country; she was embroidering a small square of cloth, not much bigger than the span of his shoulders.

'I am very rarely kind, Lady Adela. I am sure that has been mentioned to you many times today. If I say I think you are talented, then I mean it.'

'Thank you,' she said again. Benedictus nodded and began cutting his meat with neat precision. There was a strength to his hands that made something flutter oddly in her stomach; something that had nothing to do with hunger.

Adela swallowed. She had come to Windsor to start a new life, to be brave and to have an adventure, and here she was acting exactly like she always had done. Being meek and mild and not daring to say anything to anyone unless she was spoken to first. That had to stop. She had to embrace her new life, just as she had promised her younger self when she was all alone in her chamber dreaming of escape.

'How was your day?' she blurted out before she could talk herself out of it.

Benedictus paused, his spoon almost to his mouth. 'My day… It was interesting.'

'Is there anything you can tell me about?'

He tilted his head to one side. 'Most of it, no.'

'Oh.'

'It's not personal to you. I can't tell anyone, not even my priest.'

'Of course. What is it that you do all day? I mean I am not looking for specifics. I am asking in general. I cannot imagine it.'

He cleared his throat. 'Mostly, I gather information and disseminate it as I see fit.'

'Oh.' She chewed on a slice of bread. 'I'm not sure I know what that means.'

'Let's say, for example, that you had a secret, then I would be keen to find out what it was. Now, if the secret was that—' he waved his knife around '—you didn't enjoy my singing voice, then I would lose interest quickly. In fact, I would probably want you to keep any negative thoughts about my singing ability to yourself.' She looked at his face to see if he was teasing her but his lips remained straight and she couldn't tell. 'However, if your secret was that you were planning on stealing a sack of grain from the stables, then that would be very interesting to me.'

'What would I do with the grain?'

'Perhaps you would exchange it for something you wanted or perhaps you want to frame someone else for the crime. Whatever the reason, if it isn't good for Windsor, then it isn't good for me.'

She broke off a piece of bread. 'How do you get your information?'

'I have lots of people working for me. They gather facts and rumours and bring them to me. It is my job to work out what is fact and what is fiction and to act on it. With the king gone, I have other duties, too. I will be very busy until he returns.'

It was yet another reminder that he did not have time for her but she was not disheartened. He might think he had not given her much time but to her, it had been so much. No one in her family had ever given her so much undivided attention as he had during this one meal.

They lapsed into silence again. As the dinner carried on, she searched her mind for something else to talk about. Anything at all, but her thoughts stayed persistently blank as everyone around her chattered happily. She hoped no one was witnessing their awkwardness but she had a feeling everyone was watching them.

After an eternity, the meats were removed and brightly coloured food, which looked like fruit but wasn't, was placed in front of them. She prodded one with her finger; it was soft and sweet-smelling.

'Have you ever tried one of these?' Benedictus had turned to watch her.

'No. What is it?'

'It's marzipan made to look like fruit. It is one of the queen's favourite delicacies. Try it.'

She picked one up and popped it into her mouth. The sweetness coated her tongue; she closed her eyes and moaned. Never had she tasted anything so good. She wanted to gorge on them, to eat them all without stopping.

'You like it?'

She opened her eyes and looked at Benedictus. For the first time in their acquaintance, he wasn't frowning or looking stern. His lips were turned in the smallest of smiles. Her heart lurched in the oddest way at the sight.

'I do like it, very much.'

'Good. I'm glad.'

It wasn't much. Anyone listening to their conversation wouldn't think anything special had happened. But to Adela this meal was a breakthrough. She'd seen a hint of a smile on her husband's stern features and she had put it there. She was going to do everything that she could think of to see that again. She need only be bold and she would see where it would lead her.

Adela took another bite of the marzipan sweet and her eyes fluttered shut. Benedictus tried not to stare. He didn't want all of Windsor to know how hard he found it to take his eyes off his wife and they would all be watching; of that he had no doubt.

She moaned softly. He swallowed and gripped the table. What was this delirium consuming him? She was not the first woman he had spoken to, not even the first one he had been close to, but no one had ever had such a grip over his body. He tore his gaze away from her and studied his empty trencher as if it held the answer. It didn't. Nor was it interesting enough to hold his attention for longer than a few moments. His gaze slid back to Adela. She was taking her time with the sweet, savouring it as if she might not get another. What must her life have been like before he had come into it? Her family was a wealthy one and so she cannot have been deprived of luxury and yet she acted as if she had been; acted as if every experience was new to her.

He searched his mind trying to think of something to say, anything to get those green eyes looking at him again but he came up with nothing. He'd had very little practise making general conversation over the past few years; every exchange he had was to the point and had a purpose. He never needed to put people at their ease; they either could talk to him or not and he had no time for those who couldn't. Adela was different. He didn't want her to be frightened of him; wanted to hear her soft moan again. And that was not good. If she knew she had any kind of hold over him, she could use it to her advantage.

'I must leave you now.'

She turned to him, a flash of something in her green eyes that he couldn't read. 'You still have things you must do?'

'Yes.' No. Not really but he could not sit here a moment longer, the same thoughts repeating themselves over and over again. The longing to touch her; the need to hear that moan directed at something he had done; the struggle to think of something, anything, to say to her.

'You work very hard.' There was no censure in her voice; no suggestion that she was angry with him for abandoning her. That didn't stop a worm of guilt wriggling its way into his stomach.

'Yes. I am very busy.'

She turned her attention back to the tray of sweets. 'I will bid you good eve, then.'

He was strangely bereft without her focus on him. 'Good eve, Lady Adela. I hope you sleep well.'

He strode from the Great Hall without a backward glance toward his wife, worried that one sight of her would have him acting the fool in front of everybody.

Because, he knew, that if Adela gave him even the slightest encouragement that she would welcome his touch then he would not be able to stop himself from sweeping her into his arms and carrying her off to their chamber.

Chapter Five

Adela straightened her dress and stared at the door; her new resolve to be brave threatening to desert her already. She had been standing in the corridor for a large part of the morning watching men come and go from her husband's antechamber from her viewpoint partially concealed in a small recess. She needn't have bothered hiding her presence; the men who came out were often far too distracted to notice her; some had been nearly in tears; all had been paler than when they'd arrived. Now almost completely sure that her husband was alone, she rested her fingers on the ornately carved door; her heart beat quickly. Leaning against it, she pressed her ear to the wood. No sound came from within. It was now or never. She rapped her knuckles against the wood before what was left of her confidence could flee altogether.

'Enter.' She jumped as Sir Benedictus's voice boomed out. Part of her wanted to flee but there was no going back now.

She pushed the door and strode quickly into the room, her dress thankfully hiding her shaking knees.

Sir Benedictus's eyes widened slightly at her approach, the only sign that he was surprised to see her. 'Lady Adela.' He stood. 'What can I do for you?'

She sucked in a deep breath. 'We are married now. I think you should call me Adela.' She was pleased her voice came out strong and assured, as if she was used to giving instructions to men who could crush her with one hand, if they chose to do so. The statement came out exactly as she had planned.

He didn't smile but he didn't frown at her words, either. 'Very well, Adela. What is it that I can do for you this morning?'

'I want to help.' She cringed. That part of her speech had not gone how she'd planned. She hadn't meant to blurt her words out. She'd meant to approach her objective subtly; while she waited for the opportunity to speak to him she'd thought over every word she wanted to say and how she was going to say it. Not once had it come out like that. Her speech had been quite clever, pointing out the benefits of her position in court as his wife and how everyone wanted to talk to her about every little thing, but none of it had come out. There was something about this man that made what little ability she had to talk normally completely vanish. Thankfully, he didn't order her from the room for her inanity.

He scratched his cheek. 'Help with what?'

She took a steadying breath. 'I was thinking about what you said last night, about how people gather information for you. I thought perhaps...' She trailed off at the discouraging look on his face. And then she rallied. She had not come this far to give up without even

finishing one of her planned sentences. 'I thought perhaps I could do the same.' He didn't encourage her to
speak further but neither did he dismiss her out of hand.
She carried on. 'So many people want to talk to me just
because I'm married to you. Why don't we use that to
find something out?'

He rubbed his jaw. Her heart raced as she waited for
him to deliver judgement. As always, his expression was
so difficult to read. 'What do you want to find out?'

'I…' She'd only thought about getting him to agree
with her plan. She hadn't thought so far ahead as to
contemplate what she might do for him. Still, she had
come so far. 'What do you want to know?'

Benedictus watched his wife for a long moment. Her
fingers were trembling against her skirts but there was
no other outward sign she was nervous of him. Grown
men often cowered before him; this slip of a woman
could teach them something about bravery. Because
she was scared, of that he was sure. She'd been scared
since the moment she'd stepped into Windsor and he had
done nothing to help her, for which he should be heart-
ily ashamed and which he was sure he would be once
he had the time to think about it more.

In the meantime, Theo was right; England would not
fall if he spent a few moments talking with her. If she
needed something from him to feel more comfortable
at court, then he could give it to her. It might appease
his conscience, which seemed intent on berating him
almost constantly for his treatment of his naive wife.
If asked, he'd have said he didn't have scruples, that

he had no time for them but it seemed, where she was concerned, he couldn't stop thinking of Adela and how she was faring. It was damned annoying.

'Would you like to sit down for a moment?' He gestured to his own seat.

'I can sit here.' She indicated the benches.

'I wouldn't recommend it. They are not designed for comfort. Come.'

She made her way over to him; as she brushed past him he got a hint of something floral and his body roared into life. He wanted to lean down and inhale her skin. To press his lips to her delicate neck, to follow with his fingers so that he would know what her soft skin was like to the touch. He held himself still, almost shaking with the effort it took. She would likely run from the room if he tried something like that.

He reminded himself for the hundredth time that he would not touch his wife until she no longer shook in his presence. He had gone long enough without a woman; he would not die if he did not have this one even if he felt like it whenever he was in his wife's presence.

He towered over her once she was sitting; she tugged on the hem of her sleeve, pulling the material over her thin arms but not before he caught sight of the blue veins that ran beneath her smooth, pale skin of her wrists. My God, but she was delicate, like a fragile flower that could be snapped in half at any moment. A surge of protectiveness shot through him. If anyone at Windsor tried to hurt her, and someone undoubtedly would because of her link to him, then they would feel the full weight of his wrath. Something of his thoughts must have reached her because her gaze fluttered up to his and then quickly away again.

He shifted awkwardly on his feet. He was not used to trying to put people at their ease. He doubted he was doing it right now; her shoulders were too rigid to be natural. He moved away from her, giving her space to relax.

He made his way over to the bench and lowered himself onto it, expecting it to be awfully uncomfortable from the moment he sat, but he was pleasantly surprised. It was nowhere near as bad as Theodore and the rest of his knights had made out. Yes, it was a little hard but nothing like sitting on the ground during a lengthy military campaign. They were going soft, his men. Perhaps he ought to take them out on a training exercise to remind them exactly what uncomfortable was. Not that they would thank him for it but at least they might stop complaining about the benches. He leaned back against the wall and crossed his legs at his ankles. 'As you know, we are at war with France.'

She leaned her elbows onto his desk and steepled her fingers and he bit back a smile. There was something adorable about her diminutive figure in the seat of his power. 'Yes.' She nodded emphatically.

'It's been reported that French warships have been seen in the Thames.' He wasn't telling her anything secret. This rumour was rife in Windsor, but it had yet to be reported as true by anyone he trusted. Benedictus was doubtful it had really happened. It would be a bold move, one that he didn't think the French were capable of yet. However, the rumour was causing a lot of unrest, which he didn't need. The calmer people were the easier they were to appease. Once they started to panic, they started to question the strength of whomever was leading them. In this case that person was him and he didn't want a revolt on his hands. Not only would it be a lot of work to subdue but also his parents would never let him forget it if a Monceaux lost control of power, especially as he currently had control over the whole kingdom. 'I need to know who is causing this rumour.'

She blinked a few times. 'Is that it?'

'Yes.'

'It doesn't sound like much.'

He wanted to laugh at the indignant expression on her face, but he bit the inside of his cheek. It had been years since he'd felt such a bubble of amusement, but he didn't think she would care for being laughed at, not by him. 'It may not sound like much to you, but it is more important than you can imagine.'

She sat up straight at that remark. Something warm slipped under his skin, something akin to pleasure. He had other men working on this and in much more detail. It did not matter if she failed to find anything out, somebody else would but he liked knowing he had given her a purpose.

He shifted on the seat; realising he was trying to get himself into a more comfortable position, he stopped. It wasn't that the bench was uncomfortable as such; it was just, now that he thought about it, as if the seat was trying to slowly torture him. It was subtle but now he was beginning to see what his knights were talking about when they complained. Not that he would ever give them the satisfaction of knowing he might, possibly, agree with them. Theodore had once compared the bench to the rack, a slow torture that gradually got worse as time went on. If Benedictus was completely honest, the seat did seem intent on causing him maximum pain.

'How should I go about it?' She was sitting on the edge of his chair now, her eyes alight with excitement. His body, which had just begun to focus on the pain and not on her body, tightened again and he stifled a groan.

How much longer could he go on like this? He was beginning to act like a very young man with no control over his body. He closed his eyes and reminded himself of all the reasons he was holding off bedding her. She feared him; he would be akin to a monster if he tried anything with her before she was relaxed in his company. She was so thin and needed feeding up otherwise there was a good chance he would snap her like a twig. He didn't have the time to give her the care and attention she needed. Even he knew you didn't just bed a virgin and walk away. There were so many reasons and yet...and yet...he was getting to the point where holding off was becoming intolerable. Perhaps he could put his duties off for...

'I'm sorry.'

He blinked his eyes open. For one horrible moment he thought she could read his mind but then why would she be sorry? It wasn't her fault he was yearning for even the slightest touch from her. 'Whatever for?'

'I didn't mean to make your workload harder.'

He frowned. 'Why would you think that you are?'

'You had your eyes closed. You looked rather like you were resigned to something awful.'

His skin heated and he was glad he was on the other side of the room. Hopefully, she could not see the effect of his embarrassment. This was the third time he'd blushed in front of her, which was the third time he had ever blushed. It was not a pleasant experience. 'I am merely tired. That is all. I apologise. As to how you should go about it. People seem intrigued by your arrival at court. Let them come and talk to you. Report back to me anything that seems relevant. Lady Medea will be able to help you. She has done some of this type of work for me before.'

She stood. 'Very well. I will start now.'

Another bolt of amusement shot through him at her enthusiasm. He wasn't used to being amused and he wasn't sure what it was about her that was making him experience the emotion. 'You don't need to hurry. You can take your time to acclimatise to court. It must be very different from the world you are used to inhabiting.'

'It is. But I think having something to aim for will make it easier.' She edged around his desk but stopped before she passed him. Her hand fluttered to his jaw, the soft touch sending shock waves through his body. 'You should get some rest.'

He held himself very still, not wanting to spook her into dropping her hand. 'I will. When the war is over.'

She smiled gently. 'That could take a long time, Benedictus.' She froze. 'Can I call you that or would you prefer…?'

'Benedictus is fine.' It was more than fine. The way his name sounded in her soft voice as her fingers rested against his skin was almost more than he could take.

'Thank you.' Dear God. Was he so much of a tyrant that he needed to be thanked for the use of his name by his own wife? It would seem so and he was surprised by how much that bothered him. He shouldn't care one way or the other but when his wife was looking down at him with such sweet kindness in her eyes, it was difficult to remember why he always had to be so hard. 'Will I see you at the evening meal?'

'Yes. I will be there. I must show my face at least once a day or else everyone will think I have disappeared.' He saw some of the light in her eyes die and he realised he should have said that he was looking forward to seeing her during the meal. He couldn't add it now; the words would look forced, and yet he hated that he'd hurt her with his carelessness.

'Until then…' She dropped her hand and he nearly grabbed it back but he didn't. He wouldn't know what to do with it if he caught it.

'Yes. Until then.' He said nothing more as she opened the door and slipped quietly away.

Entering the Great Hall by herself was not nearly as daunting for Adela as it had been yesterday. Somehow, having a purpose gave her a confidence she had been lacking for most of her life. Or perhaps it was her conversations with Benedictus, especially the one in his antechamber earlier. For the first time since their marriage, she had felt, not his equal, not even close, but something akin to becoming that one day.

She had even touched the unyielding muscles of his jaw under the soft bristles of a day's worth of beard. Her fingertips had tingled and it had taken great effort not to skim along the outline of his face to the soft-looking flesh beneath his ear. Would he have welcomed it or shaken her off? She'd never know because she had not been courageous enough to try. She was getting braver, though. She'd dared to enter his antechamber and had come out of there with a purpose. It was huge progress for a woman who had feared her own shadow until very recently. Now all she had to do was show Benedictus that his faith in her was warranted.

It was easy to spot Medea amongst the crowds of people in the Great Hall. Her wild hair made her stand out from everyone else. Adela made her way over to her, all the while trying to listen in on the conversations she was passing. Most of it was a jumble of words, and anything she could make out made no sense.

'Adela.' Medea's smile was huge. 'How lovely to see you.' Adela's heart warmed. It seemed the woman's words were genuine. Adela had never had someone pleased to see her before and it added a lightness to her heart. 'I'd like to introduce you to somebody. Sir Hendry, come here.'

A man who couldn't be much older than Adela stepped toward her. Sunlight poured in from the high windows and hit Sir Hendry's blond hair, lighting him up like an angel.

'Sir Hendry, this is the lady everyone is talking about,

the woman who married Sir Benedictus. Lady Adela, Sir Hendry is newly arrived from Northern England and has become a knight in the king's army.'

Sir Hendry's blue eyes twinkled down at her. 'It is lovely to meet another newcomer to court,' he said. 'How are you fitting in to your new surroundings?' His voice was warm and friendly, and his face was so incredibly pleasing to the eye that women all around them were blatantly staring at him; and yet, there was something about him that reminded her of her father, something she couldn't pinpoint but which had the hairs on the back of her neck standing on end. She had to hold herself still to stop herself from shying away from his scrutiny; her father was many leagues away; she may never have to see the man again and the young knight standing before her was not him.

'Everyone has been very pleasant to me so far.' She was pleased her voice showed no sign of her instant re-vulsion. How he looked was not the man's fault.

He laughed. 'I'm sure they are. You will need to be careful. People will cultivate your friendship in order to get close to Sir Benedictus. I understand he is the man everybody wants to know and yet he manages to avoid getting close to anyone.'

She nodded. 'I realise that.' Medea and Benedictus had both said much the same thing but for some rea-son coming from this stranger, the observation felt mis-placed. It was too familiar. Perhaps because he was a stranger or maybe her reaction was completely due to Sir Hendry's eyes being the same shade as her father's.

'I do beg your pardon. I was a little blunt there. I'm

sure you've heard that before and it's not something you want to dwell on.' Sir Hendry's smile was still friendly, despite her noncommittal answers.

'Yes.'

He smiled and a woman nearby sighed. Adela shifted on her feet. This was her first opportunity to start trying to find things out about a person. He was new to court; neither Benedictus nor Medea would know anything about him. He seemed keen to talk to her and she should use this time wisely. It wasn't that she suspected Sir Hendry of anything. The haunting resemblance to her father's eyes was not his fault, although if his reasons for being at Windsor did turn out to be nefarious and she found out… Benedictus would be pleased and would see that it was worth her coming to Windsor.

But now that she'd thought about it, the pressure to make conversation wiped her mind of any words at all. Not a single thing came to mind. This was worse than her normal shyness. Her throat was constricting. She swallowed but it brought no relief.

'Are you quite well, my lady?' Sir Hendry frowned.

She touched her neck. 'I am feeling somewhat faint.'

'I am not surprised. It is so hot and crowded in here. Let me take you outside so you can breathe.'

She was about to point out that she was perfectly capable of walking the few steps outside on her own when she stopped herself. He was very keen to help her; perhaps she would relax when she was outside; perhaps the words would come after all.

Chapter Six

It wasn't quite time for the evening meal to start. Benedictus normally arrived once everyone was already sitting down to enjoy it but tonight he found himself striding down the corridors at an unprecedented pace. He willed himself to slow down. If he arrived too soon, he would have to spend an age talking to people about trivial things as he made his way through the Hall. It was better when everyone was already seated; striding through the Hall to the top table was an effective way to remind everyone who was in charge. It always worked. People stopped to stare at him and conversations slowed as he passed by. He didn't enjoy being the centre of so much undivided attention but it served a purpose, and so yes, it was better for him to arrive later rather than earlier.

For some reason his stride picked up again despite his stern words to himself. It seemed he was impatient to get there this evening. He wasn't hungry, so he couldn't lie to himself that he was keen to get to the food. There was something else driving him on and unfortunately, he knew what it was. He wanted to see his wife, wanted to talk to her, to discover the way her mind worked. She had surprised him earlier when she'd come to see him. He hadn't expected her to want to be involved in his world. She seemed far too meek for such a proposition and yet she had come to his antechamber and talked to him as if she believed in herself completely. She was at turns brave and terrified and he couldn't work her out.

And there was the other thing. The constant longing to touch her, to see what her soft skin felt like under his fingertips, to know what it was like to taste her mouth and to hear her soft moan as he explored her body.

He paused. Thinking about kissing his wife just before he was about to stride into a room with close to a hundred people in it was not a good idea, especially as those hundred people would all be looking at him because they always did. If only one of them could see a visible sign of how much he wanted his wife then that was a mortification he did not want to contemplate. He waited for a moment, forcing himself to think about all the problems he'd had to deal with throughout the day, willing his body to calm down.

When he was sure he wasn't going to embarrass himself, he rounded the final corner and came to an abrupt stop. There, on the arm of some man, a man so handsome he looked like he had fallen from heaven, was his wife. Jealousy hit him like a punch to the gut. He glanced down, half expecting to see a fist buried deep inside his stomach.

Adela was smiling up at this person, her smile so

wide and open. Benedictus had never seen her smile like that before, which was probably his own fault. He had hardly made her welcome, barely tried to put her at her ease. He should have done so because her smile transformed her face. She was breathtakingly lovely, so astonishingly beautiful that he was left winded. She laughed at something the young man said and Benedictus experienced the overwhelming urge to rip the young man's arm off and throw it into the Thames.

He strode over to the couple, his fists curled.

Adela turned at the sound of his approach and her smile faded and the fist buried deeper into his gut. 'Sir Benedictus. I wasn't expecting to see you yet.' Benedictus resisted the impulse to growl. 'Sir Hendry, this is my husband, Sir Benedictus. Sir Benedictus, I have discovered that Sir Hendry is like me. He is new to court. We are comparing our experiences of Windsor.'

Only years of training allowed Benedictus to school his features so that they remained passive as he took in the young man. Sir Hendry was nearer his wife in age than Benedictus was and, damn the man, he had the looks to go with his youth. Of course Adela was going to want to spend time with a man who looked like that. What woman wouldn't? Especially one whose husband had barely spoken to her since their wedding ceremony was completed and who was so focused on what he was doing for the kingdom that he did not have time to talk to her let alone woo her.

'It is an honour to meet you, Sir Benedictus. I have heard much spoken about you.' Sir Hendry seemed like a personable person, the wretch. It would have been much better if he was loathsome.

Benedictus nodded to him. It was all he seemed capable of right now. Where was his normal calmness and why could he not access it? What was it about this situation that was bothering him so much? And most importantly, why was Adela not stepping away from the man?

'The meal is about to begin,' was all he could manage. 'Shall we?' He held out his arm to Adela and she finally stepped toward him, slipping her arm through his. As always, her touch sent ripples of pleasure through him. He clamped his jaw shut, trying his best to ignore them. This whole situation was absurd.

He nodded to Sir Hendry and entered the Great Hall without saying another word.

Her fingers rested lightly on his sleeve, but he felt her touch everywhere. This was getting worse than ridiculous. He should bed his wife, get her with child, and then this incessant yearning would stop. He could go back to his normal self and how young knights looked would cease to bother him.

There was nothing sweet-tasting in this evening's food and Adela merely picked at it. Benedictus would have to have a word with the kitchen. Adela clearly had a sweet tooth and if the food didn't appeal to her then he would do something about it. He rubbed his brow; perhaps it wasn't the food but the company she was keeping. Maybe if she sat by someone like Sir Hendry, she would be eating and laughing. He took a deep swig of wine.

'How did your mission go today?' he asked. This was

the only common ground they had, and he would exploit it until he could find something else to talk about; surely, there was another topic they could discuss.

'I think it went well.'

'Do you have anything to report?' Damn it! He sounded like he was interrogating one of his knights. Had it really been that long since he had made conversation with someone who wasn't working for him that he was out of practise? He thought back but he couldn't remember the last time he'd had a social interaction for pleasure. When he was a young squire, he could remember laughing with his fellow knights about something but that had been more years ago than he cared to think about.

'It's possible,' said Adela. 'I have heard something that sounds strange, but I would rather wait until I am sure before I say anything. I don't want to incriminate someone who is completely innocent of anything other than saying the wrong thing to the wrong person.'

Benedictus nodded slowly. She'd surprised him again. 'I appreciate that. Most people tell me all the trivial detail they have discovered, thinking I want to hear it all. I only want to know what is relevant. How do you know Sir Hendry?' He winced. Where had that last question come from?

If she noticed the bluntness of his questions, she didn't comment on it. 'Medea introduced us. He was very attentive.'

Benedictus took a large bite of bread to stop himself from saying anything and making the situation worse. There were two reasons for Hendry's attention; neither

were good. One reason could be he was trying to get to
Benedictus through his wife, which made no sense. As
a newly arrived knight, Sir Hendry could come and talk
to Benedictus himself more or less whenever he wanted.
As far as Benedictus knew, Sir Hendry hadn't tried.

The other, far worse alternative, was that Sir Hendry
was trying to take advantage of the fact that Adela was
a young woman with a husband who was not around
very much. Men who acted like that would normally
wait until after a woman had a few children with her
husband before trying their luck but not always.

Perhaps Sir Hendry felt the same heady rush of desire Benedictus experienced whenever he was around
Adela. Benedictus put his bread down; the thought of
taking another bite making him feel sick. He supposed
he could put one of his spies on Sir Hendry and discover his motives that way but even as he thought it,
his stomach twisted. There was a thin line between
having a man followed because he was suspected of
treason and spying on him because he was attractive.
Benedictus was not going to turn into the sort of man
who was jealous of his wife and did not allow her freedom. Besides, to be jealous he'd have to care about his
wife and he didn't. These strange new emotions were
all down to the disruption in his life. He'd never had a
wife before and so of course he was going to be feeling out of sorts.

A light touch briefly brushed the back of his hand.
'Is everything well, Benedictus?'

Adela was looking up at him, her moss-coloured

eyes filled with concern. He glanced down at his hand; it was curled tightly in a fist.

He loosened his hand, flexing it and then dropping it onto his lap. 'Forgive me. I have a lot on my mind. There is nothing wrong.' He needed to get a grip on himself. It was far more likely that Sir Hendry's interest in Adela was because of her link with himself rather than because Sir Hendry wanted to bed her.

He glanced down at her. He'd thought her birdlike when they first met but that was because of her timidity. He had not taken the time to study her properly. Her large eyes were her most beautiful feature; they were so expressive. He felt that he could read her soul in them, if only he knew her better. They were framed with long, dark lashes and her soft-looking mouth… Her mouth had him thinking of things he had better not.

She was still thin. She had not been at Windsor long enough to develop any flesh on her bones and he wanted to fill her up, not because she was not attractive to him as she was but because he wanted her to be fit and well, wanted her to be happy. He wanted her robust enough that she could easily bear any children they might have. And…he was going down that route again. He turned to his food and studied it intently, trying to distract himself once more.

Benedictus knew his body wanted her but until now, he had thought this desire more because he *could* have her and after so long without, his body was desperate for release. But was there more to it than that? Her faint, floral scent was delicious; her skin was so soft-looking he was afraid he would damage it with the calluses on his fingers. If she ever let him touch her, that is.

Other men would be able to see she was beautiful, the same as he did. His heart beat faster; what if he lost her to another man before she had even had a chance to relax around him? A man who made her laugh and who had something in common with her.

Benedictus should make her desire him as much as he did her, or he'd even settle for like, but he had no idea how to do that. He had never indulged in the courtly love like his fellow knights. He'd seen no need to get a lady to sponsor his tournaments. Even though it was all often done as harmless fun, he'd been aiming for the top for as long as he could remember and had not had time for anything so frivolous. He rubbed his brow. This was getting out of hand. He was worrying about a woman and he never thought about his personal relationships with women or otherwise.

'Have you made many friends at Windsor?' he asked because if he didn't speak to her, his thoughts would spiral out of control and he'd become a gibbering mess.

'Apart from Medea, most people here are only interested in talking to me because of you, I think.'

His heart clenched. Life at Windsor was the same for him. He had no one he called a close confidant and now he had condemned Adela to the same fate. 'Do you miss your family? You could always return to them if you liked.'

The colour drained from her face; she gripped the edge of the table. 'I do not wish to return to my family. I will be useful to you. Please give me a chance.'

This was a disaster. In trying to make conversation, he'd upset her. 'I'm not going to make you do anything you don't want to.'

'Thank you.' She placed her spoon down. 'I am very tired. Please, will you excuse me?'

She stood and walked away from the table; her head bowed. Benedictus muttered a curse. In trying to talk to her, he had only made things worse and he was no further in getting her to like him than he had been at the beginning of the meal.

Adela tried to undo the bindings of her dress but her hands were shaking so badly, she was unable to pull at the threads. She gave up and lowered herself onto the edge of the bed. She had thought she and Benedictus were making progress, thought that he was finally getting to see that she could be useful, but she had been wrong. He wanted her to be gone from his life as much as he had on that first day.

She blinked back tears. Sorrow had never helped her before; she would not give in to it now. She had made progress today. She hadn't found out anything remotely useful for Benedictus but she had begun to form connections and that was a start. Sir Hendry had been more than happy to introduce her to some of his acquaintances and they had been pleased to speak to her. A couple of them had been interested in talking about France and the warships. Granted, nothing had been said that was particularly out of the ordinary. One man had started to say something and then been shushed but there could have been many reasons for that. She would keep going and when she had proven that it was worth her staying at Windsor, Benedictus would not suggest sending her back to her parents again.

She inhaled deeply and began to tug at the bindings once more, this time managing to pull them free. Tomorrow was a new day. She would find something out. It didn't matter what. Benedictus need only see a hint that she could be an asset to him and he would want to keep her with him. He wouldn't send her away. She couldn't go back to her parents' stronghold now. It would kill her to walk through those gates once more. She could not face her father, especially if he thought she had somehow failed as a wife to the man her father was so proud to call son-in-law.

She slipped her dress over her head and folded it neatly, setting it to one side.

A fresh jug of water had been left on the table and she poured some into her basin. She would wash properly in the morning but there was something soothing about wiping her face at the end of the day, as if she could wash away her problems.

She was drying her face when the door opened.

She gasped, whirling around fast, her arms coming up to cover her body.

Benedictus was standing in the doorway, holding something in his hand. He stopped when he caught sight of her, his eyes widening. The column of his neck moved as he swallowed. Slowly, so slowly, she could almost feel it, his gaze dropped to her neck, her shoulders and down further. She couldn't have moved for all the wealth in the kingdom. His gaze travelled back up and finally met hers. His dark eyes were molten, searing her with their intensity. Her fingers trembled against her underclothes, not from fear but from the sudden heat coursing through her body. A heat that was causing her skin to tighten and her breath to quicken.

He blinked and the look was gone; his normal, stern gaze back, almost as if she had imagined the whole thing. He cleared his throat. 'I'm sorry. I didn't mean to frighten you.'

She pressed a hand to her heart; it raced beneath her fingertips but she didn't think fear was causing the reaction. 'It is your chamber. You are free to come whenever you want.'

He nodded and his gaze dropped to his hand. 'I brought you some of these. You left before they came out and I remembered how much you enjoyed them yesterday.' He held out the offering to her.

She stepped closer. He was holding two of the marzipan sweets, the ones that had tasted so good when she'd tried them the day before. Her heart tightened at the sight. It was a thoughtful gesture; one she would never have thought Benedictus would make. She took one, the pads of her fingers grazing his palm, setting off a wave of delicious tingles up the length of her arm.

The sugar touched her tongue and she couldn't help her involuntary moan. She glanced up at him; his gaze was back to blazing. It was a look she couldn't read but her body responded to it, swaying almost imperceptibly toward him. He blinked and the look was gone again. She straightened. What was happening here? She didn't think she had imagined the heated look but why would he hide it from her? Did the look in his eyes mean he desired her? If so, why wasn't he doing anything about it? She knew she wouldn't object if he touched her; she'd already thought longer about those long fingers on her skin than anything else.

He smoothed a hand along his jaw; the next words he said drove any thoughts of desire away. 'I didn't mean to upset you by suggesting you should return to your parents' stronghold. As long as you want to remain at Windsor, you are welcome to stay with me.' She forced herself to hold herself upright, even as all her muscles relaxed in relief. His words weren't quite a passionate declaration begging her to stay, but they would do.

'I don't ever wish to go back.'

For a long moment he held her gaze. 'Very well.' He held out his hand. 'Would you like this other one?'

She looked down at the sweet at the centre of his large, callused palm. She did want it very much. 'Would you like to share it with me?' She took it from him and broke it in half; the two pieces were tiny. He took his half with a light brush of fingers. She wondered if he felt the same tingling sensation whenever their skin touched as she did. If he did, he didn't show it because the next moment he was turning to go.

'I shall leave you to retire for the evening. I still have much work to do.' Before she could say anything further, he was striding for the door and she was left all alone once more.

Chapter Seven

Life settled into a routine of sorts. In the morning Adela kept to Benedictus's bedchamber; she still couldn't think of them as her own, embroidering a blanket she wanted to someday use to cover the bed. Later, she would venture down to the Great Hall and immerse herself in the chatter and gossip. She was coming to recognise who was fake, who wanted information about Benedictus from her, and who was genuinely interested in becoming her friend. Only Medea and her husband, Theo, fitted into that final category so far but that was fine. It was two more friends than she had ever had in her life before and she was finding she was able to laugh freely in Medea's company. It was a joy to her.

Sir Hendry was an odd acquaintance. He was a firm favourite among the ladies of court who didn't seem to be able to get enough of his charming smile, but whenever Adela was at court he made it his business to talk to her. She couldn't decide if she liked him or not. He never said anything to offend or upset her; he was always charming and kind and yet… And yet, she was not sure of his attentions. It couldn't be that he found her attractive. Her father had reminded her often enough that it was lucky she had his wealth to her name as it was not as if she would have found a husband any other way. As the years had passed, she'd learned to shut out her father's diatribes but this one had stuck, possibly because her husband had shown no attraction toward her. Yes, there had been that heated moment in their bedchamber, but days had passed since then and nothing similar had taken place between them. She was beginning to believe she must have imagined the look in Benedictus's eyes after all.

So although Medea teased her about her conquest of Sir Hendry, Adela didn't think he was always hovering around her with romantic intentions. And yet, he never asked her about Benedictus either, not like other members of the court who were fascinated by her husband and wanted to get close to him via her. She couldn't guess at his motivation. She wanted to discuss it with Benedictus to see whether he thought Sir Hendry's actions suspicious, but that might draw attention to a man who was probably entirely innocent. Adela was always friendly toward Sir Hendry, so perhaps he viewed her as a friend although she didn't think of him as one.

Benedictus didn't count as a friend, either. He barely counted as a husband but she didn't know how to change that. Dinners were still a torture of stilted conversation and long silences. Last night they'd managed to talk about beef for some time but it had hardly been a beautifully meaningful moment. The most interesting dialogue between her and Benedictus hadn't been about them at all.

One afternoon she'd been walking in the grounds of the castle when she'd caught sight of her husband standing ahead of her. It was so unusual to see him out of his antechamber that her heart jolted. At least, she put her body's reaction down to surprise; there was no other reason for it to act in such a strange way otherwise.

She would have carried on walking, ignoring her heart's reaction and avoiding another awkward conversation with Benedictus, but she heard a feminine voice cry out, 'Please,' the word so anguished it hurt Adela's heart; the idea that Benedictus could be hurting a woman making her stomach roil.

Without thinking, Adela stepped into the nearest shadows not wanting anyone to know she was there but knowing she couldn't leave until she knew what was going on.

Before her, in the bright sunlight, a guard gripped the arm of a boy just out of toddlerhood. A woman was curled around the other side of the boy as if trying to shield him from Benedictus's gaze. Benedictus glared down at them all from his imposing height, every line of him rigid with tension.

'I caught him stealing, sir,' said the guard, shaking the lad's scrawny arm.

The woman moaned and clung to the boy. 'He didn't mean no harm, sir. He saw the coins and thought them shiny. He wanted to give me something pretty. He didn't know they belonged to someone else. He's only just a baby. Please…'

At the sound of the woman's pleas the guard's grip became so tight, Adela could make out the whites of his knuckles. 'I've told her we can't be showing special dispensation just because he's a child. Can we, Sir Benedictus? It's the hand or an ear that's got to go. An example must be set.'

Adela's knees weakened and she gripped the wall behind her. Surely, Benedictus wouldn't agree to remove a body part from a boy little more than a baby. But from the way the woman was sobbing, it seemed she believed he would. Adela had heard her husband was a hard man but acting against the child would be cruel, worse even than any of Adela's father's actions. She would never have believed her husband capable of such an action but then she barely knew him. The idea that she could be married to such a tyrant rocked her to the core of her being.

The guard tried to tug the boy away from his mother, and Adela caught sight of his face, his cheeks streaked with tears.

'Please.' The woman let go of her son and threw herself at Benedictus's feet. 'Remove my hand or ear, not his.' She held up her arm as if Benedictus would do it that moment.

'Lady Adela,' said Benedictus, addressing her for the first time. She jumped, not realising he was aware of her presence but of course he was. He knew everything. 'Please come and take the child from Thomas.'

Adela stepped out of the shadows and tried to take the boy from the guard. At first, it seemed as if she would have to fight him, but after a moment he re-

leased his hold and stepped back. Adela leaned down
and scooped the boy up into her arms, holding him
tight; his whole body trembled against her. In that moment she knew that, if Benedictus wanted to harm the
child, he would have to go through her. How she would
fight him she didn't know but she would do everything
in her power to make sure neither the boy nor his mother
were hurt.

'Thomas, I have a very special mission for you,' said
Benedictus. Adela closed her eyes. If Benedictus was re-
warding the guard then her husband must think Thomas
had performed his duties well. 'I have a band of men
in Dover, who are patrolling for French ships. I think a
man with your keen eye will do well with them.'

Adela glanced across at Thomas. His chest was puffed
out with pride and Adela, who had never experienced a
violent emotion in her life, wanted to punch him.

'Report back to your leader and then come to my antechamber for further instructions,' continued Benedictus, ignoring the sobbing woman at his feet.

'Yes, sir.' The guard spun on his heel and raced off,
the young boy and his mother forgotten.

Benedictus crouched down beside the woman, not
the action of a man who was about to mete out some
dreadful punishment. Adela held her breath as Benedictus's hand hovered somewhere near the woman's
shoulder, as if he was about to pat her on the back. He
clenched his fist and pulled his hand away before he
could make contact. He looked up at Adela, pulling a
disgruntled face. She would have laughed at the unusual
expression if the situation hadn't been so dire.

In the end, Benedictus settled for clearing his throat. The mother looked up, seemingly startled to find Benedictus so close. 'He didn't mean to steal, Sir Benedictus,' she began again. 'He didn't realise he were taking coins. He only wanted to show me something pretty. He…'

Benedictus held up a hand and the woman's words ground to a halt. Tears ran down her face and she didn't bother to wipe them away. The boy wriggled in Adela's arms and she set him down. He ran to his mother and buried himself in her arms. Adela moved until she was standing between them and Benedictus, the confined space bringing her very close to her husband. She knew he could move her with barely a twitch of his hand. Even so, she tried to make herself as tall as possible. He would have to get through her if he wanted to hurt the child.

'Thomas is a new guard who takes his duties very seriously,' said Benedictus.

Nobody said anything in response. Benedictus sighed. 'I am not going to cut any part of your son's body off, mistress. You can get up.' The woman didn't move. 'I would try and keep out of Thomas's way but otherwise you can carry on about your day.' There was still no movement from the family huddled on the ground. Benedictus's jaw clenched and Adela repressed the urge to laugh out loud; relief rushed through her, making her limbs lighter. It seemed her husband was kind but he didn't quite know how to show it and wasn't that just the loveliest thing she had ever seen.

Adela reached out and lightly touched his arm; his

muscles were coiled and tense. It was the first time she had touched him as such and she wanted to go on holding him there, exploring the muscles, but now was not the time. 'I think they may be a little frightened by the events this morning. Would you like me to see to them so that you can go about your day?'

He gazed at her for a moment; slowly, his stance softened. 'Thank you, Adela. That would be most helpful.'

He was about to walk away when she stopped him with a tug to his sleeve. 'Why aren't you punishing him?'

Benedictus looked down at the mother and son, still huddled together on the ground. 'I am not an unfeeling monster, Adela. That boy is barely more than a baby. I do not believe he took anything with malicious intent. His mother will make sure he will not make the same mistake again and he will grow up to be a helpful asset to Windsor.' Benedictus clearly believed that was enough explanation because, without saying anything else to any of them, he turned and left.

It took Adela some time to get the woman and her boy to understand that they were no longer under threat of bodily harm. It took even longer to extract herself from the mother once she realised what Benedictus had done for her family. Adela rather thought the woman would spend the rest of her life thinking Benedictus was little short of a god.

Over the next few days Adela had waited for gossip about the event to circle around the Great Hall. She'd held herself still, waiting for the inevitable criticism of her husband's compassion, but nothing had been said.

If she hadn't witnessed the exchange for herself, she would never have known that Benedictus was a man capable of empathy; never have known he wasn't carved from stone.

The knowledge changed something in her. She no longer trembled whenever they spoke to each other during the evening meals. She could even cope with the long silences that often stretched between them because she knew, or rather, she hoped that, like her, he found it difficult to express himself and that perhaps, just perhaps, they were more alike than she had first thought.

She even redoubled her efforts to find out who was spreading rumours about the French warships but she was coming up short. Benedictus hadn't pressed her and she sometimes wondered if he had forgotten he'd ever asked her to do it. Apart from those evening meals, he barely paid her any attention. That was why she was putting herself through the daily rigours at court, trying to find something to discuss with him, something more interesting than the meal before them.

Several weeks after the incident with the boy and his mother, Adela was standing in the Great Hall; she waited to be approached. She'd found she was never standing alone for long before someone came to her. Over in the far corner of the Hall, she could make out Sir Hendry; he was laughing at something someone had said to him. She knew that at some point he would come over to her. Her gaze searched the rest of the crowd but as always, Benedictus was not amongst the many people who gathered to gossip and exchange information. She felt the familiar tug of disappointment but pushed it to one side.

It wasn't long before Medea found her in the crowd. 'Sir Hendry is very easy on the eye,' she commented, watching the women fawning over him.

'Hmm.' He *was* handsome to look at, but he never made Adela's heart lurch, unlike her husband, who only had to step into a space for her whole body to shake with anticipation.

'He does pay rather a lot of attention to you,' Medea speculated. 'I know you don't believe it, but I think he is quite smitten.'

For a moment Adela thought Medea was referring to Sir Benedictus and her heart nearly burst out of her ribs, but then she realised her friend was still looking at Sir Hendry.

'Smitten! I really don't think so.' At least Adela pretty much hoped not. She didn't need that complication in her life.

'There is no need to look so defensive about this. He is always hunting you out and looking for you when you are not here. He even asked Theo whether you and Benedictus were happily married. A risky question, I thought.' Medea laughed but Adela couldn't even smile at such a thought. 'But that only backs up my theory. No one would risk Benedictus's wrath unless they were very keen to hear the answer.'

Adela twisted her dress around her fingers. 'What did Theo say to him?'

'I have no idea. I know Theo wanted to investigate Sir Hendry after that, but Benedictus would not allow it. He told Theo it was not a crime for a man to find you attractive.' Adela squirmed uncomfortably, not sure what part of that statement upset her the most. 'I am sure Theo made it plain to Sir Hendry you would not be available for an affair, so you needn't worry.'

'An affair! You think Sir Hendry wants an affair with me?' Adela barked out a laugh, despite not finding it even a little amusing. 'You must have lost your mind.'

Medea laughed again. 'It is not so out of the question. You are a pretty young woman who's married a stern older man. A man who is almost never by your side and who, everyone knows, spends most of his time on court business. There are many men circling you, but he is certainly the most persistent. If I were Benedictus, I would be worried.' There was a teasing light in Medea's eyes and Adela's stomach churned.

'Adela, I am not in earnest.' Medea reached out and touched her arm. 'You have gone very pale.'

'I would never betray my marriage vows.'

'Of course you wouldn't.'

'Why do people think that I might?'

Medea shrugged. 'You would not be the first or last person to be tempted into a liaison outside of marriage. It is not as shocking as you might imagine. Although, the man who tried to cuckold Benedictus would have to be either very brave or very foolhardy.'

'Is an affair so very normal that people are almost expecting me to have one?' Adela's heart was hammering. It had never occurred to her that infidelity was a frequent practise.

Medea frowned. 'Not everybody, no. I certainly

wouldn't and I know that Theo would never betray me but it does happen and not infrequently.'

'But…it's wrong.' She remembered the shock of finding out that her pious father, the one who lectured her on propriety nearly daily, had, not only a mistress, but also several children with the woman. She'd thought he was an aberration not the norm.

'Yes but…try and remember that most people don't marry for love and when they find it with someone with whom they find happiness, then who are we to judge?'

A cold wave washed over Adela as a sickening thought hit her. 'Do you think… Do you imagine that…' She swallowed. 'Do you think that Benedictus has a woman?'

Medea snorted. 'Oh. Sorry. I didn't mean to laugh. I see that you're serious. No, I do not think Benedictus has a mistress for even the tiniest of moments. No.' She shook her head firmly.

'Why is it so unbelievable?' Was that why he hadn't consummated their marriage because he already had someone to see to his needs? The Hall spun alarmingly. She reached out a hand and touched a nearby pillar; the cold stone anchored her but it didn't stop horrible images crowding her mind; Benedictus smiling at some faceless woman, his broad fingers running down the length of her jaw, cupping her face and dipping his head toward her lips. If it was true, Adela did not think she would ever recover from the humiliating betrayal. 'I hardly ever see him. He comes to our chambers after I have fallen asleep and leaves before I wake. I only know he's been there because his side of the bed has been

used. During the day he is always busy doing something, but he is rarely in here. The only time I spend
with him is during the evening meal and, even then,
we don't talk much and never about anything deep. I
assumed that was just his way but...' She couldn't finish the thought.

Medea was shaking her head again. 'No. Benedictus
does not have a mistress.'

'How can you be so sure? You said yourself that we
shouldn't judge those who must marry for duty finding
love outside of the marriage. That describes my marriage. I'm not convinced Benedictus even likes me.'

'Adela. A man with a beautiful young wife is not
going to go looking elsewhere for...' Medea waved her
hand in Adela's direction. 'He does not need to look
elsewhere.'

Adela shook her head. Medea's implication was
clear; she though Benedictus wouldn't stray because
his needs were being met by his new wife, but Medea
did not know all the facts. 'He has not...that is to say...
we have not.'

Medea's eyes widened as the truth dawned on her.
'Oh.'

Heat spread across Adela's skin. 'He said that we
must get to know each other first.'

'Well, that is very noble and very like him. He must
be dying.' Medea smirked. 'No wonder he is always in
a bad mood.' She nodded decisively. 'I think you should
talk to him about it.'

'About him having an affair? No, I couldn't.'

'Not about that! I really don't believe he is but if it

puts your mind at rest, I will ask Theo what he thinks. He is a very good judge of character and sees more than most. No, I think you should tell him that you are ready for the next stage of your marriage to start.'

Adela shuddered. 'I'm not sure that I am. He's right. We don't really know one another and the other thing… Doesn't it…?' Adela pulled in a deep breath. She'd wanted to know the details ever since her mother's in-adequate explanation, but getting the words out was proving incredibly hard. 'I've heard that it hurts and Benedictus is so big…'

Medea tightened her lips as if she was trying not to smirk. She looked away and Adela wished she had said nothing as her skin began to heat.

'It may hurt initially but it is worth it and…' Medea turned back to her, a mischievous glint shining in her eyes. 'Big can be good.'

Adela still wasn't convinced. 'My sisters implied it was something to endure.'

Medea scrunched her face, all trace of amusement disappearing quickly. 'Ah, poor them. It can be unpleas-ant for some women, maybe some men, if there is no love or at least mutual respect. Then the act between a man and woman is something to be got through rather than enjoyed, but for some of us…' A small, secret smile touched Medea's mouth. 'For some of us, it is one of the best parts of being married. I would imagine, al-though I know I shouldn't say and don't tell Theo that I have, that being in bed with Benedictus will be deli-ciously intense.'

Before Adela could explore what that might mean,

Sir Hendry made his way over to them and broke into their conversation. She couldn't decide if she was relieved or disappointed at the interruption. She did not know if she would have been brave enough to ask for details from her friend anyway; to find out what she meant. Her tone of voice suggested it was something good but Adela wanted more details; she wanted to know how to make it happen so that she, too, could have a special smile whenever she thought of her husband. Perhaps the interruption was for the best. There were some things you didn't share, and Adela had the feeling that Benedictus would want things that passed between the two of them to remain private. That is, if anything ever did come to pass.

Chapter Eight

Every time Benedictus stepped into the Great Hall, his wife was talking to Sir Hendry. He told himself not to care; he didn't care. There was no love between his wife and himself, so there was no reason for him to be jealous of some other male receiving her attention. Provided she was faithful to her wedding vows, then he could not deny her a flirtation with the handsome young man. If his hands curled into fists at the sight, then that was his problem and one he could master. Today was no exception.

He forced himself to stop and talk to Theodore, even as his whole body urged him to storm over and drag the golden-haired knight away from Adela.

Theodore had spent the morning talking to some of the barons who graced the Hall with their presence, and Benedictus wanted to know the outcome of these discussions. In fact, it was imperative he knew all about it. There was no need to go to his wife's side straightaway and every need to stay and listen to what Theodore had to say. 'I think Munroe is going to hand over some of his funds. He…'

'That's good.' Was Sir Hendry touching Adela's hair? Surely, the impudent pup wouldn't be so blatant in his flirtation. He must know Benedictus was in the Hall; must know that Benedictus was a superior fighter; must know that Benedictus would not accept such an obvious challenge.

'Are you even listening to me?' asked Theodore.

'Of course I am.' This was almost intolerable. If Sir Hendry moved any closer to Adela then Benedictus would have no choice but to rip his arm off.

'You could go and talk to her, you know.'

'I don't know what you are talking about,' Benedictus bit out, but he didn't take his eyes from Adela and Sir Hendry so he knew that Theodore would know he was lying.

'Mmm. I see.' Theodore paused for a beat. 'Sir Hendry is a good-looking man, or so I'm told. Quite angelic. He's causing a stir with the womenfolk at court. Are you sure you do not want him investigated?'

'I'm sure.' Sir Hendry giving attention to Adela was not a crime, even if it felt like one to Benedictus.

'You could send him to some distant outpost and be rid of him that way.'

Benedictus grunted.

'If you ask me…'

'I didn't.'

'But if you did, I don't think I would enjoy my wife talking to Sir Hendry for any length of time. Medea might realise she's made a terrible mistake in being stuck with my hideous features for the rest of her life.'

'Surely, she's already realised she's made a serious error of judgement.'

Theodore laughed. The cur was really enjoying himself at Benedictus's expense and he couldn't really blame him. He was acting out of character with all this pointless staring. They should probably continue their discussion about Munroe. That was far more important than this, whatever this was. 'I will go and speak with Adela.'

'Good idea.' Theodore seemed rather too cheerful for Benedictus's liking but he ignored him. He didn't have time to argue with his closest knight. He thought he heard Theodore laugh again but he did not turn around to check.

'Lady Adela,' he said as soon as he was in hearing distance.

She turned. A smile lit up her eyes; a smile so sweet his heart expanded. He couldn't remember the last time anyone had looked so pleased to see him. He was a fool for not coming over to her sooner.

'Sir Benedictus, this is a pleasant surprise. I hadn't thought to see you so early.'

'I came to see if you would like to dine with me in private this evening.'

A blush stole across her cheeks but her smile widened and he felt like a bore. Why had he never suggested this before? It would be far easier to talk to her when they were alone and they didn't have the eyes of everyone from the court on them. Perhaps he would manage more than several curt words for her, which was all he seemed to be able to grind out no matter how hard he tried during those long, endless mealtimes. He liked to think his awkwardness was because they were on show and not because he so lacked imagination when it came to talking, although both were probably true.

'Yes, I would like that.' His heart thudded strangely at her response. She seemed genuinely pleased at the thought of spending time with him.

'Excellent. I shall arrange for food to be brought to our chambers and I will see you there.' He turned on his heel and left without acknowledging the young, golden-haired knight. He'd deliberately ignored Sir Hendry during the whole exchange. He didn't want the knight to think he was bothered by his presence one way or another. It helped him maintain the facade even to himself.

Adela smoothed the front of her dress down as she slowly lowered herself onto the edge of the bed, jumping straight back up again as she reached the mattress. Perhaps it would be better to stand by the window. Sitting on the bed might look like she had expectations for this evening. She *did* have expectations. But she didn't want Benedictus to realise that as soon as he walked into the room. It felt like it was something she should build up to, if she had the nerve.

She wasn't sure how to take Benedictus's unusual request that they dine alone. She could count on one hand the amount of times they had been alone together. Not unless you counted the times they slept next to each other, rigidly keeping to their own sides of the bed. During those long nights, she was so painfully aware of his powerful body so close to hers. Sleeping was nearly impossible.

She paced slowly to the window. Far below her, in the fading light of the evening, people were going about their business, oblivious to the momentous occasion above.

She couldn't guess what this evening was about but Medea's words *deliciously intense*, had been rolling around her mind ever since she'd uttered them.

The door opened and Benedictus walked in carrying a trencher laden with food. A servant followed him, bringing with him two goblets and a decanter of wine, but she only had eyes for her husband. He wasn't wearing a tunic and she could make out the shape of his wide shoulders beneath clothes. She wanted to run her fingers along his collarbone to the dip at the front of his throat. What would he do if she acted on that impulse? Would he think her odd? Or would he welcome her touch as much as she craved for his?

She made her way over to the table. 'This is mostly marzipan,' she said when she caught sight of the food he had brought.

'I noticed you have a sweet tooth.' Adela's heart squeezed; she hadn't realised he'd noticed so much about her. She did, indeed, prefer sweet-tasting food. 'Thank you. I have it from here,' Benedictus told the servant as he took the wine from him.

The man nodded and left, the soft click of the door closing behind him resounding loudly in the silence of the chamber. Benedictus said nothing as he poured the rich red wine. He handed her a goblet, his fingers brushing over hers. The touch shot through her like a lightning strike. She sipped the wine, the fruity liquid doing little to settle her nerves.

'Let me cut you some apple.' He pulled a knife from his belt and began slicing the fruit. 'It might appeal to you more than the bread.' Tiny bubbles of pleasure raced through her at his words. He sounded as if he cared about her, as if he had given her likes and dislikes some thought.

He held out a slice. Her fingers trembled slightly as she took it from him.

He frowned at the sight. 'Do I still frighten you?'

'I am not frightened.' She glanced down at the apple; she might as well be honest. 'I am a little nervous.'

'Tell me what I can do to stop that. I want you to be relaxed around me.' There was a note in his voice that she couldn't identify. It was different from how he sounded around everyone else when his words were always measured and precise. Maybe he was as nervous as she was. The thought calmed her, making her feel closer to being his equal.

'Talk to me. Tell me something about you that I don't know.' She took a bite of her apple. It was delightfully sweet, cutting through the richness of the wine.

He sank down onto the edge of the bed. 'I don't know what to say.'

'I'm not asking for any state secrets,' she reassured him. 'I would only like to know more about you. Do you have any brothers or sisters, for example?'

His eyes widened slightly. 'I have one brother still alive. I thought you knew that.'

She shook her head. 'I know nothing of you. You said *still alive*. Have you lost a sibling?'

He nodded slowly. 'I never…' He stared into the distance. 'It has been a very long time since I spoke about him.'

'You don't have to do it now,' she said softly. 'Not if it causes you pain.'

He shook his head. 'It's fine. I can talk about him. I… I had an older brother, Neleos. He was clever, tough and adored. He could talk to anyone and make them at ease. He was perfect. Even my parents liked him.' Benedictus smiled wryly. 'That's a rarity for them. They value the Monceaux name over everything, but Neleos was special. They had high hopes for him.' He laughed without humour.

'What happened?'

'He was a page at the king's household. There was an accident and a wound that became infected. My parents were very disappointed to be left with me as an heir.'

She frowned. 'You have reached the highest point possible in the kingdom without becoming the king himself. How can you possibly be a disappointment to anyone?'

He shrugged. 'I suppose I am not now, although the idea has become so ingrained in their minds they are unable to act in any different way toward me.' He half smiled. 'You don't need to look so sad. I am used to it.' Adela frowned. Benedictus may say that his parents' reactions didn't bother him, but she didn't believe it for one moment. She knew what it was like to perpetually fail to live up to a parent's standard, and it was not something that made you happy.

'You parents are wrong to make you feel that way.'

'Perhaps. But they are not going to change. They thought they had everything in Neleos and then they lost him. Not that Neleos is ever spoken about. I sometimes wonder if Alewyn even remembers him. Alewyn is my younger brother.'

Adela had never heard of this brother. 'Alewyn doesn't live at Windsor. I would have met him otherwise.'

'No. He doesn't. He used to belong to the King's Knights but he left around six months ago.' A small frown settled between Benedictus's brows, and Adela resisted the urge to smooth it out with her fingertips.

'You sound like you disapprove of that. Why did he leave?'

'He met a woman and married her and I don't disapprove as such.'

If he didn't disapprove, why didn't he say his sister-in-law's name? 'As such?'

'I'm disappointed.'

'Why?'

He stroked his chin. 'Alewyn was a good knight. No, he was a great knight. I guess he still is. He hasn't stopped being one just because he left the King's Knights. I trusted him and when he left it reduced the amount of people in whom I can put my faith to only two.'

Her heart ached for him. He had lost two brothers; two people he clearly cared about deeply. She wondered if he knew how sad he sounded. 'Who are the other two?'

'Theo, who you've met, and Sir William. William is another member of the King's Knights. He is in Antwerp with the king. You will meet him soon, I expect.'

She studied him for a moment. 'You can trust Medea. She is always looking out for your interests.'

He nodded thoughtfully. 'Yes. I suppose I can trust Medea also.'

'And you can trust me.' His gaze locked with hers but he made no comment. 'That makes four people who are definitely on your side.'

'That's more than most people can say,' he said quietly. He cut her another slice of apple and held it out to her. She came to the edge of the bed and took it from him. Instead of moving away she sat down next to him, her thigh brushing his as she did so.

'What else would you like to know about me?'

Being truthful had led them to their most revealing conversation so far; she may as well continue. 'I'd like to know why we haven't consummated our marriage yet.' He jolted as if she had struck him but she carried on regardless; she had gone too far to stop. 'Is there somebody else that you are doing this with?'

He inhaled sharply. 'Are you asking if I have a mistress?'

Part of her, the part who shied away from confrontation, wanted to stop talking, but the new her, the her who was trying to be brave and truthful, willed her to keep going. 'I'd understand if you have.' She wouldn't but she would make it so that he would never know how hurt she would be. She forced herself to sound practical and calm. 'You have not married me for love. I know that the king needed the money from my dowry. If you loved someone else before you met me, then I would not hold it against you.'

Benedictus stood up abruptly and paced to the other end of the chamber, his hands clasped tightly behind his back, the line of his shoulders tense.

'Are you asking me about this because there is someone *you* love? Do you want the freedom to be with him?' He wasn't facing her but his voice was as cold as ice. If she had been having an affair then she would be terrified but at least she could answer honestly.

'No. There is no one in my heart. Even if there was, I would not betray my marriage vows.'

His shoulders relaxed slightly. 'I will not betray my vows, either. Not now, not ever.'

All the air rushed out of her at his statement and she was glad he was looking away from her because she slumped forward in relief.

'If there is no one else, why have we not…' She cleared her throat but the words she was looking for would not come. The last of her bravery was fleeing quickly.

'I told you I wanted us to get to know each other first. I don't want you to be nervous of me.'

'I keep telling you I am not afraid of you.'

He turned and walked slowly toward her. 'Then maybe it is only me who is scared.'

'What are you afraid of?' she asked softly.

He reached out his callused fingers and trailed them softly along the length of her jaw, setting off a wave of delicious tingles down her spine. 'I am afraid I will hurt you. You are so small, so delicate.' His fingers slid behind her ear and into her hair. Her eyelids fluttered closed.

'I am sure you wouldn't hurt me,' she said softly.

He dropped his hand; she immediately missed his touch. 'I wouldn't know how not to,' he whispered.

She opened her eyes and gazed up at him. His dark eyes, normally so calm, were tortured. 'What do you mean?'

The pause before he spoke seemed to go on forever. 'I have never lain with a woman.' His skin burned red but he did not turn away from her. He reached down and lightly brushed the skin of her collarbone. 'I am so desperate to be with you that I'm frightened I would forget to be gentle. I want you to enjoy it. I really don't want to hurt you. I'm so much bigger and what if I...' He shook his head. 'I want you to find as much pleasure as I do but I don't know how to start.'

Adela's heart swelled until it felt like it might almost burst. He wanted her...desperately. She wanted to laugh, to jump, and spin around in triumph. Nothing else mattered, not one thing, in comparison to this admission.

As for him never having lain with anyone else... Well...the unexpectedness of such a confession had shocked her for a moment but now something else was building inside her, something fierce and possessive. They would be one another's first and, God willing, only. She glanced at his face. His skin was burning redder than ever before. For such a proud man to admit to such vulnerability must have been hard. He had been brave and revealed all to her; she must do the same, must forget the joy at his confession and move forward. She smoothed the blanket next to her. 'Please sit.'

He lowered himself back down. She tipped toward him as the mattress sagged under his weight but she didn't straighten as her body brushed against his; nor did he pull away.

'I don't know what consummating a marriage entails,' she confessed, her own skin heating. 'Perhaps, if you explain it to me, we can work out how we can both get pleasure from it. Medea tells me it is one of the best parts of being married.'

She'd been so worried he'd laugh when she told him she didn't know what to do. Since their marriage, it had caused her much anxiety. Instead, he laced his fingers with hers. His fingers were thick and blunt and gave her the comfort she hadn't realised she'd needed. He looked down at their joined hands. 'Have you never seen a couple making love?' he asked. 'The Great Hall at night does not leave much to the imagination.'

'My father kept me mostly secluded. I was not allowed in his Great Hall unless for a special occasion when it would look odd for one of his daughters not to be present. All I know about the act is that it takes place lying down, but that is it.'

He was going red again. It was delectably adorable. Better than any of the marzipan sweets she'd tasted; better than those first heady days of freedom from her parents' stronghold.

'It doesn't have to happen lying down but I think

that's perhaps where we should start. Have you ever kissed anyone?'

'You mean like this?' she asked, leaning up to brush her lips over his jaw. His stubble was prickly beneath her lips. He tightened his grip on her hand. 'Not quite.'

He turned to her and slid a finger under her chin, tipping her face up to his. 'May I?'

She nodded, not entirely sure what she was agreeing to, but trusting him not to hurt her in any way. Not after his confession.

He leaned forward and lightly pressed his lips to hers. The touch so soft and gentle, so different from what she'd expected from him. His lips moved over hers, soft yet firm, cautious yet exploring. Her whole world became where their mouths touched and moved together. Gradually, he slowed and lifted his head. His gaze met hers, an unspoken question in their depths.

'Oh,' she whispered. 'That was lovely.'

He smiled and her heart jolted. His full smile, the one she had never seen before, was beautiful. He leaned forward and kissed her again, firmer this time and more demanding but still wonderful. Her bones turned to liquid as his arm slipped around her back, pulling her closer. He deepened the kiss. For several breathless minutes his mouth moved over hers. When he pulled away, she tried to follow him. She felt his smile against her lips. He rested his forehead against hers and gazed into her eyes.

'You knew what to do then,' she said.

He laughed and her soul filled with joy. His laughter warmed his eyes and relaxed his severe brow. She wondered when the last time was that he'd expressed joy in such a simple way.

'I am not a total novice. I have kissed women and…' He dropped his gaze, pulling away from her slightly. 'I've done some other things.'

A sharp pang of jealousy stabbed her breastbone at the thought of these mysterious other things but she pushed it aside. He was older than she was and had much more experience than she did. It was not surprising that there had been other women. It was something of a miracle that he had not lain with anyone before their marriage. 'Why have you never…?' She gestured to his body, and his cheeks tinged pink once more.

'Before we were betrothed, I nearly did. I don't want you to think I am a saint. I wanted to, very much, but I think I don't have a winning personality or a particularly handsome face.' He smiled at her, his eyes crinkling in the corners. 'No, there is no need to protest. I know I am not like the Sir Hendrys of the world.'

'You are better.' It was important he knew this. For all his handsome looks, Sir Hendry never made her heart skitter like Benedictus did.

But Benedictus only laughed. 'At sword fighting perhaps but not at matters of courtly love. I have no patience to try and woo a woman.' He shook his head. 'It doesn't matter. For whatever reason, it didn't happen. After our betrothal, it would have felt like a betrayal to bed another woman when I was promised to you.'

Her heart swelled. She was starting to like this gruff, honest man more and more. Could he really be as good and true as he made out? And why was it that he was so different in private from the man he presented at court? The man everyone else saw, the man she saw most of the time, appeared hard and cold. The man she caught glimpses of could be thoughtful, kind and loyal and was someone any woman would be proud to call their husband.

His thumb stroked the back of her hand, making her stomach squirm. She wanted to start with the kissing again but wasn't quite brave enough to press her mouth to his; besides, she needed to know something and he couldn't answer if his mouth was occupied. 'I know you have not done it before, but you know what to do.'

He grinned, a surprisingly boyish expression. 'Yes.'

'What happens after the kissing on the mouth?'

'I don't just have to kiss your there,' he said with a smile. 'I could kiss you here, for example.' He swept her hair to one side and trailed his mouth down the length of her neck. She gasped as his rough stubble against her soft skin sent sensation rushing through her. She gripped his arm; his muscles flexed under her touch. His lips followed the neckline of her dress along her collarbone. She gasped with the pleasure of it; never had she imagined anything so exquisite.

His fingers slipped from her hand and began to trace along the skin his mouth had just explored, running along the edge of her dress. 'May I take this off?' His voice was deeper, far gruffer than normal.

'Yes. Please.' Her clothes felt too tight for her anyway, as if the material was scratching against her skin. She couldn't remember why she'd ever thought clothes were a good idea. She stood and turned her back toward him so that he could easily reach the bindings.

He made fast work of them, pulling the dress off quickly, and her breath caught in her throat. His gaze ran over her, his shoulders rising and falling quickly as if he had just been running. Her fingers were trembling slightly, not from fear but from some other strong emotion. She could no longer bear not to touch him. She leaned down and brushed her mouth against his, sliding her fingers into his hair at the nape of his neck. He grunted and deepened the kiss. His hands came around her, their warmth settling against her back.

For an endless moment their lips moved together. A soft whimper filled the air and she lifted her head, surprised to realise the noise had come from her. She gazed down at him; his lips were swollen and his eyes were glazed. A giddy feeling was rising inside her, almost as if she had drunk too much wine but somehow much better. She would have laughed but his hands were tugging at her undergarments. 'I want to touch you.' His words breathed over her skin.

She nodded, not trusting her voice to come out correctly. Together they tugged the remainder of her clothes off until she was standing in front of him with nothing on.

Shyness gripped her. No one had ever seen her like this. The urge to cover her breasts with her hands was strong but the reverent look in his eyes held her still. His gaze travelled down her body; her skin tingled and burned in its wake. He lifted his head, swallowing as their eyes met. 'You are so beautiful.'

Right at that moment, with the wondrous look in his eyes, she felt it.

He licked his lips. 'We were talking about kissing.'

She nodded. 'I like it.'

His eyes flamed. 'Me, too. Did you like it when I kissed you here?' He brushed a finger over her neck and she shivered.

'I did. The feel of your stubble against my skin...' she trailed off.

'I could kiss you here.' He swept his fingertips over the curve of her breast. 'Or here.' He skimmed over her stomach. 'Or even here.' He lightly brushed over the curls at the top of her thighs.

She jerked in surprise and his hand fell away immediately. 'Why would you want to kiss me there?'

He half smiled, still looking slightly dazed. 'To give you pleasure.'

'I can't imagine that it would.'

He grinned. She didn't think she would ever get used to the way his smile transformed his face. It lit up those dark eyes and made her heart warm.

'I think you would enjoy it if I did it right. May I carry on?' He held up his hands but waited for her to nod before skimming them over her hips. 'To consummate our marriage,' he said, 'I would need to touch you there.' He was back at her curls again. 'There is part of you here, that is so sensitive, it will enjoy my touch.' There was a strange ache between her legs, which lent a truth to what he was saying, only she couldn't imagine it. 'Once you are relaxed then part of me will enter you and hopefully we will both find much joy in the union.'

She frowned, momentarily distracted. 'What part of you?'

'My…' He cleared his throat as colour blazed on his cheeks again. She loved it when he blushed. 'It might be easier if… Do you mind if I…?' He took her hand, a question in his eyes.

'I want to know everything.' If this was going to work between them, she *had* to know everything.

He took her hand and guided her down the length of his body. 'Here.'

Beneath his clothes she felt his member. It was hard and he hissed as her fingers closed over it. She snatched her hand away, worried that she had hurt him. 'I don't think that will fit anywhere in my body.'

He huffed out a laugh. 'It will but not until you are ready. First, I think we should carry on with the kissing.'

He pulled her gently onto his lap and began by kissing her mouth again. Very quickly, it wasn't enough. She slid her fingers into his hair and pulled him closer.

He grunted and deepened the kiss, sweeping his tongue in. She gasped in surprise but when he tried to pull away, she held on tightly. It was odd at first but it quickly became the most wonderful thing she had ever done.

His palm traced her waist, along her ribs and up over her breast. She moaned as his fingers closed over her nipple and tugged gently.

He pulled away from her, breathing heavily. 'I'd like to…' He lifted her easily and arranged them so that they were both lying down on the bed, facing each other. 'Is this acceptable?'

'I will tell you if I don't enjoy anything but for now, don't stop.'

He nodded and lowered his head to her breast. She gasped as his mouth closed over her nipple, the sensation so shockingly delicious that she could only lie there dazed as he showered attention on her. Soft moans filled the room and she clamped her mouth shut when she realised they were coming from her, but only moments later the sounds ripped out of her once more. She couldn't help it, not when Benedictus was making her body come alive.

His mouth began to move down her body, over her stomach. He paused, glancing up at her but she didn't utter the words to stop him. Everything he had done so far had been divine and if he said…

The first lick had her arching off the bed. The second had her crying out. Her fingers twisted the covers as sensation took over her body. Her whole world centring on what he was doing. She called out his name and the pressure intensified.

His finger nudged at her entrance. She stiffened slightly at the invasion but his mouth kept up his relentless kiss until her legs relaxed once more. He pushed a finger inside her centre and she exploded. Her back arched off the bed as she cried out, ripples of ecstasy pushing out to the tips of her fingers and every corner of her body. She was gasping, pushing her heels into the mattress. Never had anything ever felt so good, so absolutely divine. Benedictus stayed with her, gentling his licks, until the ripples of pleasure slowly faded away and she slumped, boneless, onto the bed.

'What was that?' she asked as he gently kissed his way back up her body, sending small shock waves of pleasure through her.

'That,' he murmured against her neck, 'is the reason men and women enjoy spending time together.'

He lay down beside her, pulling her against his chest. She was so sleepy, contentedly tired in a way she'd never experienced before. In the cage of his arms, she felt protected from the world. She never wanted to move again.

'There's more, though, isn't there?' Her words came out slurred, as if she'd had a little too much wine.

'There's more,' he agreed.

'Does it get better?'

'It does.'

'I'm not sure I'll live through that.'

She felt his laughter against her back and she smiled. This evening had been wonderful and not just because of all the new sensations, but because she had made her husband smile and laugh and she knew that she had the rest of their lives for her to make him as happy as he had made her.

Benedictus knew he should move, should roll away from Adela and cover her with a blanket. She was sleeping deeply now, having dropped off to sleep almost immediately after he'd pulled her to his chest. He couldn't bring himself to uncurl from the softness of her body.

Tonight had been better than anything he had imagined. The way she had trusted him, the way she had responded to him, and the way he now felt was something he had never thought possible.

Unable to stop himself, he pressed a soft kiss to her neck. She stirred in his arms and burrowed closer, rubbing against his hardness in a way that brought such exquisite torture. His body was urging him to wake her so that he could finish what he had started but his mind reminded him of his promise. He would take his time with her and it would be all the more pleasurable for him when it finally happened.

Even though it was warm for late August, goose bumps were breaking out over her arm. He lightly touched her fingers; they were cold. Reluctantly, he pulled himself off the bed. He rolled her over, pulled back the blankets and rolled her back. She was so slight, his wife. He could see her ribs beneath her skin. A surge of anger swept through him. She hadn't been treated properly by her family. They should have ensured she was fed properly. They had money enough to give her plenty of food and to make sure it was things that she liked to eat. She'd put on a little weight since coming to Windsor, but her hip bones still stood out worryingly.

He pulled the blankets back over her and tucked them tightly around her before letting himself out of the room. He was halfway to the castle kitchens before he realised what he was doing. He was fetching her more food so that she could eat as soon as she woke the following morning. He paused on the stairs. He was only doing this because it was the right thing to do and not because he was in love with her. He did care for her but not in the same way his brother cared for his wife. Benedictus was not like Alewyn. Benedictus would not give up everything he had ever worked for if Adela requested it. No, he was in no danger of that. This urge to feed her came from his need to protect those who could not protect themselves. He carried on with his journey. He would look after her, would make sure that she had enough food and that nothing bad happened to her but he was in no more danger of falling in love than he had ever been.

Chapter Nine

Adela stretched, her eyes closed against the morning light spilling in through the gaps in her shutters. She already knew she was alone. The mattress was not dipped away from her by Benedictus's weight and the air was still and silent. She hadn't expected Benedictus to still be with her when she woke. He never was. What had passed between them last night was not going to change his habits. She rubbed her chest, trying to dislodge an ache that had started up there when she'd realised she was alone.

Last night had been more than she had ever dreamed of, and she should be satisfied with that. She had woken sometime in the early hours with Benedictus curled around her, the heavy weight of his arm better than any blanket. She'd never been held like that, never felt that comfort and support from another human. She'd wanted to stay awake, to revel in the new sensation, but she'd been so relaxed it had not been long before she'd drifted off again. And now he was gone and she had to

hope the actions of last night would be repeated. She
didn't know if she could bear it if they went back to
being stilted around each other again.

She slipped out of bed, gasping as the cool air hit her
skin. She paused to look down at herself. Benedictus
had gazed at her as if she was beautiful and it had made
her feel powerful. In the harsh morning light, she could
see no changes to her body. She had the same slight
body as always with breasts that were hardly there and
a concave tummy. And yet...there was a difference.
Above her hipbone was a patch of red skin. She ran her
fingers over it, but it was not her touch she felt. Instead,
it was the rough stubble of Benedictus's beard scraping
over her skin that had her shivering in delight.

On the table was a slab of bread and a selection
of fruit. Benedictus must have left them for her. She
pulled on her clothes before biting into an apple; the
juice dripped down her chin and she wiped it away with
the back of her hand.

She was amazed she wasn't embarrassed by what
had passed between them. Benedictus had had his head
between her legs. Thinking about it should have caused
her back to curl with shame, but imagining it only had
the effect of her wanting him to do it again and again.

She wondered what her father would say to such un-
godly behaviour and then she shook her head. Why was
she giving him any thought at all? He did not deserve
to take up any of her memory; did not deserve to steal
into her best moments and ruin them. He only would
do so if she gave him the power to.

She went to pick up her sewing but the project didn't

hold its normal appeal; she stowed the fabric back under the bed and pulled herself upright. She wasn't going to spend her morning cooped up in her room like she normally did. Before she could talk herself out of it, she decided to visit Benedictus; if he was too busy to see her then she would go outside. Medea had told her that the queen had a private garden and that it was available for her to walk in and she'd yet to visit it. It was a beautiful morning; Adela could enjoy her own company in the grounds.

But it wasn't the thought of spending her morning amongst the flowers that had her rushing through her morning ablutions. It wasn't the thought of the peaceful gardens that had her practically skipping to Benedictus's antechamber. It was the thought of seeing Benedictus's rare smile; the idea that she might be able to pull it out of him again that drove her onward. This behaviour was not like her; normally so cautious, she didn't recognise the woman rushing along the dark corridors. She made herself slow down to a more dignified walk but when she caught sight of his door, she sped up again, unable to stop a smile spreading across her face.

She knocked lightly on the carved wood, entering when Benedictus called her in.

Her smile faded in the face of Benedictus's fierce frown. For a moment she thought it was directed at her, and her heart beat painfully fast; her legs itched with the desire to run away. She blinked and realised that there were several men standing around the edges of the room; all of them facing Benedictus; all of them stricken.

'I'm sorry, I'll…'

She made to slip back out the door.

'No,' Benedictus barked. 'Lady Adela, you may stay. My men were just leaving.'

Nobody spoke as the knights trudged past her, slowly emptying the room, all of them deathly pale. One, younger-looking man was blinking back tears.

'What's happened?' she asked when they were finally alone.

He shook his head. 'It doesn't matter.'

'It clearly matters to them. One of them was crying.'

Benedictus scowled. 'If it was only one of them, I didn't go in nearly hard enough.'

Gone was the gentle man from last night, replaced with the hard, unyielding knight she was more used to seeing.

She rounded the desk and he stood. 'Would you like my seat?' He gestured toward it.

She shook her head. 'I thought maybe I could sit on your lap.'

For a moment it looked like he might refuse her request, and heat spread across her face. She held herself still; she would not move away until he told her to go. They had begun to knock down barriers between them yesterday evening and she wanted to march forward, not go into retreat.

His shoulders were so tense they could probably be used to support a ceiling. Time seemed to slow and extend. Finally, he let out a long breath. 'That might be quite pleasant.' Her legs wobbled in relief. She didn't know what she would have done if he had rejected her.

He sank back down onto his chair and she clambered on. Once she was there, she wasn't quite sure what to do with herself. She had come only because her body had craved his touch. Although he'd relaxed slightly, he was stiff beneath her, his arms still on the chair's rests. She felt strangely ridiculous perched on the edge of his knees, but to climb down would be worse and so she held herself rigidly still. It was uncomfortable and it was awkward, especially as she could no longer see the expression on his face.

He cleared his throat. 'To what do I owe this pleasure?'

'I came because… I wanted to thank you for the food you left me this morning. It was thoughtful of you.'

'Think nothing of it.'

He didn't say anything further and she had nothing more to add. There was no reason for her to remain sitting here. She began to shift forward. 'I should leave you to it.'

His arms came around her then, banding around her middle and holding her in place as tightly as any rope. 'You don't need to go just yet. No one will disturb us for fear I might make someone else cry.' He tugged her toward him until she was settled against his broad chest; if she'd been a cat, she would have purred.

'You shouldn't make people cry. It's mean,' she murmured, but there was no heat in her comment. She didn't want to argue now that she had discovered her favourite way to sit.

'You don't know what they did.'

'Are you able to tell me?'

He didn't answer. Instead, one of his hands slipped into her hair; he began to pull gently on the strands. She closed her eyes and melted deeper into him, her muscles loosening contentedly. 'You like that?' he asked, keeping up the delicate pressure.

'Yes. Very much.'

'That's good to know.' She could hear the smile in his voice; he was pleased with himself.

'You're still not telling me.' She shifted so that her head tucked under his chin. This is what she had hoped for when she'd suggested their seating arrangement but had not really believed possible.

He sighed. 'It's more because I don't want to think about it rather than because it is a secret.'

'If it's not a secret, then why not tell me? It might make you feel better.' Adela was beginning to realise she had to push if she wanted her husband to talk. He wasn't used to conversing. The problem was neither was she. Together they could get better at it. She wanted to be the person he turned to when he had a problem; wanted to help ease his burdens in any way she could.

He shifted her in his arms but only to get a better hold. 'The French are sending warships along the French coast. They aren't engaging but I wanted to know where they are going. Are they trying to frighten us and then returning to their homeland or are they landing somewhere in Britain? It's something they attempted before in a place near Dover, but the operation failed, thanks to Alewyn. Do you remember me telling you about my brother?'

She nodded against his chest. She remembered every

detail he told her about his life; every detail hoarded like precious jewels.

'Right, well, after that was resolved, I knew I'd have to put men on the coast on a permanent basis. That was the group I put together. They were supposed to be the best. A few days ago they were tracking a French ship's movements but they lost sight of it. It's a disaster that I cannot condone. If the king finds out about their carelessness, then a few tears will be the least of their worries.'

'I see.' She didn't like that Benedictus had reduced someone to tears but she understood why he had done so. 'It must be difficult to run the country.'

He snorted. 'I'm not running it. The king is. I think if I was running the country, my life would be easier.'

She turned her face up to his. He was staring into middle distance. 'Why is that?'

He looked down at her. 'Because I wouldn't be involved in this absurd war with France. I would concentrate on building the wealth of the country and not fuss about land that doesn't belong to us.'

She gazed up at him and her stomach whooshed oddly. She could not believe Benedictus had been so honest with her. Surely, criticising the king was treasonous, especially said by the man closest to Edward. The level of trust he must have in her must be huge and she wasn't sure she had done anything to deserve it.

It was not what she'd expected when she arrived. She'd hoped that she wouldn't be sent away; hoped that she could see the hint of his smile, but this was so much more. She tilted her head until she was looking up at him. She reached up to touch the edge of his strong jaw. His eyes fluttered shut at her touch. Emboldened, she lightly touched her lips to his. It was a flame to kindling. His grip on her tightened; his mouth moved over hers, urgent and demanding. Her fingers tangled into his hair, pulling him closer. She moaned as his tongue swept into her mouth. His hands moved over her, tracing her jawline, the curve of her hip. It was too much and not enough.

His hand brushed her calf and she tightened her grip on his hair. His fingers skimmed the back of her knee, the soft skin of her thighs. She squirmed, trying to get him to touch where she craved him the most. He smiled against her mouth as his fingers grazed her stomach and down to the tops of her thighs. She mewled in protest when he did it again; he lifted his head slightly. 'Is there something you want?' His voice was thick and heavy and layered with amusement.

She wriggled on his lap, brushing against the hard length of him. He grunted and claimed her mouth again, his smile lost to desire. Still, he didn't touch her where she wanted, where she needed him most.

'Benedictus,' she moaned against his lips.

'Tell me what you want,' he said gruffly.

'I want you to touch me,' she breathed.

'Here?' His fingers traced the inside of her thigh.

She shook her head.

'Here.' His hand brushed along her stomach.

'Benedictus,' she ground out.

'Now you have an idea of the torture I am going through,' he murmured against the skin of her neck.

'I'm sorry. I can…' But the rest of her words were lost as his fingers brushed against the most sensitive part of her body. The part where she was craving him the most.

'Oh,' she sighed.

Her head fell back. He kissed her down the column of her neck. Her hand slipped from his hair as her whole world became the pressure and glide of his fingers. Pleasure was building quickly, centring at her core. She gazed up at him; he was watching her intently.

'When you look like that, Adela, you make me want to…'

She cried out, clinging to his body as he pressed his lips to hers once more. Pleasure spiked through her, even more intense than the last time.

How had she ever lived without this in her life?

As the exquisite sensations slowly ebbed away, his kisses gentled until he stopped and raised his head. 'I hadn't planned on doing that this morning.'

'I'm very glad you did.'

He smiled a smile of pure satisfaction.

'Can I make you feel like that?'

He swallowed. 'Yes.'

'How?'

He groaned and closed his eyes. 'I would love to spend the morning showing you but I fear we will soon be interrupted. I am surprised we haven't been so already.'

He tugged her dress back down, rearranging the fabric so that it fell to her ankles. He would have to peel her off him if he wanted her to leave. 'Please tell me what

I must do to you. It does not seem fair that I have felt like that twice and you have not. Is it to do with this?'

She brushed her hand along the hard length of him and his eyes rolled back in his head.

'Adela… I…'

She moved her hand over it, unsure of what to do but watching his face for signs of his enjoyment. He leaned his head back against the chair. With her other hand she undid the bindings of his clothes. He didn't appear to notice, or if he did, he was too far gone now to stop her.

His member sprung forward as she released it. She wanted to study it, to work out exactly how something so large would fit inside her, but she didn't want to stop touching it in case he came to his senses and put an end to this. She ran her fingers down its length and back up again. His fists clenched, his knuckles white.

'That is quite unbelievably pleasant,' he ground out.

She brushed her lips against his neck, hoping he liked it as much as she did. 'What can I do to make it even better?' she murmured against his skin.

'I…' His Adam's apple bobbed. 'I'll show you.' He took her hand and showed her how to wrap it around him. He moved with her for a moment, until she brushed his hand away. She wanted to bring him pleasure by herself. 'This is good?' she asked.

He nodded, his head thrown back against the chair, his eyes closed, and his lips parted. She grinned; she couldn't help it. It was fabulous to see this giant of a man rendered insensible by her touch.

'I will not last long,' he said.

She didn't know what he meant, only that it must be a good thing by the tone of his voice.

She reached up and pressed her mouth to his. He was breathing heavily now.

Shouting from farther down the corridor broke them apart.

'What...' murmured Benedictus, blinking in surprise.

The noise drew louder. Adela leapt of his lap, straightening her clothes. Benedictus was unmoving, his eyes still glazed despite the approaching commotion.

'Benedictus,' she hissed.

Something in his gaze snapped and then he was standing and adjusting his clothes and covering himself up. He strode toward the door, wrenching it open just as Theo appeared in the gap, Adela seemingly already forgotten.

'French warship,' Theo gasped out. 'Spotted in the Thames, farther out toward the sea. We need to go.'

Benedictus nodded. Already there was no sign of the man who'd been enjoying himself in her arms. 'Find Steward John. He will have to stand in for me until we return. I will meet you at the stable.' Theo was already running before Benedictus had even finished speaking. He turned back to her. 'I am sorry, Adela. I need to leave.'

She walked up to him, placing her hands on his chest. 'Stay safe,' she murmured.

A strange look crossed his face, one she couldn't interpret. She wished she knew him better so that she could read him. Was he sad that he was leaving her?

Did it bother him that they had been interrupted just as she was learning how he liked to be touched? If so, he gave no sign of it. He leaned down and brushed her mouth with his. 'I will.'

She followed him slowly out of the room, knowing that the safety of the kingdom was more important than the two of them, but wishing the king to the devil for his absence. The hallways were crammed with people rushing toward the courtyard. She followed along, not sure what to do with herself.

The swell of people outside was overwhelming. She hadn't realised how many people called Windsor their home until they were all crowding in one place. She spotted Medea's curls amongst the jostling courtiers and pushed her way forward to her friend's side.

'What is going on?' asked Medea. 'There seems to be a lot of shouting. Are we under attack?'

'There's a warship on the Thames.'

'Really?' Medea's eyes lit up.

'You're excited about this? Aren't you worried about Theo? About what will happen if the French reach us here at Windsor?'

Horses were being pulled out of their stables as men in full armour clattered toward them. All around them, the din increased.

Medea laughed. 'You should see Theo fight. It is the French who need to worry about him, not the other way around.'

A strange tightness was forming in Adela's stomach. She pushed herself up onto her tiptoes but she could not see Benedictus amongst the chaos. It suddenly seemed

important to see him one last time before he left. She
should have told him how happy he'd made her last
night; how cherished and cared for. How important
their marriage had become to her. How he wasn't just
a means of escape from her previous life. What if she
never had the opportunity now?

Medea's hand touched her forearm. 'You have nothing to worry about. Benedictus will be fine. I haven't
seen him fight often but he is quite something to watch
when he does. Theo often praises the man's skills. He
is not the leader of the King's Knights for nothing.'

Adela shook her head. 'If the French land, it is him
they will be interested in, though, isn't it? Because he
is the leader of the knights and currently the person in
charge of the country in the king's absence. They will
target him before anybody else.' The strange tightness
seemed to be spreading from her stomach to all parts
of her body.

'You've gone very pale. You mustn't worry. This
comes with the territory of being married to a knight.
There will always be some threat they must see to. You
will get used to this feeling of helplessness and soon it
will not affect you so deeply.'

How could she ever get used to this feeling? It was
as if her skin was too tight; she wanted to climb out of
her own body, to get far away where none of this could
affect her. She was just starting to understand Benedictus; just starting to hope that this marriage might be
more than a convenience for both of them; just starting
to understand why Medea looked so coy when she spoke
about what happened in the marriage bed. To lose him

now would be terrible and not just because she would have to return to her parents.

The crowd roared and there was a surge forward. Medea and Adela were swept along, squashed between others. 'He's here,' muttered the woman closest to Adela. 'He's going to save us.'

Adela stood up on tiptoes again but she could not see what was causing the heated reaction. And then, Benedictus swung up onto his horse and the crowd roared. In his knight's armour, he was bigger than ever. Here was another version of her husband. This was a man fired up on passion; a man who looked like he could battle the French single-handedly and win; a man everyone saw as a hero.

He faced the band of knights who had gathered to see off the French. Benedictus raised up his hand; the crowd gradually quietened, waiting for his words.

'Today we face our enemy.' His voice boomed across the courtyard, and Adela's heart swelled even as her stomach twisted with fear. 'Today we show our adversaries that they cannot come into our land whenever they so please. Today we show them what it means to be English.'

The men roared as one and the crowd cheered.

Benedictus whirled his stallion around and kicked it into motion. The knights left the courtyard in a thunderous cloud of horses clattering and people cheering as they followed, streaming out of the gates to watch the men ride away.

'That was very dramatic,' murmured Medea as they were swept along by the crowd.

'Yes. It was another side of Benedictus. One I have not seen before.'

'Oh, he knows how to talk when he wants to.'

'He just rarely wants to.'

Medea laughed. 'Did you speak to him about…you know?' Medea waggled her eyebrows.

Adela laughed. 'I did.'

'And…?'

'And…' Adela found she didn't want to share the details with her friend. What had transpired between her and Benedictus was private, not something to be gossiped about. 'Things are progressing.'

Medea laughed again. 'I am pleased for you, especially as that look on your face suggests that the progression is very good. I would hate for you to miss out on such an integral part of wedded bliss.'

Adela's cheeks heated. She kept her gaze on the departing men, who were now so far away she could not make out the individual parts of their faces. She could still tell which one was Benedictus, though. He was out in front, leading the charge, the sun glinting off his armour. And then he was gone, disappearing behind a bend in the river and out of sight.

The crowd watched for a moment longer but there was nothing more to see, and gradually they began to return inside the castle walls, the collective mood reminiscent of a celebration.

'Why is everyone so happy?' Adela asked as the last of the stragglers disappeared and it was only her and Medea left.

'People have been braying for French blood for

months. They are hoping now is the time for it to be spilt.'

Adela shuddered. 'I do not understand why they are so keen on bloodshed. The people on the boat will be husbands, fathers, and sons just like our men. How can they not see that? Are they not worried that our knights will fail? It is not definite that we will win. How many men will be on that ship? If they disembark, who's to say which of our men will return to Windsor?' What if it was Benedictus who didn't return? She pressed her hand to her stomach. She was going to be sick.

'You are going to have to hide those views if you are to survive at court, my friend. Come. I can see this has upset you. I will show you one of my favourite places in the world. It's somewhere Theo and I visit when the heat of the day becomes too much. It's calming and far away from anyone else.'

Medea began walking away from the castle.

'Are you sure this is allowed?' asked Adela as she followed.

'Why wouldn't it be?'

'Because…'

But Medea wasn't waiting for an answer to her question; she just strode away from the safety of the castle walls as if it was an everyday occurrence. Perhaps, for her, it was.

With every step away from Windsor Adela kept expecting to be stopped. She kept glancing backward, awaiting the call. If her father were to see her now, he would be purple with rage. In his eyes, a woman should always be at home waiting on the needs of the menfolk whether there were menfolk there or not. But nobody called them back and soon the two women were down by the water's edge, birds calling overhead and the sun beating down on them.

Medea came to stop by a large willow tree. 'You could bring Benedictus here when court life gets too much for you both. Only…'

'Only?'

'You had better make sure Theo and I aren't here first. That could be embarrassing for all of us.' Medea laughed and made her way over to the water's edge. It was flowing slowly here. Adela followed her and dipped her hand into the cool water.

'Medea?'

'Yes.'

'How do you make a man…?' She trailed off, not quite able to find the words to explain what she meant.

'You cannot leave that sentence there. I am absolutely dying to know what it is that you want to know. Ah, there is no need for your cheeks to redden like that. I shan't tell anyone what is spoken between us.'

Adela still couldn't carry on. Her lips were paralysed with mortification. She wished she'd never begun. Medea lightly touched her arm. 'I know how hard it is to find another person to talk to. Before you, I could only truly talk to Will's wife and now she is in Antwerp with him. It is lonely being married to such powerful men. We have each other. Now, tell me what it is that you want to know.'

Adela smiled, her heart lightening. 'I've never had anyone to talk to before. My sisters were older than me and married and sent away before I knew they were people to be missed, and my father kept me away from most other people. He wanted me pure of mind for my husband.'

'What a fool your father sounds.' Adela laughed and Medea grinned in return. 'No matter. You can talk to me about anything.'

Adela inhaled deeply. 'I want to know how to pleasure a man using…' She held up her hand.

Medea sat down at the river's edge, patting the dried mud next to her. 'Sit down and I will tell you everything I know.'

Chapter Ten

The brief visit to the river was to be Adela's only re-
spite over the following days. She tried to recall the
lightness she'd felt as she'd laughed with her new friend
but as the time wore on and the men still didn't return,
it was hard to remember ever being happy as fear for
Benedictus pressed down on her.

The excited mood of the inhabitants at Windsor
slowly ebbed away to be replaced with a restless en-
ergy. The people needed to see their men returning
with a victory or even a Frenchman at the gates; anything to stop them from exploding into a fever pitch of
group anxiety.

Adela trailed her fingers over the soft wood of Benedictus's desk. She didn't know if she should be in his
antechamber without him. He had never forbidden her
from entering but she had always done so when she
knew he was already there. This space was private. It
was where he conducted his most secret meetings and
not somewhere a husband and wife could relax. But

this is where she felt closest to him; she could almost smell him; almost see his fierce look of concentration.

She sank onto one of the benches. They were as hard and uncomfortable as Benedictus suggested. Perhaps she could make something to soften them slightly. Embroidered cushions stuffed with hay might make them more palatable and it would give her another activity to fill her day.

She'd made no progress on finding out whether anyone at court had dubious connections with France. With the able-bodied men away from Windsor, all the remaining inhabitants could speak only about what might be happening to them and, because Benedictus was the most prominent of all the men, he was talked about the most. It didn't seem to matter to the women that Adela was his wife. They speculated about almost everything about him; about how good a fighter he might be to how many Frenchmen it would take to bring him to his knees, and what the French might do to him if they did. Gruesome images played on her mind in a continuous loop. The only place she felt truly calm was here, in Benedictus's private space.

The door to the antechamber swung open. As if all her thinking about him had finally conjured him, Benedictus stood in the doorway: dusty, tired but whole. For a moment she was frozen on the spot and then she was running. Benedictus opened his arms and she flew into them, landing against his chest with a sharp *thwack*.

'You're alive!'

She heard his snort of amusement and regretted not being able to see his smile, but she was not going to let go of him. He was solid and unharmed and in her arms and that was perfect.

'I don't think,' he said, laughter lacing his voice, 'that anyone has ever been this pleased to see me.'

'I thought you might die,' she said into his chest.

His arms tightened around her. 'It's disheartening to know you think so little of me. I've been known to be reasonably good at being a knight and to being able to win a fight or two.'

She tilted her head up then to look at him. A small smile played around his mouth, the fine lines around his eyes crinkled, and something in her heart shifted.

'You look tired.' She reached up and lightly touched the deep purple shadows beneath his eyes.

'I am.' He paused, looking surprised. 'Don't mention that to anyone else please.'

Adela didn't question his request. He was a private man who would not like to show weakness. 'Have you slept at all?'

'No.'

'Was there truly a warship in the Thames?'

'Yes.'

Her heart thudded painfully. 'Did you engage them?'

'No. When they saw us riding toward them, they turned and began to make back out to sea. We gave chase and made sure they left the estuary. I have left some of my men there. They are to report to me if the French try again. I doubt they will anytime soon but we must be prepared.' He rubbed his eyes.

'Why do you think they will hold off for now?'

'They were not expecting such a strong reaction from

us. With the king in Antwerp they probably thought they could swan into the country and into the seat of power. Now they know it will not be so easy.' He dropped his arms and she took a step backward. 'I trust you have been well in my absence.'

'Yes.' She didn't know how to say that she had not been completely well. There had been a hollowness in her chest, which appeared to be filled now he had returned. She didn't know if he would welcome such a sentiment. They were more relaxed around each other than they had ever been, but there was no hint that he returned her growing attachment.

He moved over to his desk, groaning as he sank down into his chair. 'Have you seen Steward John?'

'No.'

'I suppose it is too much to think he will come and see me with a report of all that has been happening in my absence.'

'You cannot think about carrying on with work business now. Surely, you need to rest.'

His mouth twisted. 'I cannot rest. If I'm not seen to be doing my duty…' He shrugged.

'I understand.' She didn't. She couldn't fathom why finding out what went on at the castle was more important to Benedictus than his health. She did understand that this was his way and just because they had spent time exploring one another's bodies, it didn't mean she could change him. His duty came first and everything, *everything*, else came second. But what she didn't understand was that no one seemed to be helping him. Was it because he put up walls between himself and the rest of the world? Or was it because nobody cared to look deeply at him? Was she the first person to notice how much of a strain this constant burden was having on him? And there was a part of her, a part that she tried to push down, that was a slice of hurt that he wanted to carry on with his work more than he wanted to spend time with her. She knew it was too much to ask of him. Theirs was a marriage made from political and financial reasons but even so…

A swift knock at the door and their time together ended as quickly as it had begun. Steward John let himself in. She would not be able to talk to Benedictus now. He would be all court business, and who knew when she would see the softer side of him again. She turned to look at him before leaving. Any trace of amusement was gone from his features; he was the hard knight, the one in charge of England and who would work himself to death if the situation required it. She let herself out of the room without another comment.

It was evening again. There was no sign of Benedictus at the meal but there was much talk of him. He had been a hero, it seemed. He had ridden through the day and night, urging the others on. When the ship had come into view, it had been Benedictus who had led the charge toward it, never appearing to flinch or swerve from his target.

The French had held steady for a moment but Benedictus had thundered toward them and they soon turned their boat around. His bravery, his speed, and his strength were all talked about, but no one seemed

to notice he wasn't there to celebrate the victory. Adela
sat alone at the top table, a strange mixture of pride and
pity swirling within her as she tried to force the meal
down while also looking content to be alone. It was a
hard act and she wasn't sure she was mastering it, not
if the pitying looks Medea kept shooting her were anything to go by.

After a while she could take it no longer. She spoke
quietly to one of the servants and then slipped from the
Great Hall without encountering any resistance.

The corridor outside Benedictus's antechamber was
quiet. She pressed her ear to the door but no deep, grav-
elly voices sounded from within, and she knew that
John the steward was eating with the rest of the court.
Benedictus must finally be alone.

She stepped inside and stopped as cold horror washed
through her. Benedictus was slumped over his desk, his
head resting at an awkward angle. She dashed over to
his side, letting out a shaky breath when she saw he was
still breathing. He was alive but sleeping so deeply. She
touched his shoulder; he didn't move.

'Benedictus.' She shook him harder. He only grunted
in response. 'Benedictus. You can't sleep here. You need
to get up.'

'Adela,' he muttered.

'Yes, it's me. Come on. Get up. I'll help you to your
chamber.'

There was no response.

She leaned down and lightly pressed her lips to his
jaw. His four-day growth of beard was soft under her
lips. She ran her mouth to the soft skin of his neck and

kissed him again. His pulse beat steadily against her, and she breathed him in.

'Adela,' he murmured. 'I dream of you.'

Her heart leapt at his words but she pulled herself upright and kept her tone practical when she said, 'You aren't dreaming now. You are sleeping on your desk. If you don't get up, your muscles will be in so much pain you'll wish the French had finished you off.'

His eyes cracked open slightly. 'Adela.' He frowned, lifting himself a little. 'How long have you been here?'

'Long enough to know you are done for the day. Do you think you can stand, or should I call someone in to help?'

'Of course I can stand.' He pushed himself upright, stretched and then winced.

Her hand fluttered to his shoulder. 'Are you already aching?'

He grimaced. 'It's like I've been in a torture chamber all day.'

'If you can make it to bed, I promise to rub out all those kinks in your back.'

He smiled and her heart skittered. His smile was truly lovely. 'For that, I will brave a thousand French warships.'

'One was enough, thank you. I have been out of mind worrying about you.'

He frowned sleepily. 'You have? I told you I would be fine.'

'That didn't stop me. Anything could have happened.'

He rested a giant hand on her arm. 'You will be taken

care of if I die. I have made provisions for you. Do not think you would have to go back to your family.'

'That was not what was troubling me,' she said lightly, unwilling to let him know just how much she was coming to care for him. Not when he'd given no indication he felt the same way. 'It's time for you to stop stalling and get moving. Otherwise, I *am* going to get someone to help me carry you up the stairs to your chamber. I don't care if that offends your dignity.'

He groaned. 'I didn't realise I had married a bossy wife.'

He stumbled against the desk and she slipped an arm around his waist. 'I prefer to call it *supportive*.'

She thought he might pull away from her, might be too strong-willed to accept help, but he slung his arm around her shoulders and allowed her to tug him out of the room. As they made their way along the long, winding corridors, his heavy weight pressed down on her. She tried to hide how much it affected her but it wasn't long before she was panting with effort.

'I'm sorry.' He tried to lean away from her but he stumbled and she tugged him close.

'It's fine. We will make it together.'

They began the heavy ascent up the winding staircase to his chamber.

'Did you sleep at all during the last four days?' she asked.

'I must have done. No one can stay awake for that long.' He stumbled over a step.

'You cannot have slept much. You are almost drunk with tiredness.'

After an eternity, they made it to the top. Adela was breathing heavily now, not even able to hide it; Benedictus's eyes were half shut as they staggered to a stop. 'It's only a few more steps to your chamber.' Whether she was trying to encourage herself or him, she wasn't sure.

'You must stop calling it that.'

'Calling it what?'

'Your chamber. I mean my chamber.' He let out a growl of frustration. 'I mean that it is both of our chamber. Call it ours.'

She smiled, her heart lightening. 'I will from now on, if you promise me to keep going.'

'It suddenly seems impossible,' he confessed.

'Imagine if one of your knights finds you sleeping right here. It will not do any good for your formidable reputation if someone finds you asleep like a baby in the corridor.

He grinned and her heart turned over. Sleepy and smiling he looked nothing like the imposing giant of a statue she had met on her wedding day; the man most people saw when he spoke to them. Instead, he looked adorable.

They managed the last few steps together. Inside the chamber, a bowl of stew steamed on the table. They staggered around the edge of the bed and he sank down, leaning against the wall with his legs propped up on the mattress. She brought the bowl of stew to him.

He blinked at it owlishly. 'What's this?'

'It's stew.'

'Yes, but what's it doing here?'

She froze, her hand outstretched toward him. 'You

missed the meal and so I thought you might want something to eat. Did I do wrong?'

'No. It's just…' He took the bowl from her. 'I'm used to being the one who does the caring, not the other way around.' His gaze reached hers; an unreadable emotion flickered in the dark depths of his eyes. 'I am grateful.'

He wolfed the stew down in several large bites. She took the bowl back off him, wishing she'd thought to ask for more for him. He obviously had eaten as little as he had slept, but by the time she had returned the bowl to the table and turned around, he was already asleep.

It was the first time she'd been awake when she was able to study him without him being aware of it, and she fully intended to make the most of it. She picked up one of his hands; it was heavy in her grip. Long fingers ended in blunt nails, scars criss-crossed over the back, a deep one running along the edge. She turned his hand over to look at his palm. She slowly traced the rough calluses, beginning to understand him a little better. His life had been hard and he had faced it alone. No wonder he was so stern all the time. She dropped his hand and moved to his boots, unlacing them and tugging them off. She undid the ties of his tunic but would have to wait until he rolled over before she could slip it off his arms; he was far too heavy for her to move by herself.

A soft knock at the door disturbed her from her work. She pulled it open only a slit. Theo was standing on the other side.

'I'm looking for Ben.'

'He's asleep. I do not want to wake him for anything less than life-threateningly urgent matters.'

Theo gazed at her for a moment and then a warm

smile spread across his face. 'It was a happy day when Ben married you. Very well. I shall say that he is not to be disturbed.'

Adela shut the door. Benedictus hadn't stirred during the exchange. She hoped she had done the right thing and that he would not be angry with her for interfering when he woke. Even if he was, she knew she had done the right thing. She could not let him carry on working in the state he was in now.

She slipped into bed and curled into his side, listening to his deep breathing. For the first time in days, she slept soundly, too.

Light from the window woke her. She had forgotten to close the shutters the night before and now the sun was streaming into the room. She blinked. Something was different. She rolled to one side and encountered a wall of muscle. Benedictus had not stolen away while she was still asleep.

At some point during the night, he had shed his tunic and now all he wore was a thin undergarment. The muscles in his chest were so clearly defined through the material he might as well be naked. She wanted to reach out and trace the lines of them but something about the way he was breathing told her he wasn't asleep, and she wasn't sure how he would take such a touch.

She tilted her head upward and looked at him. He was awake and watching her.

'Good morning,' she murmured. 'How are you feeling?'

'Like I need to sleep for the entire day but I should get up and carry on.' Despite his words he didn't move.

'How are the kinks in your back?'

His mouth pulled up at the corner. 'It feels as if I have been in a fight and lost.'

'I promised to rub them out for you last night.'

'You did.'

'But I suppose you had better get on with your day.'

He laughed, his eyes crinkling at the corners. 'I suppose I should.' Still, he didn't move.

Her heart began to flutter. 'If you'd like to stay a little bit longer then I could do it for you now.'

'Hmm.' He appeared to give it some thought. 'It might be difficult to run the country if my back continues to ache like this. I wouldn't be able to concentrate on anything.'

'Indeed. So I suppose you could say that it is essential.'

He nodded seriously. 'I suppose you could.'

She smiled, happiness bubbling up inside her. This was all she had ever wanted; to be able to do something for him. She reached up and lightly touched his undergarments. 'I think it would work better without these on.' She hoped she sounded calm and not desperate to touch his skin.

'Ah, well, if you think so.' He sat up and tugged the rest of his clothes off; the muscles in his arms bunched. She couldn't tear her eyes away from the movement. She'd caught glimpses of his forearms, enjoyed watching them as he moved, but the rest of his arm was magnificent. She reached up and traced the curve of his biceps. She laid her hand flat against the muscle; she could not fit her hand around it. She brought up her other hand but together they couldn't encircle it.

'Impressive,' she murmured.

He laughed huskily. 'Thank you.'

Her fingers followed the line of his shoulder until she reached his collarbone. There was a smattering of hair across his chest. Without thinking, she took some of it between her fingertips. It was soft. She tugged lightly and he rumbled deep in his chest.

Her throat was suddenly dry. She could spend all day studying him but she had promised him a massage. She slipped from the mattress and made her way to his side. 'You should lie on your stomach.'

She was surprised when he did what she said without comment. The room settled into a heavy silence. She hovered over him, taking time to study him some more. He was all defined muscle with no hint of fat. His back was corded but criss-crossed by dozens of scars, some of them tiny, others a little thicker. She wanted to ask him about each one, to learn their story and how they had made him the man he was, but she held her tongue. This moment was about bringing him pleasure, not about reliving his worst moments.

She leaned over him. 'Tell me if I hurt you.'

'I really doubt that you could.' She pinched his skin. He laughed. 'I have felt much worse.'

She looked at the scars again. 'Of that I have no doubt.'

She reached out and skimmed a hand along the length of his back. He shuddered at her touch and she smiled. She returned to his shoulders and began to knead the tight muscles coiled there. He groaned and she kept going, thrilled to be able to touch him as much as she wanted and that he welcomed it.

Benedictus had died and gone to heaven. That was the only explanation for this exquisite torture. Adela's hands were all over him and his body was burning up with sensation. He wanted it to go on forever; he wanted it to stop so that he could cover her body with his own; he never wanted to leave the room. He would give up everything that he owned, his position in life, and everything he had ever strived for to lie here with her hands upon him forever. Slowly, Adela worked her way down the length of his back until she was at the very base. His fists tightened as she dipped lower only to return her attention to the curve of his spine.

And then she stopped moving, resting her hands lightly against his skin. He told himself not to be disappointed as she finished. She had given him more pleasure than he had ever experienced. He could leave now and carry on with his day. He only had to will himself off the bed and it would happen.

She slipped from his back and he closed his eyes. That moment of bliss was enough. It would sustain him for the rest of the day. The rest of his life, if it had to. He had no reason to feel bereft now that her touch was gone. He clamped down the odd urge to beg her to carry on; he never begged anyone for anything.

The warmth of a damp cloth running off his back had him jolting in surprise. He bit his lip to stop himself from groaning with pleasure as she moved over him, softly running the cloth down the length of his legs and back up again, washing every part of his skin.

'Turn over.' He froze, almost afraid to do as she asked. If she looked into his eyes, she would know what level of control she had over him. She'd know that she could very easily make him vulnerable; that all it would take was her touch and everything he had striven for would fade away. 'Turn over,' she repeated. This time her tone had bite. If asked, he would have said he hated being told what to do; would have denied himself rather than comply, but a bolt of need shot straight to his centre and he was helpless to do anything other than follow her command.

He rolled over onto his back and gazed up at her. Her dark hair was loose around her shoulders and falling in waves down her body. There was a look in her eyes that had his heart pounding, but before he could try and interpret it she traced the cloth along his collarbone and down to the centre of his chest, resting above his pounding heart. She must be able to feel how hard it was beating but he was too far gone to be embarrassed about her realising just how much power she had over him.

She continued to trace the lines of his chest, down over his stomach and around the tops of his legs; the sensation so exquisitely delicious he clamped his lips together to stop himself from calling out her name. Any movement was beyond him now. The entire French army could arrive at the gates of Windsor and he would let them take control so long as nobody disturbed him in this endless moment.

The lightest of touches grazed against his length;

he closed his eyes tightly. She passed over him again, firmer this time. He clenched his teeth. It was embarrassing how ready he was for this, how he knew he would not last very long if she carried on. And then she held him like he had shown her and began to move in a rhythm that had him calling her name and urging her on, telling her how good she was making him feel and how he never wanted her to stop.

The first lick of her tongue had him bucking off the bed, and then there was nothing as sensation overtook him and he could do nothing but feel. It was moments before his release built inside him, curling his toes and arching his back off the bed. He tried to pull away from her but she didn't move, and all too soon he was spilling inside her. The ecstasy went on and on until he could no longer remember his name or his reason for being. There was only Adela.

After, he slept deeply and without dreaming.

Awareness came back to him in slow snatches. The *clunk* of something being moved on the table, the *swish* of fabric, a small sigh and then darkness again.

Later, he blinked awake to the sound of splashing water. Adela was standing by the table, her back to him, pouring water into a bowl. She dipped her fingers into the liquid and then flicked them dry.

'Adela,' he croaked; he cleared his throat. She turned to him, her eyes wide. 'How long have I been asleep?'

'It's midday.' She took a tentative step toward him. 'Are you very angry?'

She looked afraid and his heart sank. What had she done? 'Why would I be angry?' he asked cautiously.

'Because I have let you sleep so late. I thought about waking you but the shadows beneath your eyes were so dark. And I…'

Should he be angry? He didn't think so. He had not slept so late since… He thought back; he had never slept so late and all manner of things could have happened in his absence. But for the first time in his life, he could not bring himself to care. 'I would be a complete boar if I was angry with you for taking such good care of me.' A blush spread across her cheeks; an answering heat warmed his own. 'I meant with the food and the letting me sleep, not…' He waved his arm around as the heat began to increase. She giggled and the sound was so joyful he couldn't help his own smile. She made him feel things; things he had not felt in so long, perhaps ever. When she laughed or smiled, his heart was lighter, softer almost, as if it was expanding. 'I do mean that, too. I am grateful for the other thing, too. Where did you…? How did you know…? What made you think to do that?'

Her cheeks turned a darker red. 'I wanted to know if I could make you feel the same way you made me feel. I asked Medea for…uh…for some pointers while you were away. That was one of the things she talked about. Did you like it?'

The thought of Adela learning how to please him had him hardening once again. He swallowed at the memory of her moving over him. When he glanced over at her, he realised she was waiting for his response, her hands clasped primly in front of her. 'I enjoyed it very much,' he said. The words sounded oddly formal. He tried again. 'It was the best thing that has ever happened to me. I can only hope you will let me return the favour today.'

'Benedictus!' She fanned her face and he laughed.

'You look so different when you are happy,' she said, walking toward the bed. She brushed the hair from his face and his whole body tightened. He wanted her to touch him again, to feel her hands all over his body, and yet he did not know quite how to ask. This was all so new, so tentative yet beautiful, so deliciously sinful, that he was almost afraid to say the wrong thing in case he ruined it. He, who was afraid of nothing and no one, was worried about upsetting the new balance the pair of them had found.

He reached up and tugged her down toward him until he could brush his lips over hers; she opened to him eagerly and he groaned. He gave her a firmer tug and she tumbled on top of him.

This. This was worth not spending the morning on trivial matters of the state. Running over arguments and decisions with people who could barely hide their dislike of him. The soft press of her lips on his was enough to make him undone.

A knock sounded at the chamber door.

She froze, her mouth on his. He wanted to ignore the interruption, to pretend they were somewhere else, to forgo his duties for just a moment longer. But he knew that he wouldn't. He could already feel the familiar weight of responsibility pressing him down, the shackles that so rarely left him, not even in this private moment.

'I told them to come only if it was an incredibly urgent matter,' she said against his skin. She slipped off
him before he could say anything and he almost groaned
at the loss of contact.

'I'm sure whoever it is believes their issue is life or
death, but it will be inconsequential, no doubt.' Despite
his words, he was already moving, heaving himself
from the bed. He could not ignore a summons. His role
in life meant that he did not have that luxury.

'Please will you answer it? I will get dressed.'

She scurried to the door while he pushed back the
covers. He found his clothes neatly folded on a chair
in the corner of the room. She was very organised, his
wife, as neat as a knight on a military campaign. He
should get her to train some of his men on how to keep
their belongings ordered. He smiled at the thought of
his diminutive wife bossing around an army of knights.
He could picture it all too well. She was meek and mild
until the situation required it and then she was bold.
Theirs might have been an arranged marriage but he
had been lucky. They might not have the devoted love
his brother had found with his wife but hopefully they
could form a friendship and, if they were able to satisfy
each other in bed as well as it appeared they did, then
their future looked pleasant.

He pulled his tunic on as he heard Steward John's
voice on the other side of the door. He rolled his eyes;
the man was an over-the-top fusser. No doubt whatever the cause of the interruption was entirely trivial.
He fastened the ties of his tunic, glad that Adela had
washed him. He'd been grimy and exhausted from his

time on the brief campaign but now he was rested and clean. Yes, marrying Adela had been an excellent practical decision.

Adela should head into the Great Hall. Now that the men were returned, the gossip would be in full swing again. If she was going to be of use to Benedictus, then this would be her opportunity. She was beginning to piece some things together. There was a group of people discontented with Benedictus's rule but she was only hearing second-hand whispers. The same names kept cropping up but she had no proof and would not accuse anyone without it.

She should head into the Hall and get talking. Her feet had other ideas. They took her straight past the entrance and out into the courtyard. A light, late-summer breeze played with her hair as she weaved her way through the busy workers. She stopped at the gatehouse. She wanted to step outside, to walk down to the river and feel the cool stream washing over her fingers. She wanted space to think, to remember each touch, each sigh, each moment, she'd shared with Benedictus.

But she could hear her father ranting about how a woman should not be alone, and her courage failed her. Frustrated with herself, she headed toward the queen's gardens. She still hadn't managed to walk between its walls, and the lure of quiet privacy was calling to her.

'Lady Adela.' Her stomach sank as she turned to see Sir Hendry walking toward her, his permanent smile fixed on his face. Why was it she found this smile so odd when other women of the court were constantly

sighing over it? She found her husband's stern features
so much more appealing and yet she could not explain
why. 'You weren't in the Great Hall this afternoon. Are
you well?' His forehead was creased in a small frown.
He seemed genuinely concerned about her health. A
wave of nausea swept through her; perhaps Sir Hendry *was* smitten with her. Goodness, what would she
do about it if that turned out to be the truth?

Even if Benedictus was the stern, unapproachable
knight he appeared to be to everyone else but her and
they never became any closer than they were now, Adela
still wouldn't betray her marriage vows. It didn't matter
if other people did this when faced with a loveless marriage; she was not one of them. She didn't wish to hurt
Sir Hendry, though. Despite her earlier reservations, he
seemed like a pleasant man. He was very attentive and
never had a bad word to say about anyone. She would
hate for him to be developing feelings for her; feelings
that she would never return.

'I am well. Thank you for your concern. I merely
wished to spend some time alone.' She hoped he would
take the hint and find somewhere else to be, but he fell
into step beside her.

'Your husband was very impressive when confronting the enemy, Lady Adela. I don't believe the French
will return to England anytime soon. They were completely cowed by his might and aggression.'

Adela glanced at him. He appeared completely sincere in his praise. Surely, if he was interested in her as
a woman, he would not praise her husband so resolutely.
His words would only serve to make her prouder of her

husband. He was a confusing puzzle but not one she wanted to spend much time thinking about.

'I would have liked to have seen Sir Benedictus in action,' she confessed.

Sir Hendry straightened. 'Would you? How strange. Most women would shy away from conflict.'

Adela snorted. 'We see fighting all the time. Men love to show off their prowess at jousts and tournaments.'

'It is not the same. The fighting you see at court is for your entertainment. The French are a fearsome enemy.'

'Have you seen the French fight?' She couldn't imagine when he had done so as he came from the north, far from the enemy's shore, yet he sounded so certain. Yet, if the French were that good, why were the English considered to be so much better?

Sir Hendry stared into middle distance. 'I do not need to see them to know. The art of war is no place for women.

Adela swallowed down her irritation. Benedictus might be stern but he was never patronising. Still, she didn't want to upset Sir Hendry by arguing with him. 'No. Indeed. In truth, it is not that I want to witness an army at war. I do not want to see blood and death, but I would like to have seen Sir Benedictus and to know that he was safe.'

'You care for Sir Benedictus, then?' His glance toward her was swift; she would have missed it if she had not been looking straight at him.

The glance rattled her although she didn't know why. 'Of course I care for him. He is my husband.' Even as she finished speaking, she wondered whether it was more than that. If their marriage was taken away from her tomorrow, would she miss Benedictus for himself and not just the freedom and protection his name offered her? She wasn't sure. She knew she had enjoyed their time together in the bedchamber. He showed a different side to her then. He was much more bashful, more considerate, and more likely to smile and laugh. But when he wasn't… He was so wrapped up in court business that he had no time for joy. He was stern and unapproachable and could barely manage to have a stilted conversation with her while they ate dinner. It was as if she was married to two completely different people. She knew which version of him she preferred but it was the one she got to see the least and yet the thought of being parted from him… Her stomach twisted. No, she did not like that idea at all.

'Can I take it from your silence that it is not as straightforward as all that?'

She folded her arms across her chest. 'Sir Benedictus is a good man.'

'Yes. Of course he is. Anyone can see how hard he works for his country. But does that make him a good husband?'

Adela stopped, desperately uncomfortable with the way this conversation was going. 'I don't think it is appropriate for us to discuss this.'

Sir Hendry squinted down at her. 'I apologise. I had not meant to be so blunt. I look at you and I see a young woman tied to an older man and it makes me sad. I do not mean to offend you in any way.'

There was nothing flirtatious about Sir Hendry's

words. If it had been Medea saying these things, Adela wouldn't feel disconcerted. As it was, she didn't know quite what to say to the man. She knew how her marriage must look from the outside. No one saw Benedictus and her when they were together in private. During the meals they must look awkward together, but without giving the details of their private time, she could not reveal the details of her marriage. 'Thank you for your concern. My relationship with my husband, however, is not something I wish to discuss.'

Sir Hendry nodded and his smile returned. 'Let us talk about something else, then, because I do not wish to put you out of sorts.' He paused. 'Before we do, I would just like to say that I do hope that you feel you could talk to me. We arrived at court at the same time and I feel we have a connection. I would hate to lose that because of my thoughtless words. Please know the motive behind my words is kindness, nothing more.'

His blue eyes were full of earnest. She thought perhaps he did mean well but she wanted to get away from him all the same. Not for the first time, she wished she had not been so friendly with him on her first day at court. If she hadn't been so keen to be of use to Benedictus she would not have invited Sir Hendry's attention, and then she would not be in this predicament. She didn't think he would leave her alone today until she had assured him that their friendship was still intact. 'You must not worry. I have not taken offence and I regard our friendship as much as I ever have. I would, however, like a little time alone. Not—' she held up a hand before he could say anything '—because I am upset with you. Rather, it's been a long couple of days and I do not think I am the best conversationalist at present. I'm hoping to have some time in quiet reflection in the queen's gardens.'

'Allow me to escort you there and then I will leave you in peace.'

She would have preferred it if he'd left her alone straightaway but it was not far to the gardens and so she said nothing. Sir Hendry kept up a steady stream of conversation as they meandered past the busy buildings that made up the courtyard at Windsor. She nodded and agreed when there was a pause in his monologue. She was glad when he left at the garden gates, relieved at last to be alone. She hoped she had said all the right things, that he was reassured that all was well between them, but she couldn't find it in herself to care desperately, and presently he went out of her mind entirely.

She wandered about the herb beds, not really seeing the fragrant leaves. Her mind was back with Benedictus and the blissful morning they had spent together.

Chapter Eleven

For the first time in his life, Benedictus could not concentrate. He tugged on his cuffs, hoping to pull his attention back to the task at hand. It was not the best time to have his mind wander. The French warship in the Thames had been a direct insult to the English seat of power. Edward would probably want to retaliate and Benedictus should no doubt write a detailed report on the incident to be sent, at haste, to Edward in Antwerp.

On top of that, several border disputes had erupted among some lesser barons, and he really needed to deal with that before the situation got out of hand. He didn't want to have soldiers fighting civil battles when he had France to worry about.

None of the pressing issues were commanding his full attention. Right now all he could think about was Adela. He wanted to be back with her, moving over her body, listening to her soft sighs. He wanted…

'And yet,' blustered the baron in front of him, breaking Benedictus from his fantasy, 'Hadleye still had the audacity to…'

'Enough.' Benedictus slammed his hand down on his desk and the two bickering barons jerked backward. Landlan's mouth hung open as if he was about to continue talking but fortunately, no sound came out. 'Landlan, you will not make any further incursions onto Hadleye's land.' He held up his hand. 'No, I don't want to hear any more. Hadleye, you will stop taking able-bodied workers from Landlan. I do not want to see either of you here again, but if I do, you will both be stripped of whatever land you have and I shall divide it between the knights who are currently serving King Edward without complaint.'

Hadleye's mouth spluttered open. 'You can't speak to us like that. You are not the king.'

Benedictus's fist curled. 'As far as you are concerned, I am. If you would like to travel to Antwerp and regale King Edward with your pitiful woes, you can go to the trouble and the expense. I would not waste my time, if I were you. I think you'll find his judgement is the same as mine.'

It took a little more grumbling but finally, the two men were gone. Benedictus rubbed his brow. He would have to remember to ask someone to check up on those barons in the next couple of months. If they were still quarrelling over such trivial matters, Benedictus meant what he said: he would strip them of their lands. He almost wanted them to carry on. Forcing their hands would be a powerful message to anyone else who thought they could seize more land in the king's absence. Still, it was a headache he didn't need.

Benedictus glanced down at his report for Edward.

He flexed his hand and picked up his stylus, curving his fingers around the detested device. He hated writing, had never really enjoyed it, but it had become harder for him in recent years. A cut by a dagger during the defence of the king had left him with limited movement in his writing hand. He could still wield a sword as well as he had ever done but the finer movement needed for forming his letters was a gruelling slog.

He should get a scribe to do it for him but he didn't trust anyone to get the facts down correctly, and it was important for Edward to know every detail. He scratched out a few more words before a cramp had him shaking out his hand.

He read over the first line four times before leaning back in his chair. It was no good; all he could think of was Adela, the way her hands had felt as they explored his body; the way her mouth had made him lose his mind. He groaned and lowered his head to the desktop. This was a problem. He would have to do something to get her out of his head and get his focus back on important matters.

A knock at the door had his heart racing. He scowled at his body's unwanted reaction. The chance of Adela being outside his antechamber was not high. She did not visit him often and, even if it was her, there was nothing for his heart to get excited about. It was his body that craved her, not the organ in his chest.

'Enter,' he called out.

Even before the door fully opened, the hairs on the back of his neck stood to attention. His hand strayed to the dagger tied to his waist. His fingers brushed the hilt but he didn't pull it from its scabbard. Killing the man entering was more bother than it was worth.

Benedictus stood. 'Good afternoon, Father.'

His father didn't acknowledge his greeting, only striding into the antechamber as if he owned the place. Benedictus gritted his teeth and made no comment. He'd discovered some years ago that standing when confronting his father was the best approach. It reminded the old man that his son was taller and broader than he was now; that he would be less able to intimidate his oldest surviving son. That there was still a small chance that his father could daunt him was annoying and something which Benedictus would rather die than admit to. Benedictus ran the country; that his father could cause any disquiet in him was an appalling embarrassment, but the man had many years of practise and seemed to know exactly what to say to set Benedictus on edge. Benedictus knew his father drew pleasure from Benedictus's discomfort, although he was far too superior to admit it.

'I've arrived at Windsor to hear you are the hero of the moment,' said his father, nearing the desk. From anyone else this would have sounded like a compliment, but his father's sneer suggested otherwise; although for the life of him Benedictus could not think what he could have done wrong by confronting the French and successfully driving them out of the country. He was no doubt about to find out. 'Don't you think it is beyond you to go galloping about the country chasing after some rogue sailors? You are acting for the king. It is time you acted like one.'

Benedictus forced himself not to show any reaction to his father's words, despite them grinding against his skin. 'I did exactly what King Edward would do in the same situation.' He made sure his voice sounded bored and indifferent by their exchange. Over the years he had learned this was the best approach when dealing with both his parents. He walked around the desk and stood directly in front of his father. How typical of the man to think that the French in the Thames were not a threat to England's safety. His father did not believe that anything could destroy the might of the English. He was as blinkered in the belief of the English's strengths as he was about everything else.

'To what do I owe the pleasure of your visit?' The sooner Benedictus knew, the sooner he could get rid of him.

'Your mother and I understand that you have finally honoured our decade-long agreement with the Valdu family and have married their youngest daughter. We have come to Windsor to meet your new wife, as you did not bring her to visit us.'

A chill ran down Benedictus's spine at the thought of Adela around his poisonous parents. The thought that they might cut Adela with their verbal assaults made Benedictus want to throw things. He put his arms behind his back. This meeting would have to happen sooner rather than later, although he would have preferred much, much later. He would try to control the situation so that Adela had minimum amount of time in their company. 'Very well. We shall dine together this evening.' He walked his father to the door. He would

escort him to the Great Hall and then go and find Adela.
He would have to warn her what she was in for. He ignored the way his heart picked up in pace at the thought
of seeing her again. His body's reaction meant nothing.
He was merely reacting to the arrival of his parents.
And yes, the increased pulse did feel different, closer
to happiness than irritation, but his heart couldn't be
acting in such a fashion because he was going to see
her; that would be absurd.

Benedictus was standing outside the gates to the
queen's gardens when Adela finally decided to leave
its tranquil paths. She was so surprised to see him; she
came to a complete stop. 'Oh, have you been waiting
long? If I'd known you were here, I would have come
straight out.'

'No.' He was frowning deeply, his shoulders hunched,
a far cry from the happy man who had left their bedchamber earlier.

'Is something wrong?' She slipped her arm through
his. He regarded it for a moment as if she had placed
a foreign object there. She held her breath, thinking
he might take his arm away, but in the end he merely
turned back toward the castle buildings with her walking beside him.

'My parents have decided to pay us a visit,' he said
solemnly. 'They are waiting to meet you.'

'Oh.' Her heart sank. She had heard rumours of these
people. They were ruthless and full of their own importance. It was something she knew she could not run

from but meeting them was not something she wanted to do.

'It will be an ordeal, I'm afraid. We are going to dine in my antechamber, so that not everyone will be watching the exchange. I will not allow them to speak ill of you.'

A lump formed in her throat. 'You think that they might?'

'I know that they will.' He glanced down at her. 'They speak ill of everyone and everything. It will not be personal but it will be unpleasant.'

This did not sound good. Although…she had survived her father's near constant disapproval so she could manage one meal. 'Will they stay at Windsor for long?'

'I doubt it. They do not care to stay at Windsor when the king is not here and will probably return to the family stronghold within days.'

They were getting dangerously close to the castle now. She slowed her steps; he copied her. 'Why is that? I would have thought being in Windsor when their son was in charge would be something to revel in.'

A small, unhappy smile tugged at his lips. 'Ah, but then they would have to follow my rule. Far better to know that a Monceaux is in charge in order to lord it over their dependents than submit to my decree.' He took her hand and squeezed it. 'They are not soft people. They will not try and make you feel at ease. They will not gossip or laugh or ask about your day. They will try to find a weakness and then poke at it until you either stand up to them or cave.'

'Why would they do that?'

'Because they believe it is better to be strong and unyielding rather than caring. It makes you tougher and that creates superior leaders. The Monceaux family was born to rule.' Adela couldn't tell from Benedictus's statement whether he agreed with his parents' beliefs or not. He didn't clarify any further and they had reached the steps leading to the castle's inner rooms. 'My advice would be to show as little facial expression as possible.'

'Let me change before I meet them.' Suddenly, it was important that she meet them wearing her nicest gown. It wouldn't make much difference to the way she looked but it would give her confidence to know that, despite their faults, her parents had been wealthy enough to clothe her well.

'You don't need to. You look lovely enough as it is.'

Her heart lightened. Benedictus would not pay her a compliment if he did not mean it. 'I will be quick.' Without thinking she pushed herself up onto her tiptoes and brushed a light kiss across his mouth. His eyes were wide as she stepped away from him but she didn't regret it. It appeared she was not the only one who had unpleasant parents. If he was as desperate for attention as she was, then a kiss was not something to regret.

Chapter Twelve

Dinner was worse than Benedictus had predicted. Adela, in her deep blue dress, was like a delicate spring flower just waiting to be trampled on by an ox.

His desk had been transformed into a dining table and they sat around its edges as food was placed in front of them. Nobody spoke. In the short few moments Adela had been in the chamber, she had reverted to the woman he had met on his wedding day: meek and mild. There was no spark in her eyes, and he knew her fingers were trembling, even though she was hiding them under the table. He wanted to pull her into his arms but he didn't. When he was a child, he'd tried to protect his younger brother from their parents. It had only made the situation worse. They had picked on Alewyn more because Benedictus tried to defend him, thinking that Alewyn, their giant of a son, needed toughening up.

And now was not the time to think about Alewyn as the familiar hurt at his absence tugged at his stomach. When his younger brother had left the King's Knights,

Benedictus had been angry and the brothers hadn't parted on good terms. Benedictus knew it was his fault, not Alewyn's. He'd thought about travelling down to see Alewyn and his new wife to apologise and try and make amends, but his pride wouldn't allow him. Sitting here, in stony silence with people that reminded him so strongly of Alewyn, made him long for his brother in a way he hadn't thought possible. For so long it had been the two of them against their parents, and now Benedictus was left to deal with them alone. And that shouldn't feel like a desertion but it did.

'What did your parents teach you of household management, Lady Adela?' asked his mother, breaking through the thick silence.

Benedictus forced himself not to roll his eyes. It was typical of his mother to go straight into a difficult question without leading in with the social niceties. Across the table Adela shot him a look of pure panic.

He cleared his throat. 'Mother, I think…'

'Lady Adela can answer for herself, Benedictus.'

Benedictus clenched his jaw. He wouldn't allow anyone else to speak to him in such a manner. He only tolerated it from his mother because she had birthed him but he wasn't sure how long he could hold his tongue.

'My parents didn't teach me anything of household management.' Adela's voice sounded so small, and Benedictus hated his mother in that moment.

'Then you had best come to our stronghold immediately so that I can begin your education. We cannot have the next Lady of Monceaux unable to wield any control. There is much to learn.'

Adela paled and dropped her gaze to the trencher before her. Benedictus had heard enough. 'Lady Adela will stay with me at Windsor.'

His mother's back stiffened. 'That is foolish. The girl must learn. I understand that you would like to get her with child as soon as possible. You need an heir and you have left it late in life to get started. But if she hasn't caught already then it is of no matter. You can visit her at Castle Monceaux.'

A horrible mixture of shame and embarrassment swept through him. Adela couldn't be pregnant no matter how much he might wish it. And he was not about to visit his wife at his parents' stronghold like a stallion covering a mare. Across the table, red splotches had appeared on Adela's neck as she stared down at her food, the very essence of misery. He didn't want his mother to see Adela's distress and so he said the first thing that came into his mind.

'I cannot travel to visit Castle Monceaux whenever the need takes me.' Flames coiled in his stomach. He should have phrased that better. Humiliation pushed him forward. 'The affairs of state are too important for me to leave for any reason. You cannot expect that of me.'

His mother was shaking her head. 'If she truly knows nothing then our family's stronghold will fall into disarray the moment your father and I depart this world. The Monceaux family name is an important and distinguished one and...'

'This is not a matter up for debate. Lady Adela will stay with me.' He didn't normally use that tone of voice with his parents. It was one he reserved for the young pages and squires at Windsor, but his mother had left him no choice. Adela was not strong enough to withstand his parents' relentless bullying; he would not put her through the ordeal of having to stay with them for any length of time. He would help her learn the household management when the time came for her to do it. He was not about to let his wife leave him; not now, not ever.

Silence reigned. The food on Adela's trencher remained uneaten. Heat flooded through his body at the sight. He would take food to their chamber later. He would relax her and then she would eat and he wouldn't have to worry that she was not getting enough food.

'She's not much to look at.' For a moment Benedictus paused, a hunk of bread not far from his mouth. He could not believe his father had spoken those words about Adela in front of her. But he had and he seemed to have more to say on the subject. 'I suppose her substantial dowry makes up for her skinny frame. Although, the Monceaux family has yet to benefit from that financial incentive. I wonder if such a body can bear a healthy Monceaux heir.'

Benedictus could take no more. He stood. 'Lady Adela and I are leaving now. You will never again speak to, or about, my wife in such a manner. I trust you will be gone from Windsor tomorrow. It would be embarrassing if I had to have you removed. Lady Adela.' He gestured for her to stand. Her eyes were wide. She pushed back her chair and stumbled to her feet. He wanted to pick her up and sweep her from the chamber, but he

waited for her to make her own way to the door. He
didn't want her to show any weakness in front of his
parents. He knew she was strong and he wanted them
to see it, too; see that they had tried to belittle her and
yet she was still able to leave the room with her head
held high. He followed her out, rage coursing through
him as he strode through the corridors. He was shaking
so badly he didn't realise she was trembling until they
were not far from their chamber door.

'I'm sorry,' he said, coming to an abrupt stop.

'It is not your fault,' she whispered.

His heart clenched. It was his fault. He knew how bad
his parents were. Hell, he'd lived through it, built a pro-
tective armour around himself, and shielded his brother
from the worst of it; he knew exactly what they were.
He also knew how sensitive his wife was; how little she
had been exposed to people like his parents; how tough
she tried to be but how soft and gentle she was really.
He should have kept her away from his parents until
she had toughened up a little or even kept her away forever. Forever would have been better. They were so...
His father... My God, how could he have spoken about
Adela like that and in front of her?

Anger bubbled up inside him again as fierce as he
had ever felt it. Only years of making practical, ratio-
nal decisions in the face of an impending crisis stopped
him from turning around and connecting his fist to his
father's face.

What his father had said about her looks wasn't even
true. She *was* beautiful; maybe not in the way of the
traditional courtly beauty but in the flash of her un-

usual eyes and the curve of her rare smile, there was no one more attractive to him. Then there was her steely backbone, the one she kept hidden for most of the time, but the one he was privileged to see. She was worth far more than her dowry and if her father couldn't see that, he was a fool.

Benedictus flung the door to their chamber open and strode inside. Fine, so he wouldn't storm back to his father and punch him; such actions were beneath him. That didn't mean he couldn't demand that the man leave right now; that his father not even spend the night in the same fortress as Adela. He didn't deserve the hospitality Windsor had to offer. He didn't even deserve…

A brush of a hand across his back pulled him from his thoughts.

'I'm sorry,' he said again. 'My father should never have said those things to your face.'

She half smiled. 'It is better that than say them behind my back.'

'True but…'

'You must not be angry, Benedictus. Your father's words and actions should not dictate how you feel after you have seen him.'

How strange that she should be the calm one. He was always the voice of reason and yet he was finding it so hard to reach his normal composure. 'He was cruel.'

She shook her head. 'He was practical and he said what he thought. You are very like him.'

He reared back as if she had punched him. 'I am nothing like him. I would never say such despicable things to any person let alone someone who was now my daughter.'

She moved away from him and began to undo her braid. He had never seen her undo her plait before, and he found he could not tear his eyes away from her nimble fingers as they threaded through the strands of her hair. 'I didn't mean that you are cruel,' she continued. 'Only that you will put your duty before other considerations. You are practical. So are your parents.'

'My behaviour is entirely different to theirs. My duty concerns running the country. Their concern is the stewardship of some land and the quality of the Monceaux name. The two roles are incomparable and, even if they were, they don't give my father the right to talk down to you like that.'

Her braid was completely undone now, her hair falling in waves around her shoulders. He longed to run his fingers through it, to feel its softness against his skin, but he wasn't sure if she would welcome his touch, not after the way his parents had treated her. He could not read her mood; her fear from the encounter in his antechamber was gone, to be replaced by complete calmness, and he could not understand it.

She tilted her head to one side, watching him closely. 'Do you know what I decided about my father recently?'

'No?'

'That I would no longer allow him to control my mood.'

He stepped toward her as if pulled by an invisible cord. 'What do you mean?'

'For the longest time, what my father thought about

me governed every aspect of my life. One day recently I was walking toward the Thames with Medea and I heard his voice criticising me and my actions. Yet, he wasn't there. I thought, why am I letting a man, whom I don't respect, crowd my thoughts? You, Benedictus, have never told me what to do, have never made me feel as if I am trapped, even though you have the power to do so. After I'd been here a while, I realised then that the fault was with him and not me. You have given me the freedom to try and find my own likes and dislikes. It was that freedom that made me decide I would no longer allow him to dictate my moods.'

He swallowed. His heart felt as if it was swelling with her words even as he was not sure he deserved her praise. 'As simple as that, eh?'

She shook her head, some of her hair spilling forward onto her chest. 'No. It wasn't simple. He still enters my thoughts with annoying regularity. He was there tonight agreeing with everything your father said, but I am working on getting rid of him and I will continue until I no longer think of him at all.'

Benedictus took a strand of her hair between his fingertips, needing to touch her. 'What did your father do to you?'

'My father is a pious bully who punished me for even the smallest perceived misdemeanours.'

The rage, which had been subsiding, surged through him once more; his jaw clenched. 'What punishment?' If that shallow, pompous, disgrace of a man had harmed her in any way, Benedictus would hunt him down and throw him in the darkest pit he could find where he would leave him for all eternity.

She smiled. 'There is no need to look so fierce. He never hurt me physically. Well, not unless you count hours spent on my knees praying for forgiveness for any small discretion.'

Benedictus growled. 'I count that.'

'The irony is that he was the very opposite of pure. I found out, not that long before you and I married, that he had a mistress. That the children of that union were allowed to do as they pleased. I could see my half brothers from my chamber window, running around the courtyard with all the freedom of the world. My full sisters were also kept sheltered but they married young and escaped my father's rule. I do hope the men they wed allowed them their liberty.' She shook her head. She had no way of knowing. It had been many years since she had last seen either of them. 'For years my father forced me to remain separate from everyone else. I was to be kept pure for you, because he values purity in women above all things.'

Benedictus's heart pinched. He could have put a stop to that if he had married Adela sooner. 'I did not need you to be pure. I wish he had not kept you separate. You must have been lonely.'

She smiled sadly. 'Yes. I was. Very lonely. I believe the worst thing that could happen to me now would be to go back to that. I could not bear to return to the tediousness of those long, lonely, endless days. Now that I have had a taste of companionship, it would be a punishment that I don't think I have the strength to live through again.'

Benedictus tugged on the hair he was holding, gently, because he knew how much she loved it when he did so. Rage was surging through him, making it almost difficult to keep his movements controlled, but he would do it for her. 'I will never let you be alone again. Never keep you locked up away from everyone. You have my word on that.'

'Thank you. I have never thought that you would. You have given me freedom and I am more grateful than you will ever know.' She rested her palm above his heart, her fingers warm and steady through his shirt. 'It's over and many people have faced much worse.'

He covered her hand. 'You are my wife and...'

Anything further he'd been about to say was stopped by the touch of her lips against his. The touch was feather-light, barely a brush. It chased everything out of his mind, the tension melting away from him as quickly as it had arrived. He leaned into her, capturing her mouth with his, pressing deeper. She let out the quietest moan and he was undone.

He buried his hand deeper into her hair and pulled her closer. Her sharp inhale caused his body to harden. Later, he wouldn't be able to recall exactly how it happened. Clothes fell to the floor and yet he didn't remember lifting his mouth from hers to pull them off. Her hands skimmed over his skin; every brush sending shots of desire shooting through him.

Any control he'd ever had disappeared completely. He barely knew his name; all that mattered was her,

her soft skin, her mouth moving against his. She was
stumbling onto the mattress, pulling him down on top
of her. She grunted as his full weight fell on her.

'I'm sorry.' He tried to lift himself but her hands
tightened on his arms, digging into his skin.

'No. I like it.'

If he'd been capable of words, he would have told
her how full his heart was with her, how his body was
only content when he was with her and how he never
wanted this moment to end. But he was beyond speech.
He kissed her desperately, trying to convey with his body
what he could not say.

Her nails scratched his back, the sweet pain shooting
through him, urging him on. He rolled over to his side,
taking her with him. She grumbled in protest until his
fingertips skimmed the underside of her breast. Then
there was only the whispering of their shared breath
and the feel of her hands moving over him.

This was bliss, paradise. There was nothing else like
it.

Her hand skimmed over his length and he groaned,
the sensation almost unbearably perfect. He lifted his
head. 'I want you so badly. I think I might die from it.'

She laughed and he felt the answering joy bubbling
up in him. He had never felt like this, never known it
was possible to laugh with a woman in such a way.

Her gaze met his. Her eyes were dancing with
amusement and some other emotion he didn't recognise. 'Then you had better take me,' she whispered,
and his heart stopped.

'Are you sure?' He almost didn't want to ask but he

knew that he had to. He wanted her to want this as much as he did.

She huffed out a laugh. 'You are not the only one who is desperate.'

Her words robbed him of breath. She smiled and his heart soared. He'd had no idea there could be such joy in a moment like this. He had imagined this moment more than he had thought about anything else. He had imagined it tender but serious, exciting but cautious. He had never considered that she would be happy, that she would want him as much as he wanted her. She rolled onto her back, gently tugging him with her. Tension curled from the balls of his feet, rolling through him fast and intense like flames against kindling.

Barely daring to breathe, he moved over her, propping himself up on his arms, taking almost all his weight off her. He wanted to gaze into her eyes while he did this; wanted to know what she was thinking and feeling as he finally made her his.

He entered her slowly. It was exquisite torment but he would do anything not to cause her pain. He could see the moment he hit her barrier. Her eyes widened. She bit her lip. He held himself still. 'Do you want me to stop?'

Please, God, don't let her say yes.

She shook her head. 'Go on,' she said hoarsely.

He pushed through the final barrier. She gasped, becoming rigid beneath him. Benedictus held himself still. 'Oh,' she breathed. 'That was even odder than I was expecting.'

He laughed, unable to stop himself. She ran a hand

through his hair. 'You are very handsome when you smile. You should do it more often.'

Right now that did not seem like an impossible request. 'Anything my lady wants,' he murmured, leaning down and brushing his mouth against hers and again, until he could feel her relax around him. He began to move slowly, achingly slowly, exquisitely slowly, never wanting this moment to end and then quicker as she pulled him to her, her fingers pressing against him, urging him on. His release was building, quickly, centring his whole body and mind on where the two of them were joined. He held on. Desperately not wanting to finish until she had; knowing how important it was for them both that she enjoy it. Her nails dug into his shoulder, her eyes glazed, and her lips parted. She cried out his name and then she shattered around him, the sensation so delicious he followed her, unable to hold back as he tipped into oblivion.

Chapter Thirteen

The early-morning sun was streaming through the window. Adela's arm was thrown over Benedictus's chest. He was drowsily stroking her skin. Neither of them had spoken in some time. She was bone-tired, but she didn't want to sleep. The lazy mornings, when Benedictus didn't rush off immediately to his duties, were like precious gold to Adela. They happened rarely, but when they did she savoured them like others did a fine wine.

The end of August had slipped away, giving way to a golden September. Benedictus still spent most of his time working on matters for the kingdom and while Adela would have loved to have spent some time with him during the day, she knew she had to be grateful for what she had right now. It was more than she had ever dreamed possible.

'Now I know why nobody gets much done,' Benedictus murmured.

She laughed. Out of the corner of her eye, she could see his answering smile. It was still a rare enough sight that the curve of his mouth made her stomach flip oddly, even after two months of marriage.

'You have a beautiful laugh,' he said, turning over onto his side.

'I think maybe you are in a good mood. Anything would sound appealing to you right now.'

He pulled her to him and pressed chaste kisses to her neck. Despite herself, she shivered. The feel of his stubble against her skin was delicious. She felt his response against her stomach. 'You can't possibly want to do that again. I don't think we've slept at all.'

'I *do* want to make love to you again, yes. But... I should leave you to recover. You must be feeling tender?'

She laughed again, thrilled that he still didn't appear to be in a hurry to leave. 'I like the way you made that into a question.'

She gently nudged him until he flopped onto his back. 'I would have thought you would want to get on with the business of running the country.' Even as she kissed the planes of his chest, she wished she hadn't mentioned it. She didn't want to remind him of his duties.

'You're right. I have much to do.' Her mouth reached his stomach and his hand threaded through her hair; his breath hitched, giving lie to his words.

'There must be many people already waiting to see you.' She was playing with fire now but she sensed she was winning; he wasn't going anywhere soon.

He grunted as her hair brushed over his length, and she grinned in triumph. It was a heady feeling this, knowing that the kingdom could come knocking on the door and he wouldn't answer, so caught up was he on where her mouth was heading next.

Sometime later he climbed out of bed, groaning as he looked back at her. 'Can't you get dressed? At least then I won't have to leave you looking like this.'

She rolled onto her stomach and watched as he began to wash himself, his movements precise and controlled.

'I think I will stay like this all day.'

He half smiled. 'You are a cruel temptress.' He began to pull on his clothes and a pang of sadness hit her chest. This slow-starting morning had been an unexpected gift and now it was over. She could see the mantle of responsibility already weighing on him.

'I am teasing you. I will get up myself shortly.'

'What will you do today?' He picked up a hairbrush and began pulling it through the tangled mess of his hair. There was something private about watching him put himself together, even more so than the night they had spent in one another's arms. He was changing from her man to the public figure he presented to everyone else, and only she got to see the two sides of him.

'I have been making something for you, so I will work on that for the rest of the morning and then later, I shall head to the Hall and see whether there is any gossip worth hearing about.'

He paused, the brush still in his hand. 'Is there anyone in particular you will speak to?'

She sighed and rolled onto her back. 'Medea is the

only one worth talking to. Everyone else is obsessed with nonsensical gossip. Most of which is rubbish.'

He cleared his throat. 'What about Sir Hendry?'

'Sir Hendry?'

'He seems quite taken with you.'

She pushed herself up to sitting, suddenly embarrassed that she wasn't wearing anything. 'What are you saying?'

'Nothing.' He placed the brush carefully down on the table.

'It doesn't sound like nothing.'

He pushed his hand through his hair, messing it up as quickly as he'd straightened it. 'I'm not saying anything important. It's not uncommon for knights to fixate on married women. I'm not accusing you of anything. I just… I can't help but notice that he has a marked interest in you. That is all.'

'He's an odd character.' She pushed herself off the bed and reached for her underclothes. She would wash when Benedictus had left but she didn't want to have this conversation while she wasn't wearing anything. 'He appears wherever I go. At first, I thought he was interested in you, but he rarely asks anything about you and he never discusses France, unlike everyone else at court.'

'What does he talk about?'

'Other people at court, his home. He asks me questions about myself but nothing too intrusive.'

Benedictus snorted. 'It sounds to me as if he is taken with you.'

'No. I am sure he is not interested in me.'

'How on earth can you tell?'

'He never looks at me the way you do.'

Benedictus's stance softened. 'And how exactly do I look at you?'

'As if you are hungry.'

He stepped toward her. 'You've got that right.'

Perhaps the moment would have turned into another round of lovemaking but a knock at the door had them both freezing.

Benedictus muttered a curse, strode over to the door and flung it open. Adela scurried over to the other side of the chamber. She had no desire to face whoever had disturbed their peace. There was a muttered exchange and then Benedictus stepped back toward her. 'I'm afraid I am going to have to go. My absence has already caused a stir and some minor barons are threatening some sort of coup.' He rolled his eyes, kissing her quickly. 'I will look forward to seeing you later.' There was enough heat in his eyes to convey exactly what he was contemplating.

Within a few short moments, he was gone.

She stared at the space in which he'd been standing, mulling over their conversation. She hadn't realised Benedictus was even more than vaguely aware of Sir Hendry's existence or that he knew she and the knight spoke daily. She supposed she should have. Benedictus knew everything that went on at court, so why not that?

That Benedictus was jealous of the time she spent with another man was something that shouldn't please her, but a small tendril of something was curling around her heart at the thought. It was making her hope that there could be something more between them that, in time, he might think of her first before anything else. She knew he enjoyed making love to her and it was an unexpected joy to her that she felt the same, but they had never discussed feelings and she had no idea whether Benedictus was fond of her or not. Based on their interactions that took place in the public eye, she would say that he had no more regard for her than he did any of those who worked for him. It was only in private that he was different, paying exquisite attention to her body.

Perhaps she and Benedictus were lucky. It was obvious that not every couple enjoyed what they had. To think of last night as a chore was so ridiculous as to be laughable. Nothing had ever given her greater joy than to be joined with her husband. If that made her inconstant as her father suggested, then inconstancy was so much better than being pious. If that was all she ever had from Benedictus, then it was more than most people could say about their marriages.

She smiled and pulled her sewing out from under the bed. She was making cushions for Benedictus's antechamber. He'd not asked her to do it but nobody really wanted to sit on hard benches. She was sure it would make his meetings with his knights go smoother. Each cushion cover was bringing her much joy. She'd created scenes from each season. She was leaving summer for last. For her, summer was the season of new beginnings, of finding hope from despair and finding joy where it was least expected.

Chapter Fourteen

September bled into October, the strangely warm days continuing even though the nights were now considerably longer and colder.

One afternoon she and Medea headed down to the Thames to lie beside the water and cool off, for once not bothering with an afternoon in the Great Hall.

'You're glowing,' said Medea, her head propped up against the trunk of a willow tree.

Adela stretched. She was lying flat on her back in the shade, watching the browning leaves of the tree as they swayed gently in the breeze. 'I am happier than I thought possible.' It was true. Despite worrying that she might be beginning to feel more for her husband than he did for her, life was far better for her than it had ever been before.

'It is more than that, I think,' countered Medea.

'What do you mean?' She tilted her head toward her friend. Medea was wearing a small, secret smile. The one she always did when she was pleased with herself.

'I think you are with child.'

Adela placed a hand on her stomach. It was as flat as ever. 'No. I think it is too early for that.'

'Oh, really?'

'Yes. I have only been married...' She closed her eyes to think. It was not long. They had married at the beginning of August and now it was the middle of October. 'It is only just over two months.'

'When did you last bleed?'

'Not long after we were married but I am not regular. I may not bleed again for weeks yet. Really, Medea, it is too soon.'

'Well,' said Medea, leaning forward and waggling her eyebrows. 'Benedictus has been a lot more relaxed in recent weeks, so I know that you have been engaging in baby-making activities.'

'Medea!' The two women peeled off into giggles.

'Do you really think that?' asked Adela when they had finally calmed down. 'Does he seem better? More relaxed? I have not known him long enough to be able to judge properly.'

'I have known him for a couple of years now. Theo has known Benedictus since they were children. Theo says he has never known him so happy. I do believe he has even smiled a couple of times in the last few weeks, which is more pleased than I have ever seen him.' Medea reached across the small space and squeezed her friend's hand. 'It was a good day for everyone when Benedictus married you.'

Adela smiled and returned the pressure. They lapsed into silence. Adela was pleased that Benedictus appeared to be happy. It matched her own feelings. There were only moments, small but definitely there, when she couldn't help but wonder if his happiness was truly because of her. Oh, she had no doubt he was happier because of the nights they spent together and obviously those moments needed her to be there. Benedictus adored her body; of that she was absolutely sure. He had spent weeks learning every way to bring her pleasure, touching and tasting every inch of her skin until she was writhing with ecstasy. To see her awash with desire seemed to drive him wild. There were times when it appeared he could not get enough of her; the days that followed were always a blur of sated tiredness; days she couldn't understand how Benedictus could work when she could barely keep her eyes open.

What she was not sure of, and what gave her moments of disquiet throughout the day when they were apart, was whether it was *she* who was making him happy or if it was her *body.* If it was only her body, then surely any woman would do. He had never told her that he had a particular regard for her; never expressed any feelings of love or affection for her.

Yes, Benedictus had defended her to his father. The intensity of Benedictus's anger at her mistreatment by the vile man still sent a thrill through her but she couldn't decide if Benedictus's fury was because he cared for her or because of his innate character. He was a knight after all, and to become one he had sworn to protect those who could not protect themselves. Was his reaction to his father chivalric instinct or something else? She couldn't be sure.

Their time together was as deliciously intense as

Medea had predicted, but was it anything special for him? Really, this shouldn't matter. They were married. He would be faithful; she was sure of that. But she feared she had given him her heart and that he hadn't given his in return. And somehow that mattered. She wanted his love and not just his desire; wanted to know that he would put her first above everything else, not because he was a knight but because she meant everything to him. She knew, deep down, that this was not the case. He had as good as said so when his parents had questioned him on that terrible day in his antechamber. He had forcibly made it clear that he would put his role before his marriage but things had changed since then, hadn't they? They had spent long nights together and they often talked but neither of them mentioned love or anything close to it. It was the only dark blot in a world of happiness.

A rustling in the leaves that surrounded them warned her that she and Medea were no longer alone in their secluded spot.

She pushed herself upright and stifled a groan when she saw Sir Hendry's golden head of hair pushing through the leaves.

'I'm sorry to disturb you, ladies, but I was seeking shelter from the sun and I couldn't help but notice you were here in this delightful shade.'

Sir Hendry still hadn't lost the knack of finding her when she didn't want to be disturbed. The handsome knight seemed as taken with her as ever. She was beginning to reluctantly agree with Medea and Benedictus that the knight was interested in more than just friendship with her. It was the only explanation for his dogged attention.

Recently, she had decided to be less friendly toward him, in the hope that he would move on to someone else, but her distance only seemed to be making the situation worse. The more she moved away from him, the more he wouldn't leave her alone.

Medea didn't help. She found the whole thing very humorous and encouraged Sir Hendry on the misguided assumption his attention to her would make Benedictus jealous, and that that was a good thing much to be desired. Adela couldn't understand why. She did not want to make her husband uncomfortable. She had lived all her life under the shadow of negative emotions. She did not want to bring them into her marriage. Besides, the only time Benedictus had seemed disgruntled about Sir Hendry's attention it had been a deeply uncomfortable conversation and Adela didn't want to repeat it.

Medea greeted Sir Hendry with undisguised amusement while Adela tried to think of a good reason to return to Windsor. Sir Hendry was becoming a nuisance with his constant attention. Adela wished she'd never encouraged his friendship. She'd been so keen to see if she could learn something from him that she had been far friendlier than perhaps she should have been, and he had clearly taken it the wrong way. She'd found out nothing from him and so the whole exercise had been completely fruitless.

'I think I will return to the castle.' She pushed herself to her feet. 'I have been absent too long and Sir Benedictus will be wondering where I am.' This was not true.

Benedictus didn't seek her out during the day and probably didn't think of her until the evening, but it would
hopefully remind Sir Hendry that she had a powerful
husband who cared about her well-being.

'Excellent. It shall be my pleasure to escort you.'
Adela wanted to throw something at his thick skull.
Why could he not take the hint and leave her alone?

Medea lounged against the tree trunk. 'I hope you
don't mind but I shan't come with you. Sir Theodore
said he would try and join me here. It seems a waste of
the last of the summer sun to return to the castle just yet.

Adela ignored her twinge of jealousy. Theo sought
Medea out at least once a day just so that they could
spend some time together. He was not so tied to his duty
that his wife came second to it.

Adela pushed the branches aside and set up a brisk
pace back along the path. To her annoyance, Sir Hendry kept up with her. His conversation was so banal it
made her want to jump into the Thames just to have
something interesting happen. He spoke mainly about
the unseasonably hot weather, not seeming to mind that
her comments in response were noncommittal. The familiar walls of Windsor came into view and she sighed
in relief. Sir Hendry could not follow her to her chamber. There were too many guards around that area, protecting the most important part of the castle from even
the other residents. She could make her escape and be
done with him for today.

'You must be excited to meet your brother-in-law,'
said Sir Hendry as they stepped past the gatehouse.

Adela frowned. 'I'm sorry. What did you say?'

'Your brother-in-law, Sir Alewyn. You must be looking forward to meeting him. I've heard he is the biggest knight who ever lived and one of the most fearsome fighters.'

What a strange thing to talk about. Adela had not given any thought to meeting Benedictus's brother. 'I suppose so.'

'Are you planning to eat with him in private later? Only I noticed you did that when Sir Benedictus's parents visited.'

Coldness seeped through Adela's veins at Sir Hendry's words and what they implied. Benedictus's brother was here, at Windsor, and Benedictus hadn't told her about his unexpected arrival. True, Adela didn't see much of her husband during the day, but he could have found her for something so important. He had waited outside the queen's gardens to tell her that his parents had come to visit but this, it seemed, did not warrant the same gravitas. And yet…if he truly cared about her, wouldn't he have come to find her? They had grown close, hadn't they? Close enough that his estranged brother coming to Windsor warranted him informing her, if not by himself then at least sending someone else to do it. She didn't want to read too much into this. She knew how busy her husband was, and she had been outside the walls for a little while now. There was no reason for her to be upset and yet she couldn't help it; she was.

They stepped through the imposing gates and Adela walked away from Sir Hendry after only a perfunctory dismissal. She wended her way through the various outbuildings, heading toward the castle's inner sanctum.

Her goal was to track down Benedictus, even if he was meeting with someone of consequence, then he could spare her a few moments to tell her something of this importance.

She came to an abrupt stop just outside the stables. A giant of a man with thick eyebrows was talking to Theo. Despite his relaxed shoulders and broad smile, there was a distinct resemblance to Benedictus. This had to be Alewyn.

Theo spotted her first. 'Lady Adela, how lovely to see you. Have you been with Medea down by the Thames?'

'Yes.' She glanced at the tall giant. There was a pause while the men waited for her to say more.

Theo glanced between the two of them. He cleared his throat. 'Have you… Have you met Alewyn?'

She shook her head. Theo muttered something under his breath, which sounded a lot like a string of curses directed at Benedictus. He cleared his throat again. 'Alewyn, please allow me to introduce Benedictus's wife, Lady Adela.'

If she hadn't been so dumbstruck at meeting a man who looked so similar to her husband in some ways and so vastly different in others, the effect on Alewyn would have been comical. His eyes went wide and his mouth dropped open. He closed it, only for it to fall open again. 'Wife,' he croaked. 'Benedictus has married!'

A shooting pain hit her heart at Alewyn's evident shock. In the slightly more than two months since their wedding, Benedictus had not thought to inform his brother of the life-altering event. Everything she had told herself about Benedictus beginning to care for her slipped away in the overwhelming evidence that she wasn't important enough in his life to inform his brother about her existence.

Alewyn appeared to collect himself, finally closing his mouth and looking more composed. He stepped toward her, his hands outstretched. 'It's a pleasure to welcome you to the family, Lady Adela.'

She placed her hands in his, still not able to conjure up any words. His grip was firm but not rough and his eyes, so similar in colour to Benedictus's, were kind.

'What is going on here?' Adela jumped, pulling her hands out of Alewyn's light hold. She turned to find Benedictus glaring at them both from a short distance away. Theo muttered something and disappeared, leaving the three of them standing in an awkward circle.

Benedictus's shoulders were rigid, his hands curled into fists. The sight didn't frighten her as it might once have done. Instead, a flicker of irritation ran through her body. What right did Benedictus have to be angry? Neither she nor Alewyn were doing anything wrong.

'I was meeting your wife for the first time,' Alewyn said, seeming to be the most relaxed out of the three of them, but she had seen his face when Theo had announced who she was. Alewyn must be as hurt as she was that he had not been informed about his brother's change in circumstance.

Benedictus stepped closer to Adela but before he could reach her side she shifted slightly away. His eyelids flickered, the only outward sign he noticed her action. 'I was going to introduce you both later.'

Alewyn nodded. 'Of course.' Adela said nothing. She was too busy assimilating the fact that Benedictus had definitely known his brother was in Windsor and hadn't come to let her know. The two men were regarding each other steadily. 'I'm sure you have much to be getting on with. I didn't mean to interrupt any of it,' said Alewyn eventually. His words were polite, but a muscle ticked in Benedictus's jaw all the same.

'You know that I am busy.' Benedictus, normally so sure of himself, sounded defensive.

'That is exactly what I am saying.' Alewyn turned and smiled at Adela. 'I am delighted to have a new sister and, as I don't have any pressing business this afternoon, I would be pleased to spend some time getting to know you.'

'You don't have to do that,' Benedictus growled.

'Why don't we let Lady Adela decide.' Alewyn's warm gaze never left hers.

Perhaps if she hadn't learned of Alewyn's arrival from Sir Hendry, or if Benedictus had taken the time to inform his brother about their nuptials, she might not have wanted to spend time with her brother-in-law. Normally, she wouldn't want to do anything to make her husband feel uncomfortable, but he had wrong-footed her and she was not feeling very charitable toward him. 'I would very much like to spend time getting to know you, Sir Alewyn.'

'Excellent. Please call me Al. Now, I know of a great place to go, if you'd like to accompany me.' She took his proffered arm and walked away. Neither of them sent a backward glance at Benedictus.

Benedictus grunted and tried to focus once more on what Steward John was saying but his mind kept slipping back to his brother and his wife. He could picture

them laughing and talking together all too easily. He
trusted them. He knew that they would not flirt with
one another, that there would be no romantic intentions
on either side, but that didn't seem to help his jealousy.
Benedictus knew that they would get on well, that there
would be no awkwardness in their exchanges. Alewyn
would have no trouble thinking of conversation to put
Adela at her ease.

Al! Benedictus shook his head. What was it with his
men and shortening their names? First Theodore and
now Alewyn. Not that his brother was one of his men
anymore but still… It was a ridiculous habit.

'I think we are done now, Sir Benedictus,' said
Steward John. Benedictus rubbed his forehead, loath
to admit he didn't know whether they were done or not.
He'd not listened to a word John had said for some time.

'Very well. Thank you, as always, for your report.'

John sniffed and Benedictus resisted the urge to roll
his eyes.

John stood to go. 'Is there any word on when King
Edward is returning?'

'None.'

John visibly sagged but made no further comment
as he let himself out of the antechamber. Benedictus
closed his eyes and leaned back in his chair. In his latest missive, Edward had given no hint as to when he
would return to the seat of his power. Even if the king
returned tomorrow, the chances were high that Edward would swan off to France and leave Benedictus in
charge again. Three months ago Benedictus would have
thought nothing of it. Two months ago he would have
been proud to serve the king in such an important role,

but now… Now he was tired. No, that wasn't true. He must be honest with himself. He was impatient with the time he spent on the king's business. He wanted it to be his arm his wife walked off holding. Hell, he wanted to be Ben to her, even though he hated the shortened version of his name. It sounded much more relaxed than the stuffier Benedictus and, although once he would have ridiculed the idea, he now wanted to be Ben to his wife.

He understood why Alewyn had walked off with Adela. Benedictus hadn't sent word to his brother that he'd married. Benedictus could use the excuse that he did not enjoy writing but there were other ways of getting the news to him. Once, the brothers had been close, so close there were no secrets between them, but time had eroded that. No, he couldn't blame time entirely. The nature of his role had made secrets Benedictus's reality. The more he'd kept from those closest to him, the more isolated he'd become until he was alone. And when Alewyn had left the King's Knights, Benedictus had not held back on making his disappointment known, and now their rift seemed almost insurmountable. So yes, he understood why Alewyn had walked away from him, but why had Adela?

Another knock on his door had his eyes tightening. He'd had enough for today. He wanted nothing more than to retire to his bedchamber and pass time with his wife, but he could never allow anyone to know that. He pushed himself upright. 'Enter.' His wife appeared around the edge of the doorway and his heart skipped a beat.

'Adela.' He stood and made his way over to her. He

brushed his lips over hers but she held herself still. He lifted his head. 'Are you well? Has anybody hurt you? Because if they have…' Dear God. He did not know what he would do but it would not be pleasant.

She pushed herself away from him and moved to his desk. She moved some things around but Benedictus didn't think she was seeing anything. Her shoulders were drooped and he wanted to flatten worlds. Whoever had made her feel this way would pay dearly. 'Who has hurt you?'

'You have hurt me, Benedictus.'

Blood pounded in his ears. 'How is that possible?'

She sighed and walked to his window, gazing out at the courtyard outside. 'Why did you not tell your brother about our marriage?'

'I…' He paused. How could something so trivial have caused her to look so desolate? 'I didn't think it was relevant.'

She spun around, her eyes glinting. 'Our marriage isn't relevant?'

'No.' He swallowed. 'That's not what I meant. Our marriage is very relevant to us, obviously.'

'Obviously,' she repeated faintly.

'It wasn't relevant to my brother.'

'Right.'

She did not seem appeased by his reasoning. Somehow this conversation was unravelling away from him. He could see that in the turn of Adela's mouth and yet he wasn't sure how to make it right. 'The last time Alewyn and I spoke, it was on less than amicable terms. He left me.' Benedictus shook his head. Good grief. What was

wrong with him? He didn't care that his brother had left
him. 'I mean he left the King's Knights. We had both
sworn our loyalty to the king. We were supposed to be in
this together until we died, and yet he met some woman
on a mission and suddenly this life wasn't good enough
for him anymore.'

Adela folded her arms. 'By *some woman* are you referring to his wife?'

'They are married now, yes.'

'Did you go to their wedding?'

'I was busy.'

She nodded slowly. 'Of course you were.'

What did her tone of voice mean? She sounded sar-
castic but she knew how hard he had to work. She knew
he was vital to the smooth running of the country. She
had never complained about it before. 'I wasn't unavail-
able to go to it because I was at some pointless tournament, jousting and competing.' His voice was risen
now. He took a deep breath, willing himself to calm
down. He and Adela didn't need to fall out about this.
'I wasn't on a hunting expedition. I wasn't drinking and
feasting. I was trying to run the country.'

Her arms dropped to her sides. Taking this as a good
sign, he stepped closer to her.

'I understand that, Benedictus, but you could have
taken a little time to get to know your sister-in-law and
make amends with your brother.'

'There are no amends to be made.' She raised an eye-
brow. He rubbed the back of his neck, an uncomfortable
sensation creeping up his spine. Yes, Alewyn's desertion of the King's Knights could have felt like a personal

blow to him. Benedictus had protected Alewyn since they'd both been children and Benedictus had thought they would watch each other's backs until they died. But he hadn't allowed himself to feel sad. Personal feelings were a weakness he could not afford to have. This was not a personal hurt. It was about disappointment over being let down by one of his best knights. 'Alewyn was the one who left.'

She stepped toward him, brushing a bit of lint off his sleeve, and he breathed a sigh of relief. He had made her see reason and now the crisis was resolved. 'Alewyn seems like a good man, Benedictus. He loves his wife. Did you know that he is going to become a father? His wife is heavily pregnant. He came here to tell you that you are going to be an uncle.'

Something strange seemed to be happening in Benedictus's chest. It was both expanding and squeezing at the same time. Perhaps he was ill. 'They're going to have a baby?'

'Yes.' She placed both hands on his chest. 'I said that we would go and visit them after the baby's birth.'

He shook his head. 'I can't spare the…' He trailed off as sadness filled her eyes.

She reached up and rested her palms against his chest. 'Since this marriage, I haven't asked you for anything. I am asking for this.'

'But…'

'Please.' Her fingers flexed against him. 'It would only be for a few days.'

Alewyn's new stronghold was on the south coast; perhaps he could combine a visit to his brother with checking on the soldiers stationed there. After the disaster of his men losing sight of the French boat and it ending up in the Thames, it was probably a good idea to turn up unannounced to see how they were faring. If he could tie that in with making Adela happy, then it was a good idea. 'Yes. We can arrange a visit to Castle Brae after their baby is born.'

She smiled, her body relaxed against his, and the muscles in his back loosened. He slipped his arms around her and pulled her close. Her faint floral scent hit him and he inhaled deeply. He loved the smell of her, adored the way it clung to them after they had made love; he wished he could somehow bottle it so he could keep it with him.

Benedictus's arms were around her, shielding her from the world. Her head rested on his chest, the steady beat of his heart sounding in her ear. She'd meant to stay angrier with him for longer but once she was touching him, all her irritation drained away. Even if he hadn't agreed to a short visit to his brother's stronghold, she probably would have forgiven him for his churlish behaviour earlier.

He had not acted well toward his brother, who was clearly a decent man and did not deserve Benedictus's reproach for his actions. Alewyn was allowed a life that made him happy, and Benedictus should not blame him for that. Yet, the desperate sadness she had seen in Benedictus's face when he had let slip that, by leaving the King's Knights, Alewyn had left Benedictus alone spoke of a different story. Oh, she had no doubt

Benedictus believed, completely and utterly, that he was angry at Alewyn because he had left their tight-knit band of brothers, but she knew differently. Benedictus was hurt because, rightly or wrongly, he thought that Alewyn had left him personally, and that had hurt him deeply, although she wasn't sure whether he would ever realise that himself. For someone so in tune with the mood of the castle and the wider country, he didn't seem to understand himself.

Adela was slowly beginning to learn her husband's ways. To see that beneath his hard exterior there was a man who thought and felt things strongly; who wanted people around him but didn't seem to know what to do with them when they got close. He might resist but she was going to make sure that things between the brothers were resolved; to show him that having his brother back in his life would make him a happier man.

Benedictus's fingers slipped into her hair and he began to tug on the strands in the way he knew made her nearly boneless with bliss.

'Do you have anywhere you need to be?' he murmured.

She laughed against him. 'Of course not.'

'Can I persuade you to spend a little time with me?'

'Hmm… What exactly did you have in mind?' She ran her hands down the length of his back, smiling against his chest at the noise he made as she did so. 'Do you want to talk about the price of grain, perhaps? Or maybe—' she slid her hands round to the front of his body, over the planes of his chest '—you want to talk about the ongoing feud between the kitchen workers and the stable boys. I hear that has escalated recently.'

Her fingers began to work on the ties of his tunic, managing to get them loose enough for her to slip her hands under the fabric to the warm skin beneath. He inhaled sharply but she ignored his reaction.

'Do you want to know what the stable boys have done?' she asked as her hands slipped over the muscles of his stomach.

'They can go hang for all I care,' said Benedictus, claiming her mouth in a brutal kiss.

All thoughts of teasing him were gone in an instant. Together, they stumbled toward his desk. He raised her onto the edge and then he was lifting her skirts, pushing the fabric aside until he found her centre. She moaned as his fingers skimmed over her. She tilted her head back and his mouth moved over the length of her neck, sucking and biting the sensitive skin, claiming her as if he was starved for her. Her breathing quickened. This was a different side to him; this was a frantic, heady race to fulfilment.

He freed himself from his clothes and pushed inside her in one fluid movement. Her nails dug into the skin of his back. His teeth grazed her jaw. The edge of the desk bit into her thighs as he moved over her. Sensation built rapidly as his pace quickened, sharpening until it was nearly painful.

'Adela,' he growled against the skin of her neck. 'Tell me you're nearly there. I cannot...' His teeth sank into her collarbone and she cried out, her hands pulling on his hair.

'So close,' she called, unable to form a complete sentence.

His hand came between them, finding the place she was most sensitive, and pressing hard against it. She erupted around him, calling out his name without caring who could hear. He kept up the pressure as he found his own release; the sensation went on and on until she was whimpering against his lips.

Finally, he stopped and she collapsed against him.

They stayed where they were, breathing heavily, leaning into each other.

'I guess that answers that question,' she said when her heart rate returned to normal.

'What question was that?' His voice was almost slurring as if he'd had too much ale. She loved him this way, drunk on their lovemaking.

'That the marital act does not have to be performed only lying down.'

He barked out a surprised laugh, his arms tightening briefly around her. 'I would be more than willing to find out the various ways the marital act, as you call it, can take place.'

'I'm sure you would.'

He leaned down and kissed her. It started out soft but deepened quickly. She felt him stir against her leg. She pulled her mouth away. 'You cannot possibly want to do that again. I feel as if I need to sleep for a week.'

'I find,' he murmured as his lips connected with hers again, 'that I cannot get enough. As soon as we finish, I want to do it again and again. When we are not together,

I imagine all the ways we could be doing it. It's almost impossible for me to concentrate on anything else.'

A flicker of triumph touched her heart. 'Perhaps you can show me some of the things you imagine later.'

'I'd be more than happy to show you now.'

She smiled. 'We'll miss the evening meal.'

'I'm sure I can arrange for food to be sent up to our chamber later.'

'In that case…'

It was only much, much later, as Benedictus slept next to her and even the great castle settled down for the night, that she recalled his words once more. With his skin still flush against hers and the glow from their time together still coursing through her, she hadn't questioned his words of desire, but now they repeated in a continuous loop.

She pushed his heavy arm off her and slipped out of bed. The nights were turning icy-cold now and she pulled on her undergarments as a protection from the chill. The fire was burning low. She crouched down next to it, prodding the embers with the poker. Benedictus had said that he could not get enough. In the moment, her heart had thrilled. The idea that he wanted her all the time was more potent than a barrel of ale. But now, as the words repeated themselves again and again, she really understood what he had been saying. He had not said that he could not get enough of *her*. When it came down to it, he was referring to their sexual relationship. And yes, he may spend his time thinking about having sex with her but he was not thinking about *her* exactly. Not in the way she thought about him.

Almost her every waking moment was spent considering Benedictus in some way. Of course, she thought about the moments they were together during the night and now she would have some memories of during the day to remember, too, but that wasn't all she was focused on. She worried about him when they were not together. She wondered whether he was hungry or tired, whether the tasks he had to do were boring him or whether he was interested in the work that took up the long hours of the day. She worried about whether he was comfortable or whether she should make him some different clothes that would allow for more ease of movement when sword fighting. In short, she thought about him all the time in many different ways. A cold chill swept through her that had nothing to do with the temperature of the room. That they felt very differently about each other was obvious.

She loved him. Desperately. And without any hope that he loved her back.

Chapter Fifteen

Autumn turned into a cruel winter and Adela still did not bleed. Benedictus commented on her fuller figure, seemingly pleased that she was eating enough for her ribs to finally disappear behind soft flesh he loved to explore every evening. The idea of parenthood never seemed to cross his mind, or if it did, he kept it to himself. Adela believed he did not think of it. She tried not to think about it, either.

She did not want to hope that the child she had longed to love for so long had finally taken root inside her. If she hoped too much and then discovered that her body was doing its normal thing of bleeding many months apart for no reason she could fathom, then the heartbreak might be too much to bear.

As Christmastide approached, so did the imminent birth of Alewyn's child. They had not discussed Benedictus's brother since his visit. Adela had been putting off reminding Benedictus of his promise to her. The only time she and Benedictus had come close to arguing had been when she had confronted him about his relationship with his brother. Since then, she had done little to upset their equilibrium. The shocking knowledge that she loved her husband had kept her from pushing him away by discussing anything that might upset him. She knew it was weak but she did not want to live in a world where he was unhappy with her for any reason.

She realised that made their marriage unequal; that it meant he held all the power while she had none but there was nothing she could do about it. Before she'd even thought about protecting her heart, it was too late.

But Benedictus had promised her the visit and it was the only thing she had asked of him. It was not even as if she wished to go herself. She liked living at Windsor; valued the friendship she had with Medea; enjoyed laughing with her and Theo about the ridiculousness of life at court, and adored the quiet, private moments with her husband.

To upset that and travel to a place she did not know, to meet a woman whom Benedictus clearly resented, was not something she was keen on doing. But it would be good for her husband; good for him to take a break from the relentless pressure at court and to fix his relationship with his brother. Steward John, for all his fussiness, was capable of looking after the goings-on in Windsor for a few days.

She waited until the evening, when Benedictus was drowsy and satisfied from making love to her, before she brought it up again.

'My dear,' she said, stroking the length of his arm. She had taken to calling him that because Benedictus now seemed too formal for the amount of time that had passed between them and yet, *my love*, which was what she wanted to call him, was too revealing.

'Mmm,' he mumbled, his eyes closed, his breath fluttering over the skin of her breast.

'When will we travel to Brae?'

'Where?' he muttered on the verge of sleep.

'Brae, your brother's home. You said we may go when your niece or nephew is born. It will be any day now. I thought we could spend a few days at Christmas with them.'

He lifted his head. 'Christmas?'

'Yes.' She was getting frustrated at how the conversation was going. Perhaps she should have brought this up when he was more awake, arguments be damned.

But Benedictus was waking up now and shaking his head. A knot was forming in her stomach. 'I cannot be away from court at Christmas. There will be much feasting. I will be expected to be here to oversee it in the place of the king.'

The knot tightened. 'I had heard that the king will be home by then.' She didn't believe the rumour even as she'd tried to hold on to the hope of it.

Benedictus rolled onto his back, his furrowed brow not encouraging. 'I wouldn't believe a thing you hear in the Great Hall. Almost all of it is complete nonsense. I doubt the king will be home then and if he is, there is even more reason for me to be here.'

Adela tamped down her rising anger. It would do no good to argue with him. 'Very well. We can go for the start of the New Year.'

Benedictus snorted. 'If I am not here for the Feast of Fools, there is no telling what I will return to. No, I will have to be here to oversee that, too.'

She gritted her teeth; it was getting harder to be unaffected by his words. 'After that, then.'

'The weather will not be favourable for a visit to the south coast of England during the winter. We could get trapped for days in some dingy village along the way, and I cannot afford to be away from Windsor for more than a few days.'

She sat upright, moving away from the distracting warmth of his body. 'When would you like to go, then?'

There was a long silence; she clamped her lips shut, forcing herself not to fill it. Eventually, he answered. 'When the weather turns warmer.'

'And when exactly do you foresee that happening?' She couldn't help it. She was cross now and it was showing in the tone of her voice.

'Maybe in June.'

'But not definitely?'

He turned to look at her. 'What do you mean?'

'You said, *maybe in June*, which suggests that you do not plan for it to take place at that time.'

He sighed. 'Why does it even matter to you? It is not as if you know Alewyn well. You only spent one afternoon with him and you have never met his wife. Why the big concern about their offspring?'

'Offspring!' She pushed herself up into sitting. 'This child will be your niece or nephew. Are you not in the slightest bit concerned about their welfare?'

He sat up, too. 'Adela, I am not sure what I have done

wrong here. I said that we will go and visit my brother, his wife, and whatever child they have but you know, having been married to me for nearly five months now, that I cannot just drop everything. At the moment my life is very busy. I cannot help that. When things calm down, I will be able to arrange a visit.'

'Things will never *calm down*, Benedictus. You take too much on yourself. You are allowed to spend time with your family. Allowed to have some time for yourself, for me, and yet you never seem to want to.'

'I have plenty of time for you. We spend every evening together.'

'We spend every evening between the sheets!' Her blood was boiling now. She had asked him for this one thing. She had thought he was a man of his word but perhaps he had only told her what she wanted to hear at the time. Had only wanted to placate her so that she would not deny him when it came to matters in the bedroom.

'That is what I meant. I devote every evening to you.' His puzzled calmness was only infuriating her more.

'You devote every evening to the piece of anatomy between your legs.' That wasn't entirely fair. He had mapped out her skin with the tips of his fingers and his mouth. He knew how to make her sigh with delight and squirm with pleasure. He was never selfish; never slaked his needs with no thought to her, but her blood was up and she wanted him to understand that she wanted more from him; wanted to feel a connection that didn't start and end in the marriage bed.

'I see,' he said, pushing back the bedcovers and rising from the bed. 'I am sorry my attentions are so abhorrent to you.'

'That is not what I am saying and you know it.'

'I don't know it. I thought that we both enjoyed what transpired in this chamber. I thought that you understood that I must devote my time to my role here at Windsor, and I thought that I was doing the right thing in making my evenings all about my time with you. What more do you want from me?'

'I want your companionship.'

He blinked at her. 'I give you everything I have to give. I am not like my brother. I will not confess my undying love for you and give up everything I do just because you ask it of me. I am sorry if that is what you are hoping for because it is not something I am capable of giving you. You have had the best of me. I thought that was enough. Now I see that I was wrong.' He started pulling on his clothes.

A pit was opening inside her. 'What are you doing?'

'I'm going back to finish all the work I abandoned to spend time with you this evening.'

She said nothing more as he pulled on his boots and strode to the door. She didn't call out to him as he flung open the door and strode through it, and she didn't utter a sound when the door slammed shut behind him. She stared at the space where he had been for a long time. That he had left told her everything she needed to know about his interest in her. If he cared for her at all, he would not leave because he knew that she hated to be alone; knew that it was the worst possible punishment for her; he knew and he had done it anyway.

Chapter Sixteen

Adela tried to sleep but it refused to come. With every creak of the castle, she thought Benedictus was returning to her but the morning broke, cold and wet, and he still hadn't reappeared. She could barely manage to drag her brush through her long hair and, instead of the elaborate braid she normally wore, she put it all into one thick braid.

The cushions she'd been working on were nearly done. She pulled them out from under the bed and laid them on top of the mattress. The seasonal themes seemed childlike now and she wondered if she'd ever show them to Benedictus. She was particularly embarrassed about the summer one, which was a celebration of their marriage, and at which she could now picture him scoffing. She refolded them and put them back where she'd found them. She did not have the enthusiasm to do any more to them today.

She let herself out of the chamber. Her feet nearly took her to Benedictus's antechamber. She hovered by the turning. It would take nothing for her to go in and apologise to him. Their relationship could go back to how it always was and she could forget about his promise to visit the only member of his family who seemed decent, but something held her back.

She didn't want to say sorry for an argument she didn't feel was her fault. She wanted him to understand her point of view; to see that what she was asking wasn't unreasonable; that her request came from a place of love. If that meant a day apart from him, or even longer, while he thought about it, then so be it.

Outside, a harsh wind whipped through the courtyard. The coldness pricked her skin like a thousand tiny needles. She turned to go back to her chamber to fetch her new cloak and walked straight into Sir Hendry. 'Oh, I'm sorry. I didn't see you there.' She moved to go around him but he stepped in front of her. She laughed, although she didn't find the situation at all amusing. 'We seem to be getting in one another's way.'

She stepped to the side again. Sir Hendry blocked her way. Really, it was time to stop being polite to this man. Hopefully then, he would finally leave her alone. 'Sir Hendry, I am cold. I need to get some warmer clothes on.' The wind swirled around her skirts, plastering them to her legs as if emphasising her point.

'I can't allow you to do that, Lady Adela. I had planned to do this at a later date, but now the opportunity has presented itself, I am going to press ahead.' His hand encircled her arm and gripped her tightly. She gasped in surprise and tried to pull away. He smiled oddly and tightened his grip. 'There is no point in struggling. I am far stronger than you and you will only hurt yourself in the process. Come along.'

'No. I am not going anywhere with you.' She tried to dig her heels into the ground, but she might as well have been a leaf in the breeze for all the difference it made to him. With only his hand on her arm, he managed to half lift, half drag her toward the castle gates.

'I had hoped to charm you into this,' he said conversationally as if they were standing in the Great Hall discussing something inconsequential as they had on many a long afternoon. 'It would have been a lot easier for you, and more enjoyable for me, if you had come with me willingly. Just think. We could have spent many nights cuckolding that ugly husband of yours. You would have had an enjoyable time, up until the end.' He shrugged. 'But for reasons unknown to me, you are the first woman I have met who is immune to my looks.'

'I… I don't understand.'

'Oh, it's fairly simple. I am taking you to France with me as a hostage. I'm loyal to the French cause. Edward has no right to enter our country and take our land. He needs to be stopped by any means possible. Edward's queen would have been preferable but as she is not here you're going to have to do.'

Adela's heart slammed in her chest. 'You have lost control of your mind.'

'I assure you that I have not. I have been planning this for many months. It was decided from the moment of your marriage to the second most important man in the kingdom.'

That anyone thought she was important enough to

take was unfathomable. 'Benedictus may be essential to the king but I am not on a par with the queen. This will not stop anything from happening.'

'Your imprisonment will slow things down and that's all we need. Negotiations about your release will take years.'

She stumbled. 'Imprisonment?'

'Yes. You need not fear for your life. We are not heathens. Not unless King Edward refuses to negotiate and even then, you will be kept in luxurious confinement.'

'No.' She shook her head. She could not go back to that half-life again; would not be able to cope with that slow death. 'You will not get past the gates.' She hated that her voice shook but the idea of being kept in solitude, possibly for years, had taken everything from her.

Sir Hendry laughed and her stomach tightened. 'The guards have seen us come and go together. It will not be anything to remark on. Besides, some men loyal to me are on duty right now. They will say nothing.'

'I will shout out. Someone faithful to Benedictus will hear me.'

His lip curled. 'Ah, but will you? I have a knife and, at this stage, I am not afraid to use it on you. I have wasted months of my time in Edward's backwater court. Something has to happen, and killing the wife of the self-righteous Benedictus is not something that would trouble me.' Sweat beaded down her back. They were so close to the gates now and he was right; no one was paying them any attention. Surely, her horror was written all over her face.

'I am willing to risk my life. It would be better than

coming with you.' She meant it. She would rather die than be locked up for days or years without end.

He laughed again. 'Is that so?' A sharp point dug into the side of her stomach. 'This wouldn't kill you, at least not straightaway, but it would probably end the life you are carrying within you.'

Ice flooded her veins. 'I'm not pregnant.'

'Ah, but I think you are. You are certainly bigger than when you arrived at court, and I haven't missed the way you touch your stomach when you think no one is watching you. You may not be sure you are with child but are you willing to risk it?'

She closed her eyes. Sir Hendry was right. If there was even the smallest chance there was a baby growing inside her, and for some time now she had held on to this private, desperate hope, she would not risk a cut to her stomach.

They were passing through the gatehouse now and no one was stopping them. Her head pounded violently. This was really happening; it wasn't some nightmare she could stop. She was being taken somewhere, France probably, by Sir Hendry and no one was coming to save her. Nothing in her life had prepared her for something like this.

Outside the castle walls the wind was even harsher. She shivered as it cooled the sweat against her skin. Sir Hendry either didn't notice or didn't care. They walked until they reached the river, its banks swollen by the recent rain. The knife stayed against her abdomen. Every step had her imagining the horrors awaiting her when they finally reached the river, but all they came to was a horse stood tethered to a tree.

'I thought you hadn't planned to do this today,' she said as tried to dig her heels into the mud; anything to slow them down, but her boots slid over the soft mud and Sir Hendry carried on unimpeded.

'I have a new horse waiting for me every day in case I have to flee.'

The magnitude of what was happening hit her. Sir Hendry was not working alone. He was not a delusional man who had impossibly grandiose ideas. This was part of a well thought through plan. There must be a network of people supporting him. Horses that needed to be stabled and fed and changed daily. 'Who is looking after the horses?'

Sir Hendry smirked. 'As if I will tell you the names of everyone involved. Needless to say, there are more people working against the king than your husband will ever know. However, thanks to Benedictus we aren't able to take the quicker route and travel down the Thames to be picked up by a ship. He has the length of the river guarded and we would be spotted before we got very far. It will be a longer and more uncomfortable journey for you, but we will have to travel by land and catch a ship off the coast of Dover.' Sir Hendry said all this as if Benedictus was the unreasonable one.

Adela made no comment. She had to hope that this overland journey would work out well for her. The longer she stayed in England, the better the chance that Benedictus would be able to find her. That was if he looked. After their row last night, Benedictus might think that she had left him. Other people might think it, too. Sir Hendry was more handsome, more personable, more courtly, than her austere husband. It would not take too much of a stretch of the imagination for people to believe she had run away with him, and that might be what Benedictus would hear. No, surely he would not believe such a rumour, not even after their terse argument.

She barely noticed as Sir Hendry threw her unceremoniously onto the horse. All she could think about were the words she and Benedictus had exchanged and the look on his face as he'd left.

Chapter Seventeen

Benedictus had tried to sleep on the floor of his antechamber, which he knew to be immature behaviour. Especially when he had a perfectly good bed with his beautiful wife in it only a few corridors away. Sleep had remained elusive and as the morning stretched into afternoon, he felt the ache of having been far too stubborn to return to his comfortable chamber just to prove a point. He was a fool and he deserved the physical pain he was experiencing.

He rubbed his shoulder. He should have gone to Adela, pulled her into his arms and apologised for upsetting her. He'd only reacted in the way that he had because what she had said had hit him hard. He loved their evenings together. If he had his way he would spend all day with her, but he couldn't and he'd really believed she understood that. To find that she didn't, had broken a little piece of him.

Even so, he wanted her happiness above all things. If it really was that important to her that she meet Alewyn's child, then it would be nothing for him to arrange for her to visit Brae. She'd have to do so without him but that was not a serious issue, even though his stomach roiled at the thought of being without her for a week or two. Perhaps he could arrange things so that he could spend a day or two there with her, maybe in the middle of her stay. Yes, that was what he'd do. That was the right course of action. The decision made, everything inside him relaxed. All would be well between him and his wife.

He'd go and find her now and suggest that they do exactly that. It was a compromise that would benefit them both and would assuage any guilt he felt over not giving her attention during the day. Not that he felt guilty. He had nothing to feel guilty about. Yes, it was true that most of the time he spent with Adela was in bed but when they were together, she had all of his attention. He pushed down the thought that she wanted more. She may want a union that was more like Theo and Medea's, who spent time together during the day whenever they could. But Benedictus was not Theo. Benedictus had a role to fulfil and he had to follow it through to the very best of his ability. He knew that meant he could not spend as much time with his wife as he wanted to, but the king and the country depended on him.

The door burst open and he leapt to his feet, his sword already partially drawn. He relaxed his grip when he saw Medea and Theodore standing before him but tightened it again when he took in their pale skin and drawn mouths. 'What is it?'

'It's Adela,' said Medea, and his world tilted. 'She's missing. Something's happened to her. Something bad.'

Theodore winced. 'We don't know for sure that it's bad.'

'We do, Theodore. She would never just leave of her own accord.'

Benedictus's knees turned to water. 'Leave…what?'

Medea took a step toward him. 'Adela is missing. She has been gone most of the day. They are saying, but I don't believe it… They are saying that she has gone of her own accord, but I think…'

Theodore held up his hand. 'Medea, please stop. Calm down and let me explain.'

'You will say it all wrong.'

The blood was pounding in Benedictus's ears. The only thing he understood was that Adela was gone. 'Start from the beginning.' He was surprised his voice sounded so calm when it felt like his insides wanted to burst free of his body. Surely, there had to be some mistake. Adela could not have left Windsor. Not unless she had decided to visit Brae by herself. Benedictus's blood ran cold at the thought of her travelling alone. There were so many dangers and she would not be able to defend herself. He would have to ride after her to make sure she was safe. If she really was that determined…

'Adela didn't turn up at court this afternoon,' Medea began, her voice taking on a breathless quality that terrified Benedictus. 'That's not normal, so I went to your chamber to see if she was unwell because…' She trailed off, glancing at her husband as if unsure what to say next.

'She wasn't there,' continued Theodore. 'Medea searched the queen's gardens while I spoke to the guards at the gate. They reported…' Theodore cleared his throat. 'They reported that Adela left early this morning with Sir Hendry. She hasn't been seen since.'

The antechamber spun alarmingly. Benedictus gripped the table edge, the wood biting into his hand.

When the world righted itself again, Theo was looking at him with a mixture of pity and concern.

'She would never have run away with Sir Hendry,' burst out Medea. 'She thought he was irritating. I don't care what everyone else is saying.' Theo shushed her with a wave of his hand.

Benedictus pressed a hand to his chest. His heart was beating painfully fast. He lowered himself to his seat. 'It may be true. She may have left me,' he said, his voice sounding nothing like it normally did. He glanced at Theo, who was studying the floor intently. Theo was a great reader of people. If he thought Adela had left of her own accord then what hope was there? A deep fissure seemed to open up in his heart; it was a pain unlike anything he'd experienced before. 'Tell me the details.'

Theo shuffled on his feet. 'There is nothing really to add. This morning, not long after daybreak, Adela was seen walking toward the castle gates with Sir Hendry. They were walking very closely together. Adela did not seem upset or coerced.'

'Adela did not seem upset?'

Theo shook his head, his eyes full of sympathy that Benedictus did not want to see. 'No.'

Benedictus stared at his desk, his argument with Adela swirling around his mind. Had it really been enough to drive her into Sir Hendry's arms? She had been upset and Benedictus had not handled it well. Why hadn't he gone back to his chamber and apologised? Showing a little humility to his wife wasn't a weakness. She would never betray a vulnerability of his; it wasn't in her nature. She would never betray *him*, of that Benedictus was sure, which could only mean one thing; she had not left Windsor of her own accord; not left to be with Sir Hendry, if, indeed, that was his name.

Benedictus stood. 'I'd like to speak with the guards.'

Theo looked apologetic. 'I spoke to them at length, Ben. As soon as I realised what had happened. They all said the same thing.' Theo was Benedictus's questioner. No one got to the truth better than he did. If he said the guards thought Adela was unconcerned, either she had been or she was too scared to show her emotions. He thought of her frozen and miserable on the day of their wedding and all those evenings she sat unmoving at the front of the Great Hall because she did not like the thought of everyone's attention on her. She was more likely to be frozen when frightened than crying out for help. Adela was a good person; she was kind and thoughtful and a devoted wife to a very underserving husband. Yes, she had been angry with him but she would never leave him without telling him.

Benedictus looked to Medea. She was furiously blinking back tears. 'Medea, tell me what you think.'

Both Theo and Medea looked at him in shock. He winced. Was he really so bad that people didn't think he valued their opinion? He didn't trust easily and so he usually preferred to deal with Theo over Medea; he respected her opinion, but she clearly did not realise that. Adela had told him he could trust her friend and he did. Perhaps, in future, he should make that clearer.

'Adela wasn't...' Medea shook her head. 'Adela *isn't* keen on Sir Hendry. She thinks there is something off about him. I teased her about him being smitten with her but only because I thought the way she wrinkled her nose in disgust was amusing.' She wrung her hands together. 'I'm so sorry. If I'd had any inkling he would do something like this, I would have...' She glanced at Theo. 'I don't know what I would have done but I like to think I would have stopped it. If anything happens to her...' Medea pressed her hand to her chest.

Benedictus nodded. He couldn't speak. A lump was forming in his throat the size of a fist and his heart splintered anew. If Adela was out there scared and alone he would tear the world apart to find her. And, if she had left him on purpose...he would have to find a way to deal with it.

'This isn't Medea's fault.' Theo was subtly inserting himself between his wife and Benedictus, and Benedictus's heart cracked a little more. Did his closest knight really think that Benedictus would do something to Medea because his wife had gone missing? Surely, Theo knew him better than that but perhaps not. Perhaps he really had drifted so far away from those he would call his friend that they didn't really know him anymore.

'It is my fault,' said Theo, his whole body shielding Medea. 'I know you said not to investigate the man but I should have done it anyway. I only asked...'

'Theo is not to blame.' Medea stepped around her husband. 'Theo asked around and no one had a bad word to say about Sir Hendry. I told Theo to stop interfering. He has enough to do without scrutinising someone who appeared so banal.'

'No, it's...'

Benedictus swallowed. Theo and Medea were falling

over themselves trying to protect each other; it would be funny if the situation wasn't so utterly awful. They must fear his retribution badly and yet Benedictus would never hurt either of them, not when they had both shown Adela such kindness and support. By being her friend, they had done more than he had done for his wife. He held up his hand to stop them in their flow. 'Of course it is neither of your fault. If it is anyone's it is mine for not paying close enough attention to Hendry.'

They both quietened and for that Benedictus was grateful. He needed to think. The knowledge that if Benedictus had spent more time with Adela during the day, he might have been able to stop whatever had happened today, struck him with the same force as a physical blow. He would have to analyse his own behaviour later. Now he had to get to the bottom of this.

'I'd like to speak with the guards. Theo, I would like you with me. Medea…thank you for everything you have done so far.' Benedictus winced at Medea's shocked expression but he pushed his remorse to one side. He strode to the door, focusing on his breathing. He would find Adela and she would be well because the alternative was threatening to bring him to his knees.

The guardroom was eerily quiet. None of his guards appeared to be breathing as they lined up against the wall opposite him. None of them would meet his gaze.

At the edge of the line he spotted Mattias, the young soldier Adela had felt sorry for when Benedictus had nearly made him cry. He was staring at a spot in the floor so intently, it was as if he wanted to burn it with his eyes.

Benedictus stalked toward him; the young man's throat bobbed. 'Where is she?'

Mattias shook his head.

Benedictus glared down at him, rage and desperation pulsing through him. Mattias knew something; Benedictus was sure of it. He wanted to pick Mattias up and throw him in the deepest, darkest dungeon he could find, but that would take time, which was not something he had right now. 'Where is she?' he growled.

'I don't know,' whispered Mattias but he wouldn't meet Benedictus's eyes; a sure sign of guilt.

'I think that you do know something and I also think you are going to tell me or spend the next few nights on the rack.'

Mattias groaned, his eyes glassy. Benedictus wanted to shake him; if anyone should be crying it should be him. It was his wife who was missing; his wife who was probably fearing for her life, who had no way of protecting herself. The room span at the thought of her trying to defend herself against Hendry. Adela would not be able to protect herself against him; he would be able to do whatever he wanted to her. 'Please, Mattias.' He heard the sharp intake of breath from the around the room. He never begged, but he would start now if that was what it took. 'Please, Mattias, I have to know where she is. She will be so scared. You may not like me but Adela is a good person. Please... Please help her.'

Benedictus's plea finally broke the young man, who started to sob. 'He said that they loved each other.'

Benedictus's heart quickened. 'Do you mean Sir Hendry?'

Mattias nodded miserably. 'He said that she wanted to run away with him but that you would kill them both.'

'I would never harm Adela. She is all that is good in my life.'

That only made Mattias sob harder. 'We were to look the other way when he took her out this morning, but I thought…' He sniffed and Benedictus wanted to howl. 'I thought it was strange because she wasn't wearing a cloak and, for a woman who was running away with the man she loved, she did not look happy.'

So Adela was out there, scared and alone and also with nothing to keep her warm. Benedictus's knees trembled with the effort of holding him up. Falling apart right now would not help his wife. He needed to keep going, to discover where Sir Hendry was taking Adela and what he intended to do with her. 'You said *we*. Who else knew about this plan?'

Silence greeted his question. And then a man bolted for the door. He didn't get very far before Benedictus caught him around the chest. 'You can come with me. The rest of you, get back to work.'

Mattias slumped down to the ground, but Benedictus paid him no heed. Later, he would see that Mattias be relegated to preparing food in the sweltering kitchens but first, Benedictus was going to get his wife back.

Chapter Eighteen

Adela lay on the sandy beach, curled tightly in a ball. She had stopped retching some time ago but she did not have the strength to stand. The boat ride to France had been long and arduous. Discovering she suffered badly from seasickness had added to her desperate situation. She'd already been weak from nearly two days without sleep or adequate food but now, after a body-jolting journey over the seas, she had nothing left inside her. She knew she should be thinking of escape but she was exhausted. All that filled her mind and every essence of her body was the sheer relief of being on ground that did not move beneath her feet. She tugged the edges of the thin cloak Sir Hendry had given her, trying to bring them together. The material provided only a little shelter from the biting cold but it was better than nothing.

Sir Hendry's voice travelled on the wind. Snatches of his conversation with two other men reached her but she couldn't find it in herself to care overly much about their plans. Not, that is, until she heard her husband's name.

'Are you sure Sir Benedictus will come for her? She's

a scrawny little thing and now he has his hands on her dowry, he does not need her.'

She closed her eyes. She had wondered the same thing during the endless sea crossing. Oh, she had no doubt someone would come for her. She couldn't be seen to easily fall into the hands of the French; it would send a message of weakness that Benedictus wouldn't stand for. She was even confident Benedictus would come himself. What she wasn't sure of was whether it would devastate him if the worst happened to her. There was a strange feeling in the pit of her stomach that had nothing to do with seasickness and everything to do with not knowing the answer to that question. And, shouldn't she be sure? She knew that if *he* died in battle, the light would go out in her life and nothing would ever feel the same again.

'He'll come for her,' said Sir Hendry. 'I don't think there is any love lost between them. He barely looks at her when they are together, but he is both loyal and proud. He has made a vow to protect her and he will honour that. He also will not stand for the insult of her being taken.'

'Can we rely on your men to keep their mouths shut?' Hendry's accomplice sounded worried.

'My men will be loyal to the death and will reveal nothing. The guards who work for Benedictus are terrified of him. It will not take him long to break them. Before long, he will know where we are taking her.'

'Why on God's earth would you tell them?' The accomplice sounded angry now and Adela hoped it would lead to a strong disagreement. 'He won't be far behind us.' The man's gaze darted around him as if expecting Benedictus to leap from behind a sand dune.

Sir Hendry only smiled. 'We want him to follow us, you fool.'

'Have you lost your mind?'

Hendry laughed. Adela couldn't understand why he was getting so much enjoyment out of everyone else's misery. He'd seemed so normal at Windsor; dull but normal; now he seemed like a man who had taken leave of his senses.

'If Sir Benedictus follows us, then he will not be in England. That will give our ships an opportunity to make an attack. But even better…' Hendry's grin widened. 'If we capture him in France then the possibilities are endless.'

Adela didn't realise she was crying until the salty liquid touched her lips. She wiped the tears away with the back of her hand. It had been a point of pride to her not to show Hendry any emotion she couldn't help feeling. She would not give in to her desperation now, not even knowing that Benedictus's life was in threat. He had told her he was a superior fighter. She would have to trust that that was true.

A rough hand grabbed the neck of her cloak and hauled her to her feet. She didn't protest, not even when she was pushed forward, up the beach to a waiting horse, and not when she was flung over it like a sack of wool.

Waves crashed onto the shore, the spray hitting Bene-dictus in the face, despite his distance from the water. It had taken an agonisingly long time to get the details of Hendry's plan from the traitorous guard. When they'd discovered Adela had been taken hostage and was on her way to France, Theo had immediately warned Bene-dictus against going after her himself. 'It's a trap,' he'd said. 'The French will either attack England in your absence or capture you as soon as you set foot on their soil. I will go and get her for you. You must not...'

There had been no doubt in Benedictus's mind. 'I will have to go after her. I trust you as much as I do myself but I cannot be at peace until she is safe with me once more.'

Theo had regarded him for an uncomfortably long time. 'You love her.'

'No.' He was sure he did not. He knew he would not give up his calling in life for her, like Alewyn had done when he was in love. Nor would he ever gaze openly lovingly at her, the way Theo did his wife. He was not capable of loving like that but she was his wife, and her safety was his concern. He could not think of her hurt in any way; to do so would send him to his knees, but even that was not love; he was sure of it. Wasn't he? 'I do care for her very much and I do not want her to be hurt. I also cannot be seen to let this insult to me stand.'

'I see,' Theo had said. There'd been something about his tone of voice suggesting that he didn't, but Benedictus hadn't had the time to question him further.

And now here they were at Dover, hopefully about to make the crossing into France, and every moment away from Adela felt like forever.

'We cannot sail today,' said the captain of the ship he and Theo had commandeered to take them to France.

'The longer we wait, the farther into France they will get and then there is no hope for an easy recovery.' That there was any hope for any sort of recovery was something Benedictus was clinging to like a drunk clinging to an empty barrel of ale.

'We cannot sail today,' the captain of the ship repeated. 'It is too dangerous.' He turned and walked away, his crew following desultorily behind him.

Benedictus watched them go until they had disappeared. He turned back toward the sea, for the first time in his life feeling absolutely helpless. He could go back and insist the captain take them to France. He was powerful enough to do that, but he would also never force someone to risk their life, and from the look of the towering waves, he would be asking just that.

Theo clapped him on the back. 'We know she was still alive yesterday.'

'It's not enough, Theo. It will not be enough until I have her in my arms.' Benedictus no longer cared if Theo saw him at his most desperate and, in the past few days, Theo had seen him at his absolute lowest. Theo had not left his side, had ridden with him through the night and day, and not once complained. To think that Benedictus had nearly taken his friend's loyalty for granted. He would not do that again. Discovering Sir Hendry was a French spy who'd been living in Windsor had him questioning everyone's loyalty and his own ability, but deeper reflection on his many failings would have to wait until after he had found Adela. Until that moment, getting her back was his sole focus.

'We will get you to France. Come on.' Theo tugged him back up the beach toward the town.

Together they tramped up and down the docks at Dover, their boots so full of water they might as well have been sloshing through puddles barefoot. Finally, they discovered a man willing to take them across the channel. His fee was exorbitant but Benedictus would have paid twice the amount.

From past campaigns abroad, Benedictus knew just
how bad travelling by boat was for him. Normally, he
would grip the edge of the ship's rails and stare at a
point on the horizon, fighting to keep himself from
being sick over the edge of the boat, until they reached
their destination. Anything less would show a weakness he was very keen to hide.

This journey was completely different. Unused to
travelling on such rough seas and realising that it made
his sickness so very much worse, he could only curl
himself into a ball and pray that he would not die until
he had lived to rescue Adela.

France was as cold and wet as England but at least
the ground was not swaying beneath them. Theo nudged
him on the arm. 'Not about to give up life as a knight
and become a sailor, then?'

Despite himself, Benedictus smiled. 'If I never get
on a ship again, it will be too soon.' His smile faded.
To get back on a ship, he would have to find Adela alive
and well. He was not going back to England without
her, King Edward be damned.

The nearby town proved to be more helpful than
Benedictus had desperately hoped. It helped that Theo
spoke French like a native. He quickly secured them
two horses and the knowledge that they were only half
a day behind Adela. The knowledge that she was still
alive nearly sent Benedictus to his knees.

'The tavern owner did not like the way Sir Hendry
charmed his wife. It seems the smarmy knight is as attractive to French women as he is to the women at Windsor. His appeal went down very badly with the men of
the town,' said Theo as they saddled two horses. 'He

was more than happy to provide me with all the information we wanted to know. He also said that Adela was
alive and, although clearly very miserable, did not seem
to be harmed in any way.'

Benedictus nodded but could not manage any words
in response. It was as if his insides were trying to crawl
out of his body the longer he spent away from her.

When they were finally on the road, he couldn't
relax, either. It was good that Adela was so far unharmed, he knew that, but he was coming to the realisa-
tion that even knowing she was miserable was torture.
The thought of her beautiful smile dimmed because
some man was using her as a pawn in the games between England and France made him want to tear down
mountains.

He'd known that he cared about her; known that she
had become the most important person in his life, but
what he was feeling now was threatening to overwhelm
him. Could Theo be right? Could this be love? If it
was, he wasn't sure it was something he wanted in his
life. It was too much, too overwhelming. He now knew
that if anything bad happened to Adela, he would be
destroyed.

Chapter Nineteen

The fire in the tavern was roaring but in the far corner of the taproom, Adela was not feeling the benefit. Sir Hendry had placed her away from the door while he spoke to some men in rapid French. How she could ever have believed he was an Englishman was beyond her. The deeper they travelled into France, the less it seemed possible. As the days passed, so did her understanding of the language. She spoke it, of course. Everybody did. But she'd become lazy in recent years and had only used English. Now it was coming back to her, not that she let her captors know she could understand them. If they spoke to her in French, she frowned until they converted to English. It was only a small rebellion but it felt as if she was taking some of the power back.

From what she was understanding right now, Sir Hendry was upset at the slow progress they were making. The French king had been expecting them days ago and would not be happy with the delay. Good. She had done her best to slow things down, dragging her heels whenever she was told to hurry, becoming a dead weight when they lifted her, and generally making a nuisance of herself wherever possible.

Adela tugged on the sleeve of her dress, pulling it over her wrist. Her skin was stained with mud and dirt. She could do nothing about it. She was not left alone for a moment and she was not going to wash in front of these strange men.

Her fear had finally subsided, replaced with a growing anger. All her life, she'd been browbeaten by her father and maybe she would have been more accepting of her current situation if Benedictus had treated her in the same way, but he never had. He never kept her contained or made her follow his rules. He'd allowed her the freedom to make her own decisions about how she spent each day and that freedom had given her a new confidence in herself. A confidence that the past few days had almost wiped out but enough of it was left that she knew she had to act. If they made it to the French king, she would be imprisoned and she would not live like that again. Not to mention what might happen to Benedictus if he was caught on French soil. If she could stop that from happening, then she would do it by any means possible.

She had to take charge of her destiny.

Sir Hendry moved toward her. She wiped her palms on her dress. There was no time to plan. She would have to act now.

'Get up. We are leaving.' Sir Hendry had ceased to be charming toward her a few days ago, finally letting her see the real him behind his chivalric mask.

She didn't move.

He stepped closer. 'Move.' He went to grab her arm, stepping closer still. As his fingertips brushed over her skin she moved quickly and pulled his dagger from the sheath at his waist, pressing it to his stomach.

'I'm not going anywhere with you.'

Hendry laughed and she gripped the handle tighter. 'You won't hurt me. You don't have it in you.'

'You're wrong. I will not be imprisoned again. I've spent most of my life in one room and I will do anything to avoid that fate again. So yes, I do have it in me.'

She slowly stood, making sure to keep her hand steady. For all his confident words, Sir Hendry paled, sweat beading across his brow.

'What is your plan, Adela? Are you going to stab me and then run for your life? You will not get far on your own.'

She had no plan. All she wanted was to get away, but Sir Hendry did not need to know that. 'I will manage on my own. I always have done.'

The door to the tavern opened on a rush of cold wind. She made the mistake of turning her gaze to the noise and froze. Her heart pinched. Benedictus stood, framed in the doorway. She blinked to clear her mind of the image but he was still there. For a heartbeat, everyone stared at the newcomer and he stared, too, his face a mask of shock.

Hendry recovered first. He easily grabbed the dagger out of Adela's hand and pulled her toward him. She bit her lip to stop herself from crying out loud; she would not give him the satisfaction of knowing how frightened she was.

Benedictus snarled and started toward them. Sir Hendry waved his knife in front of her, and her husband came to a complete stop.

'I don't want to hurt your wife, Sir Benedictus. I'm quite fond of her but I will if I have to. I'm going to request that you stay exactly where you are unless you want to see something happen to her.' Hendry's hand slid to her neck and she shuddered.

Benedictus's hand clenched but he stayed put. 'Give her to me and I will walk away from here with no repercussions for you.' Benedictus sounded calm but she could see the telltale tick in his jaw, which showed just how furious he really was.

She was desperate to run to him, to place her head against his chest and take shelter from the unfolding events, but she held herself completely still, barely daring to breathe.

Sir Hendry snorted. 'The moment I hand her over to you is the moment before I die. No. I don't think so. Adela and I will be leaving and you will stay here unless you want something terrible to happen to her right in front of you.' He pressed his knife to her throat; the blade nicked her and a small trickle of blood dripped down her skin.

Benedictus's eyes hardened and she shivered. 'You have insulted me, taking my wife from the stronghold in which we live. I cannot allow that to go unpunished. I will be taking my wife back to England but whether I take her alive or dead is of little consequence to me.'

Sir Hendry's grip on her loosened. 'What?'

Benedictus shrugged. 'Lady Adela has served her

purpose. She has provided the king with funds to continue with this war between our two countries and that was all that was required of her. But you…you have come into the seat of English power and have sought to embarrass me and I cannot let that go unpunished. Do what you will with Adela but know that you will not be leaving here alive regardless.'

'You think that you can best me in a fight?' Hendry sneered. 'You are an old man who does nothing but sit behind a desk all day, giving orders to those more physically able than yourself. You would not last a morning in a real battle.'

Benedictus laughed, a harsh sound Adela had never heard before. 'Would you like to test that theory right now? You will be crying for your mother within moments.'

Hendry flung Adela to one side. She crashed awkwardly to the floor, crying out as pain shot through her arm. Hendry pulled his sword from its scabbard and charged toward Benedictus. Within moments the rest of the patrons had fled in a hurried scraping of chairs and pounding footsteps until only her three captors remained. Hendry's accomplices surrounded Benedictus, their swords pulled. Adela's heart pounded in her throat as they closed in on him.

Benedictus seemed to grow, his arms thickening, and his teeth bared in a feral snarl. He whirled around and before the men could move, Benedictus knocked the sword from one of their hands, and with one punch sent that same man sprawling to the ground.

'Don't be a coward. Attack him!' yelled Hendry to

his remaining accomplice. But Adela could tell Hendry's co-conspirator was wary now, afraid of Benedictus's power.

Adela's husband smiled grimly. 'You are right to be afraid. I am a superior fighter to you in every way. You cannot win against me. It would be better for you if you ran.'

The man's gaze flickered from Benedictus to Hendry; whatever he saw in both men's expressions had him running for the door; it slammed shut behind him.

In a roar of rage, Hendry charged at Benedictus. Adela screamed as Hendry grazed Benedictus's stomach with his sword. Whether her husband was hit or not was hard to tell because he did not falter. His sword flashed as he rained down blow after blow. Adela could not tear her eyes from the bout. Even though her stomach twisted at every move, something inside her thrilled at Benedictus's skill. Here was the fearsome warrior everyone talked about; the man the French feared more than the whole of the English Army.

Hendry was backing away to the corner of the room, his movements becoming increasingly desperate; his eyes frantic. Benedictus swiped so quickly the movements were a blur. Hendry's sword clattered to the floor and his jaw fell open in a wordless scream. Benedictus stood over him, his blade close to the Frenchman's neck.

Adela closed her eyes tightly. She may not like Hendry, may have wished him to the devil since he'd captured her, but she did not want to see him die.

There was a smack of flesh hitting flesh, a chair scraped and there was the thud of a body hitting the floor.

Arms came around her and she squealed. 'It's me.' Benedictus's voice spoke in her ear. 'Everything is all right now.' He pulled her tightly to his chest.

She leaned against him. Beneath her ear, his heart beat wildly.

His fingers tangled into her hair. 'You are all right. I have you.'

She swallowed. 'Is he dead?' Her voice was raspy, as if she had not used it in days.

'No. But when he wakes up, he will wish that he was.' Benedictus ran his fingers along her jaw, her shoulder, her hip, his touch gentle. 'Are you hurt? Your neck?'

'It's only a scratch.' Benedictus muttered something so low she couldn't hear it. 'My wrist hurts from when I fell to the ground.'

'Let me take a look.' He let go of her and gently took her hand in his. She cried out when he touched a spot. 'Sorry, sorry. I'm so sorry, Adela, more than you will ever know.'

'It's not too bad. But where you touched it before… that was painful.' It amazed her that they were having this conversation. It was almost as if they were back in the chamber at Windsor and not in a tavern in France with three bodies in various states of consciousness behind them. It was almost as if Benedictus hadn't ripped her heart out when he'd told Hendry she didn't matter to him. Almost as if they hadn't argued. Almost as if she could pretend both things hadn't happened. But they had. She was going to have to think about everything that had passed at some point. To decide how much of what he had said had been a distraction and how much of it had been the truth, about how much of their argument was important and how much wasn't. Right now she would concentrate on her wrist and on getting as far away as possible from Hendry and his cronies.

'I don't think anything is broken,' said Benedictus as he inspected her arm. 'I will find something to strap it up all the same. It will be less painful for you when we are travelling. Can you stand?'

'Yes.'

He helped her to her feet. She stumbled once and he caught her before she could fall again. 'Adela, I…'

The sound of the tavern door opening had Benedictus whirling round and reaching for his sword once more. But it was only Theo, a wry look on his craggy features. 'I see things escalated while I was in the stables.'

'Where were you?' demanded Benedictus.

'Seeing to the horses, as per your request.'

'It would have been far better had you been in here.'

Theo flinched at Benedictus's words. Adela did not understand why he always had to be so sharp to people who cared about him, but aside from his physical reaction, Theo did not seem to mind. 'I'll bear that in mind for next time.' Theo surveyed the room. 'What do you want me to do with them?' He nodded to the two men who hadn't stirred.

'I don't care.' Benedictus lifted Adela, cradling her gently against his chest.

Theo's eyes widened. 'You don't care? Are you sure? Don't we need to find out why they took Adela and what they intended to do with her?'

'Do all the interrogating you want. Adela and I will ride back to the village of Yvoire and find a place to stay.

We will meet you at the crossing the day after tomorrow. The sooner we are back on English soil, the better.'

Benedictus didn't wait to see what Theo did next. He strode out of the tavern carrying Adela as if she weighed nothing at all.

Chapter Twenty

Rain hammered down on them as they rode through the afternoon. Cold seeped into Adela's bones, her whole body shaking violently no matter how tight Benedictus wound his arms around her. Tiredness dragged her every movement; she wanted to sleep more than she wanted anything.

Benedictus hadn't asked her about her time with Hendry; hadn't enquired whether she'd run away with him of her own accord or been dragged. Perhaps he knew. He must have interrogated someone to know where to find her. Neither of them said a word to each other and even though she knew that was what caused the problems in their marriage, she couldn't find the way to begin. And because she couldn't begin, she was left trying to guess how he felt about everything that had passed.

If anything, the silence between them was worsening with every league. Benedictus rode in stony silence, reminiscent of the early days of their marriage. She wanted to cross the chasm that was opening up between them but exhaustion tugged on all her senses and she couldn't find the words.

Her head bounced against his chest as she slipped in and out of consciousness, no longer able to keep fully awake. After what could have been days, she was aware of him lifting her off his horse and carrying her inside a smoky room, aware of words being spoken as Benedictus sorted out their accommodation, but she could barely concentrate on what he was saying. She must have dozed off again against his side because the next thing she was aware of was being placed in front of a roaring fire.

'The landlord is bringing some clothes for you to wear. We'll need to get you out of these wet ones before you catch a chill.' The words he spoke were the first since he'd rescued her from the tavern, and they roused her out of her tiredness. Her hands went to the ties of her clothes; she hissed as pain scorched through her arm.

'Careful,' said Benedictus, gently nudging her out of the way. His fingers, trembling slightly, fumbled over the wet knots. He paused and let out a long, steady breath. 'These need to come off.' He slipped his dagger from its sheath and cut through them. He tugged them from her body and they fell to the floor with a wet thud. Despite the fire, goose bumps rushed over her skin. He rubbed her arms vigorously before reaching over and pulling a blanket from the bed. He wrapped it around her. 'You're so cold.' His hands slipped beneath the blanket and he began rubbing them along her skin again. There was nothing sexual about his touch, nothing loving. It was all practicality. Despite the warmth of his hands, she was numb. She had longed to be away from Hendry but now that she was, there was no overwhelming relief, just an unending darkness. She wanted to sleep and forget.

Benedictus lowered himself onto the dusty floor and leaned against the wall. He stared at the bed where Adela was sleeping. He'd thought only of getting Adela back from the moment he'd discovered she was missing. He hadn't given a thought to what she would be like when he'd found her, partly because the thought that she might be harmed in any way had been like staring into a black void, and partly because finding her had consumed him completely.

When he'd seen her holding a knife to Sir Hendry, he'd experienced an intense mixture of pride and terror and he'd hesitated for the first time in his existence. That hesitation had nearly cost Adela her life. He wasn't sure he would ever be able to forgive himself for that.

He'd known he could take on the three men and win. They were nothing, merely irritating flies on a summer's day. One swat and they would go away, but seeing Adela with a blade so close to her precious body had nearly robbed him of his strength. He, who always kept calm no matter the situation, had panicked. He had said those awful, dismissive words about her lack of importance to him; the words, so reminiscent of the way his father spoke about people, had made him sick to the stomach.

Sir Hendry had believed them but surely Adela hadn't. She must know that she meant more to him than her dowry; that the thought of her hurt or dead would kill him. He knew he had never said the words; knew that they had argued about his lack of attention, but surely all he felt for her was obvious, if not by his word, then by his deed. It was finally obvious to him. He did love her. And yes, it might not be in the same way as his friends loved their wives, but it was just as true for them as it was for him. He adored her; she was his life and his love.

She was frightening him now, though. She had barely spoken since he had found her and he didn't feel as if it was like the silences in the early days of their marriage. This was a quietness that seemed to touch darkness and he didn't know how to reach her, how to pull back to the light. She was curled up in the centre of the bed, sleeping soundly, and he was glad she was resting. She'd reassured him that it was only her wrist that hurt. And yet… And yet, there was something so profoundly different about her that he couldn't help but think something must have happened to her; something she didn't want to discuss with him.

And now she was unresponsive to him, to his touch, and to his words. It was killing him to have her with him in body but not in mind, but he had no idea how to reach her, no idea how to say everything that was in his heart. Words, which had always come so hard to him, were impossible now.

He pushed himself to his feet. He had found her, so why did it feel as if she was still lost to him? That damned lump was forming in his throat once more. He swallowed but it wouldn't go away. He crawled onto the mattress behind her. She didn't wake as he pulled her to his chest, or when he whispered her name into her hair or even when tears, he would never acknowledge, soaked into her hair.

Chapter Twenty-One

A rowing boat was waiting for them high up on the shoreline. The ship to take them back to Britain farther out to sea. Even though Adela knew this boat was her way home, she still slowed her approach to it, knowing that as soon as she was on the waves, she would feel as if her world was ending until they reached the other side. Next to her, Benedictus seemed equally reluctant to reach the safety of their own people. Theo, who had joined them earlier, grim-faced but resolute, was striding toward the boat ahead of them as if the boat wasn't the embodiment of hell on earth.

'It's like being tortured,' Benedictus muttered as men began to haul the rowing boat down to the shoreline.

'Being on a boat?'

He nodded. 'It makes me very sick.' It could have been the brisk breeze that turned his cheeks red.

'Me, too.'

They shared a grimace as they began to follow the others to the sea. Before they could catch up with them,

Benedictus stopped her with a brush of his fingers on the back of her hand. 'Did he hurt you? Hendry or the men travelling with him?' He glanced down at her body and she knew what he was asking. His skin had paled and his eyes were full of emotion.

'Nobody hurt me,' she said. 'I was only to be used as a ransom in the ongoing negotiations with France.'

He nodded and appeared to be about to say something else; she waited, breath held, but the sailors were calling them onto the boat, rushing them before the tide turned and the moment was lost.

The voyage back across the Channel was as painful as the one over. Adela could only lie amongst the thick ropes coiled on the deck, her body too heavy and too sick to move. The only difference was that this time Benedictus was curled around her, seemingly as incapacitated as she was.

'Did someone just say Dover is in sight?' Benedictus's voice was barely audible over the howling wind. She was only able to hear him because he spoke directly into her ear. He sounded as pained as she felt.

'I didn't hear anyone say anything.'

'It must be wishful thinking, then.'

Adela never would have predicted that Benedictus would suffer from seasickness. She would have thought he would have willed his body into submission, forcing it to do what he commanded. And yet, he seemed sicker than she was, as if he was holding on to her not to give comfort but to receive it. As if her touch was somehow soothing to him. She rolled to face him, burrowing herself deep into his familiar chest. His arms tightened around her and she knew, regardless of what happened next, in this moment she was safe. Finally, blessedly, sleep claimed her.

It was impossible to say who helped whom onto the docks at Dover. Benedictus didn't want to admit just how much he was relying on his wife to hold him upright. Together, they staggered along the wooden planks like two drunks after a luxurious feast. Theo followed them slowly, for once not making any jokes at his expense. If anyone of his enemies saw him now, they would know it would take nothing to beat him. Put him on a boat and he became as helpless as a baby. He wanted nothing more than to find a room at a tavern, pull his wife into his arms, and sleep for the next few days.

That dream was cut short as soon as they stepped into the town.

A couple of guards jogged toward them, their chain-mail marking them out as men from Windsor before they got close enough for him to see their faces.

'Sir,' one of them called. 'Thank the good Lord that you are returned so quickly. The French have returned to the Thames. Last we heard our men were keeping them at bay, but more ships have been spotted off the coast and an invasion is surely imminent.'

Benedictus could only stare at them. It was as if the words were coming at him through a thick soup. He understood the urgency and yet his body was not reacting as it normally would. He knew he should be running, calling for a horse, and shouting out orders, and yet he was oddly frozen.

Next to him, Adela slipped from his arms and he wasn't quick enough to hold on to her.

The movement roused him slightly from his stupor. 'When did this occur?' He had only been absent for five days; surely, England couldn't fall to the French in that time. Had that been Hendry's move all along? To distract him and then take England while his back was turned? If so, the plot had worked humiliatingly well.

'The latest information we have is two days old, sir.'

Not too long ago, then. There was still hope that he could avert a crisis. 'Where's my horse?'

'He's waiting for you at the nearest stable. We've had him saddled and ready to go since we arrived in the hope that you would turn up. Sir Theo's and the Lady's are ready, too.'

Normally, Benedictus appreciated such efficiency, but today he would have welcomed the rest for the time it would have taken for the horses to be prepared. 'And provisions?'

'Also ready, sir.' The man was puffed up with pride for having done a good job.

'Well done,' said Benedictus because what else could he say? He'd trained these men to be well organised and he couldn't criticise them when they had done their job properly, even if it meant he'd had no time to rest.

'I want to go to Brae.' He turned to Adela. Her skin was still a deathly pale shade, her eyes as shuttered as they had been since he had found her.

He pushed his hand through his hair. He couldn't understand why she was returning to this argument right now. They could discuss this again when the fate of the country was not hanging in the balance. 'There is no time to make a social call,' he snapped. 'I must return to Windsor as a matter of urgency.'

She nodded once. 'That is true, but you do not need to come with me.' His heart slammed in his chest. She couldn't be saying what he thought she might be. And then her next words confirmed that, yes, she was. 'I would like to travel to Brae instead of returning to Windsor.'

What did she mean by this? He couldn't let her go. Not after he'd gone to such lengths to get her back; not when she was the only person whose company he truly enjoyed. Couldn't she see that he needed her? 'No. I forbid it.'

Something in her eyes flickered. 'Do you really?' she asked softly.

He thought about what she had told him, how her father had controlled everything and about his promise not to be like the man who had raised her and ruled her life. He turned away from his men, blocking their view of her. 'Is this really what you want?'

'Yes.' She dropped her gaze.

He cupped her cheek, tilting her face so that she had to look at him. It didn't help. He could not read her expression; could not understand the meaning behind her words. 'I have to go to Windsor. I cannot travel with you to Brae. You understand this?'

She nodded, stepping away from him so that his hand dropped to his side. 'I understand. You have your role to play. It is an important one and I would not stop you or expect you to choose me over it, but I am tired. I cannot face Windsor and everything that goes with it. You do not need me and I will only slow you down when you need to be quick. Please tell me you understand.'

Dread curled in his stomach. The only thing he understood was that she didn't want to be with him. Behind her, his men were waiting for him. He could not ride with her to Brae. He did not have the time to spare but, for the very first time in his life, he wished it wasn't so. He should tell her. It seemed important that she know, but the words would show a weakness he could allow none of his men to witness. They needed him to be strong, now more than ever. 'Theo will take you.'

'Can you spare him?'

No. Theo was one of his best men, and Benedictus needed him with him but Theo was also one of only three men Benedictus would trust with his wife. 'Yes, I can spare him. I must leave you now. Every moment I delay could have serious consequences.'

She nodded, still not meeting his gaze. He slipped a finger under her chin and tilted her face to his again. Her expression was still blank; he would have preferred anger or annoyance; at least then he might know what to do and what to say to make this right.

He leaned forward and pressed his mouth to hers. For a brief moment he thought she might kiss him back, but there was no responding movement from her and his heart splintered. He stepped back. 'I hope you like it at Brae. Alewyn will take good care of you.'

'Yes. Thank you for taking such good care of me, Sir Benedictus. I wish you good speed on your return journey.' Then she was turning away from him and Benedictus, who would have sworn that he never cried, felt tears prick the backs of his eyes. She was talking to him as if he was a stranger, and it wasn't because he was surrounded by his men, and he didn't think it was because she was in shock. It was because of him and who he was. He didn't know how to make this right and there was no time for him to even try.

Chapter Twenty-Two

Riding along the coastal path wind whipped through Adela's hair, pushing away the last vestiges of seasickness. Even though her stomach wasn't roiling anymore, she did not feel better. If anything, the heavy dragging sensation in the pit of her stomach was worsening with every league that passed.

A deep fissure had opened up beneath her breastbone as if her heart really had cracked into two pieces. The pain was constant, so excruciating it was hard to believe she could keep living.

'I need to stop for a rest,' she told Theo as they rounded another outcrop. She didn't wait for Theo's response before stopping and slipping from her horse. Theo rode up next to her and joined her, staring out over the clifftops, saying nothing.

The sea looked so calm from high above, nothing like the rolling nightmare that had made her so desperately unwell when she and Benedictus had crossed it earlier. Seagulls called to one another over the headland, oblivious to her distress far beneath them.

She'd made the right decision in deciding not to go back to Windsor. She loved Benedictus and he did not love her. To spare them both, it was better for her to have distance from him. She could repair her heart, harden it so that she could cope with a loveless marriage; make it so that she didn't love him; make it so that it didn't hurt when he walked away from her. Then they would be equal and she would no longer feel the pain that unrequited love was giving her. When she next saw him, she would be the calm and practical wife he needed and not someone who craved the attention he couldn't give her.

She'd done the right thing. And yet... The quiet desolation in his eyes when she'd told him she was not returning with him was haunting her with every league that passed. She'd been too caught up in her own feelings to pay this any attention, but now...

'I'm not asking him to put me first,' she spoke out loud as if she and Theo had been in conversation the whole time.

'I know.' Theo's quiet confirmation did not stop the turmoil of her thoughts.

'I would never have asked or expected him not to go off to defend the country from the French. That is what he has to do.'

'Yes.'

'I understand he has to work hard, harder than anyone else. I know that he must put the needs of the kingdom before mine. I don't resent that. I... I just... It just... When he... It hurts.'

'Mmm...'

'I didn't expect to love him and it isn't his fault he doesn't love me back. I am not angry with him. He told me how it would be at the start of our marriage. If there is any fault, then it is mine. I'm not sure he is capable of love.'

The wind took her words out to sea and for a long time, Theo did not respond. She almost thought he wouldn't but eventually he muttered, 'I'm not sure it's true he cannot love. I think…perhaps…that he does. And that, perhaps, he feels things far stronger than I, or anyone else, could imagine.'

Adela closed her eyes as her heart twisted painfully. 'If it isn't true then I have made a terrible mistake.' She inhaled deeply. 'I have to be sure, Theo. Completely and utterly sure, for me and for the baby I think I am going to have.' She ignored Theo's quick inhale. 'I have to know that, despite everything, he is capable of love and that he feels it for me, even if he can never articulate it, because the alternative is too painful to contemplate.'

'He begged a man.'

She whirled round to look at Theo. 'What do you mean?'

'When Benedictus realised you'd been taken, he begged a man to tell him where you were.' Theo stared out across the water. 'He did it in front of lots of his soldiers. Men who have only ever seen him as a for-midable warrior. I have never seen Benedictus act like that before. Not once in all the years I have known him, even when he was younger and not so…uptight.' He turned slowly to face her. 'Over the last few years, I have found it difficult to relate to him. So have all of us who knew him as a young man. He has become harder and more closed off. He pushes those who want to be close to him away. I thought it was a combination of the way his parents are and the pressures of the role he has undertaken. I thought it had reached a point where his hardness was set in stone and could not be changed. He has cut off his relationship with his brother and that made me think he had become an unreachable tyrant, but now I am not sure…' Theo trailed off, turning his gaze back out to sea.

Adela's heart clenched. Benedictus was aloof but she'd never thought of him as a tyrant. He was too thoughtful, too kind, and too loyal to be an absolute ruler. He would never want the complete authority of a king. He may show a certain face to the world but that was not all there was to him. He was deeply sad about his relationship with his brother, even though he would not admit it to anyone, even himself. She could see that he felt deeply about that, even if no one else could. Perhaps that was her answer. Maybe he did love her; she just needed to take a deeper look at him.

In leaving him, had she made things worse? More to the point, could she return to him knowing that he might never love her as she loved him? Knowing that, if he did come to care for her in that way, he would never be able to show it? She pressed her hand to her chest; whatever decision she made, it had to be the right one for her.

Chapter Twenty-Three

The celebratory mood of the makeshift campsite was entirely at odds with the way Benedictus was feeling. His men slapped him on the back as he walked through them in the fading light of an autumnal dusk. The soldiers were almost drunk on the recent victory, which was normal when a win had not been assured from the outset. When Benedictus had arrived the French were gaining the advantage. Full of rage, Benedictus had shown them no mercy and now his warriors were full of praise for him, for the way he had driven the French from English waters; the way he had seemed fearless in the face of their advance. The praise was misplaced. He had been trained to fight since he could walk. The aggression and the force needed to overpower an enemy was second nature. He had barely been thinking of what he was doing. His mind had been consumed with thoughts of Adela and the knowledge that she would not be at Windsor when he returned. The rage coursing through him had nothing to do with the advancing enemy and everything to do with the anger he felt for himself.

He shouldn't be surprised that she'd left him. That was what everyone did. And he didn't even blame her. She deserved someone who could show her how much he loved her, even if he wanted to rip the world apart at the thought of her with someone other than himself. He wanted her to be happy above all things and if being apart from him allowed her this, then he would learn to accept it, not resent it.

He was glad when he finally reached his tent. He could go inside and stop the pretence that he cared about his win against the French. Hopefully, he would sleep. If he slept, he could, for a short period, forget.

The interior of the tent was dark. He blinked as his eyes adjusted. A movement at the back of the tent and his tiredness vanished in an instant. He held his breath. Yes, there it was, the soft exhale of someone who didn't belong in here. His hand strayed to the hilt of his dagger.

'Benedictus.'

He froze. 'Adela?'

'Yes.'

There was the rustling of skirts and then the brush of a finger over the back of his hand. His heart stuttered at the contact, unsure whether it was real or if he was already dreaming.

'You're here.'

'Yes.'

He blinked and gradually shapes came into focus. He could just make out her edges in dim light. He reached up and traced the length of her jaw, the soft skin beneath her ear, her neck.

Adela let out a shuddery breath and slipped her arms

around his waist, pulling him close until they were flush against each other.

'Why are you here?' He felt her flinch and her arms loosened. He tightened his grip before she could move away. 'It's not that I want you to go.' Now that she was here, he would not repeat his mistakes. He might never have flowery words or be able to perform gestures of courtly love but he could be honest. And if he was honest, perhaps he could convince her to stay with him always. 'I thought you were going to Alewyn's castle.'

'I was but then I thought of how tired you must be, and I remembered how the last time you went to fight the French and how you didn't eat or sleep properly, and I thought perhaps you needed me here. Come, I managed to get you some food, because I'm sure you haven't thought to fetch some for yourself.' He allowed her to tug him deeper into the tent, her concern lightening his heart. 'There are some blankets near here.' She bent and he could hear her patting the ground. He should say something but there was a lump constricting his throat and no words would come. 'Ah, here they are. Come and sit beside me.'

There was something comforting about following orders rather than giving them, and he gave in to the sensation. A warm bowl was thrust into his hands and he began to eat, automatically spooning the tasteless stew into his mouth. There was so much he wanted to say and yet he did not know how to begin. Even though they were alone, this was already turning into one of those awkward dinners where he couldn't talk to the one person to whom he had the most to say.

He'd barely settled his spoon back in his empty bowl and Adela was taking it from him and setting it to one side.

'This can't be comfortable,' she said, tugging at his chainmail. 'Let me help you take it off and then you can get some sleep.'

He caught her hand. 'No. That's not what I want to do.'

'Oh. Well…if you would like, I can leave you to call in your men. I am sure you will want to debrief them on today's events, although I really think you should rest.'

His eyes had adjusted to the light enough that he could see her head was turned toward their clasped hands. Her voice sounded practical but her shoulders were drooped and his heart clenched at the sight. She was sad and it was because of him, because she thought he cared more about his duties than about her.

'I don't want to speak to my men. I want to talk to you.'

She looked up at him then, her lips parted in surprise. He wanted to lean down and capture them with his own, but he knew that was where he had gone wrong in the past. He had tried to show her how he felt by using his body, but she had no idea at the depth of his feelings, and so now he had to find the right thing to say.

'Adela, I am not good with words.' He huffed out a laugh; that was an understatement. 'I can give orders, I can sum up political strife, I can solve an argument between warring barons with a few simple phrases, but when it comes to matters that mean a great deal to me… the words…they get stuck.' He touched his chest and he saw her nod. He thought she might understand but he did not want to leave it there. He had to make it clear she knew how he felt about her. He never wanted to experience the pain of her leaving again. 'I want you to know that you are everything to me.' He heard her soft gasp but he pressed on. 'I will never be a man to whisper poetry in your ear or perform acts of courtly love, but I need you. I need you so much.'

'Oh, Benedictus.' She closed the gap between them and pressed her mouth to his, and he could have taken it further, given in to the desire that always seemed to simmer between them, but he wanted to talk, to know that she really understood and to see if, just possibly, she felt the same way.

He pulled his head away from her. 'As much as I'd like to keep doing that, I think we ought to stop before we get carried away.' He slipped his arms around her and tugged her close. 'I don't want you to think I am dedicating our time together to the anatomy between my legs, as you called it.' He hoped she could hear the smile in his voice because he didn't want her to think he resented anything she had said to him.

'I shouldn't have said that. It was mean and it implied that I didn't enjoy our time together, when it is one of the greatest joys of my life.'

His heart squeezed. 'Mine, too. But I think I understand what you were trying to say to me that night. You want there to be more to our marriage than what goes on in the marital bed.'

'There already was more. I just didn't realise it until I stopped to really think. I know that you cannot speak your feeling easily, Benedictus. We are alike in that respect. Neither of us has had much practise. Together, we can learn.'

Together: he liked the sound of that. 'You are not going to Brae, then?'

'I would still like us to go together. And before you protest, I will understand if you cannot go but I want you to be honest with yourself and with me. Is it because you have too much to do or is it because you are angry with Alewyn for leaving you?'

'I… He…' Benedictus started but couldn't finish.

'You can tell me the truth, my love.'

Benedictus's heart jolted. She had never called him her love before. It amazed him how much he liked it, how right it felt. He was her love, and she was his and that made everything else easier. 'I am upset that Alewyn left me. It feels as if everyone does.' His voice sounded small even to himself. A part of him thought that he should be embarrassed by such a confession, but the bigger part of him was relieved to finally admit the truth to himself. He'd been lonely and it was only when Adela had walked away that he'd truly realised it.

'He hasn't left you, my love. Alewyn is still the brother you have always had. I know that if you could relax the walls you put around yourself, then you would find that all your brother knights would be pleased to be close to you once more.'

Before today, he would have said her request was impossible. Before entering the tent, he would have said that he didn't want to do what she suggested, but with her by his side, perhaps anything was doable. 'I will try but I fear I have become so entrenched in my ways I do not know how to stop. It is only with you that I feel relaxed enough to be myself. For you, though, I will try and change.'

She laid a hand on his arm. 'No, that's not what I want. I want you to be yourself. I don't want you to be any different. I love you the way that you are. If you can see it in yourself to relax, then…'

But Benedictus had stopped listening. 'Say that again.'

She paused. 'I want you to be yourself… Is that what you…'

'No, not that. You said you loved me.'

She cleared her throat. 'I do.'

He slipped his fingers along her jaw and into her hair, tilting her face until she was turned to him. This close, he could see into her eyes. He wanted to be looking straight at her; wanted her to be able to see him. 'I love you, too.' The smile that spread across her face was worth more than all the gold in the kingdom. He pressed a kiss to that smile, joy bubbling through him, lighting him up from inside. 'I wish I could marry you again. This time I would show you in words and deed how much I feel for you. I would order the finest feast and no one would doubt for one moment that I was the happiest man in the world to become your husband.'

He felt her laughter tremble through her. 'No feast. We are not good at feasting.' Her lips brushed over his lightly, her hands running up the length of his arms. 'Let us make our own vows in private, right here, right now instead.' She inhaled deeply. 'I promise you, Benedictus, that I will not leave you again. That I will always be by your side, no matter what life throws at us. I vow to you that I will always be honest with you, even when I don't think you'll like what I have to say. I swear to you that I will love you, no matter what lies ahead in our future and that you will never have cause to doubt my love.'

Benedictus swallowed. Words were hard for him but his wife had laid her soul bare; he could offer her the same. He ran his thumb along the delicate edge of her jaw. Her pulse pounded under his fingertips. 'I promise you, Adela Monceaux, that, though it may sometimes appear differently, you will always be my first thought. That with every breath that I take I will love you and care for you until the very end of my days. I vow to you that I will always be honest about how I feel no matter how difficult that is for me, and I swear that you will never have reason to doubt my love.' He brushed over her lips once, twice, and then again, deeper this time.

'I have something else to tell you,' she whispered as his mouth trailed down the length of her neck.

'I think I already know.' His hand traced the small swell of her belly. 'There may be someone else for us to love sometime in the spring.'

'It's frustrating how you always know everything,' she gasped as his mouth moved lower still.

'Not everything,' he said, moving his hands over her body. 'I'm not sure, for instance, whether you like to be kissed the most here…' He pressed his lips to the soft skin of her neck. 'Or here.' He moved to the base of her throat. 'Or somewhere else entirely.'

'I think you should spend some time finding out,' she murmured breathily.

He laughed against her skin. 'I shall do just that.'

Epilogue

Benedictus stared down at his daughter's tiny face. Only a few hours old and he was already so desperately in love with her he knew he would take down kingdoms if she needed him to.

Beside him on the bed, Adela dozed lightly, her hand flung above her head.

Their daughter stirred and Adela's eyes fluttered open. 'Is she all right?' she murmured.

'Just stretching.' It always amazed Benedictus how in tune Adela was with their children; she instinctively seemed to know when one of them needed her and she always gave them her full attention. They were never in any doubt that their parents loved them with all that they had, but he worried that she was giving too much of herself. 'I think this beautiful girl should be our last.'

Adela smiled sleepily. 'You say that every time.'

'Six children is more than enough for anyone.'

Adela rubbed his arm. 'You just don't enjoy the labour. I'm sure you'll forget in time.'

Benedictus frowned. 'I hate seeing you in pain.'

She smiled, slightly more awake. 'It is getting easier every time.'

'For you, maybe.'

She laughed tiredly and he grinned. He loved the sound of her happiness. Even after all these years, it gave him a deep satisfaction that he could bring her joy.

'Do you need to go and relieve Theo from his duties?' Adela murmured, her hands moving as if to take hold of their daughter.

'I'm sure he can manage for a while longer. I think he is getting tired in his old age. He seems to prefer sitting in my antechamber with his feet up rather than patrol Windsor looking for treasonous plots.'

Adela's grin was wide, even as her eyes flickered shut again. 'If only you hadn't used those cushions, my love. Now everyone thinks you are going as soft as your benches.'

Benedictus smiled down at his daughter. None of his knights would ever accuse him of softness, although with Adela's influence he had unbent slightly. The first step he'd taken, all those years ago, was to use the cushions his wife had made to make his antechamber a more comfortable place for his men to meet with him. He still expected his knights to dedicate their lives to their roles and would never count those who worked for him as his friends, with the exception of Theo. Theo, who was his brother in all but name, who knew the best and worst of him and who would take that knowledge to his grave, as Benedictus would do the same for him. Theo, who wasn't tired or old but who would want Benedictus to spend this time with his family and who would work extra hard to ensure Adela and he had some peace and quiet with their newborn daughter. Theo, who he trusted absolutely and who would be more than irritated if Benedictus did appear right now to relieve him from his extra duties.

The door burst open and Benedictus didn't flinch. Gone were the days when he would automatically reach for a weapon, always assuming the worst. A young girl stormed in, her eyes flashing with indignation. 'Uncle Alewyn says I must let Alaric win the tournament sometimes because he is only four and because I should be looking after my brothers and cousins and not winning against them all the time, but I don't think that's right, is it, Papa? I should win because I am the best.'

Benedictus bit the inside of his mouth to stop himself from laughing. His oldest child, beautiful and fierce Ida, was going to be beating his best-trained knights within a year or two, but for now she was thankfully still his little girl.

'You must always be kind, Ida,' said Adela from the bed.

'Has the baby arrived?' cried Ida, all thoughts of defeating her younger relatives gone in the excitement.

'Yes, come and meet your sister.' Benedictus held the baby out for Ida to see.

Ida gasped, reaching down to delicately trace the baby's tiny fingers. 'She's so beautiful. I will go and get the others. They will want to see.' Ida was gone before either of her parents could object.

'Are you feeling well enough to see everyone?' Benedictus asked.

Adela pushed herself upright. Benedictus tried to study her subtly; strands of damp hair still clung to her forehead, and faint shadows rested beneath her eyes. His heart squeezed; how was it possible to still love someone this much after all this time? If anything, his love was getting stronger with every passing year.

'I know what you're doing,' she said as she settled back against the cushions.

'Me?'

'You are worried I am going to break. You should know by now I am not as fragile as I look. I'm fine, Benedictus. I would tell you if I wasn't.'

That was true. In the early days of their reunion they had been unfailingly honest about what they were both feeling. It had led to a few tense moments but now he could honestly say that he knew his wife better than he knew anyone, and she him.

There was no further time for introspection as every nook and cranny of the chamber filled with children, some of them his and some of them Alewyn's, all of them clamouring for a moment with the newest member of the family. It was loud, chaotic, and messy. It was perfect.

* * * * *

*If you enjoyed this story, make sure to read
the other books in Ella Matthews's
The King's Knights miniseries*

The Knight's Maiden in Disguise
The Knight's Tempting Ally
Secrets of Her Forbidden Knight

*And why not check out her
House of Leofric trilogy?*

The Warrior Knight and the Widow
Under the Warrior's Protection
The Warrior's Innocent Captive

COMING NEXT MONTH FROM

HARLEQUIN
HISTORICAL

All available in print and ebook via Reader Service and online

THE NIGHT SHE MET THE DUKE (Regency)
by Sarah Mallory
After hearing herself described as "dull," Prudence escapes London to Bath, where her new life is anything but dull when one night she finds an uninvited, devastatingly handsome duke in her kitchen!

THE HOUSEKEEPER'S FORBIDDEN EARL (Regency)
by Laura Martin
Kate's finally found peace working in a grand house, until her new employer, Lord Henderson, returns. Soon, it's not just the allure of the home that Kate's falling for...but its owner, too!

FALLING FOR HIS PRETEND COUNTESS (Victorian)
Southern Belles in London • by Lauri Robinson
Henry, Earl of Beaufort and London's most eligible bachelor, is being framed for murder! When his neighbor Suzanne offers to help prove his innocence, a fake engagement provides the perfect cover...

THE VISCOUNT'S DARING MISS (1830s)
by Lotte R. James
When groom Roberta "Bobby" Kinsley comes face-to-face with her horse racing opponent—infuriatingly charismatic Viscount Hayes—it's clear that it won't just be the competition that has her heart racing!

A KNIGHT FOR THE DEFIANT LADY (Medieval)
Convent Brides • by Carol Townend
Attraction sparks when Sir Leon retrieves brave, beautiful Lady Allis from a convent and they journey back to her castle. Only for Allis's father to demand she marry a nobleman!

ALLIANCE WITH HIS STOLEN HEIRESS (1900s)
by Lydia San Andres
Rebellious Julián doesn't mind masquerading as a bandit to help Amalia claim her inheritance—he's enjoying spending time with the bold heiress. But how can he reveal the truth of his identity?

YOU CAN FIND MORE INFORMATION ON UPCOMING HARLEQUIN TITLES, FREE EXCERPTS AND MORE AT HARLEQUIN.COM.

HHCNM0323

Get 4 FREE REWARDS!

We'll send you 2 FREE Books plus 2 FREE Mystery Gifts.

FREE
Value Over
$20

Both the **Harlequin® Historical** and **Harlequin® Romance** series feature compelling novels filled with emotion and simmering romance.

YES! Please send me 2 FREE novels from the Harlequin Historical or Harlequin Romance series and my 2 FREE gifts (gifts are worth about $10 retail). After receiving them, if I don't wish to receive any more books, I can return the shipping statement marked "cancel." If I don't cancel, I will receive 6 brand-new Harlequin Historical books every month and be billed just $6.19 each in the U.S. or $6.74 each in Canada, a savings of at least 11% off the cover price, or 4 brand-new Harlequin Romance Larger-Print books every month and be billed just $6.09 each in the U.S. or $6.24 each in Canada, a savings of at least 13% off the cover price. It's quite a bargain! Shipping and handling is just 50¢ per book in the U.S. and $1.25 per book in Canada.* I understand that accepting the 2 free books and gifts places me under no obligation to buy anything. I can always return a shipment and cancel at any time by calling the number below. The free books and gifts are mine to keep no matter what I decide.

Choose one: ☐ **Harlequin Historical**
(246/349 HDN GRH7)
☐ **Harlequin Romance Larger-Print**
(119/319 HDN GRH7)

_____
Name (please print)

_____
Address   Apt. #

_____
City   State/Province   Zip/Postal Code

Email: Please check this box ☐ if you would like to receive newsletters and promotional emails from Harlequin Enterprises ULC and its affiliates. You can unsubscribe anytime.

Mail to the **Harlequin Reader Service:**
IN U.S.A.: P.O. Box 1341, Buffalo, NY 14240-8531
IN CANADA: P.O. Box 603, Fort Erie, Ontario L2A 5X3

Want to try 2 free books from another series! Call 1-800-873-8635 or visit www.ReaderService.com.

---

*Terms and prices subject to change without notice. Prices do not include sales taxes, which will be charged (if applicable) based on your state or country of residence. Canadian residents will be charged applicable taxes. Offer not valid in Quebec. This offer is limited to one order per household. Books received may not be as shown. Not valid for current subscribers to the Harlequin Historical or Harlequin Romance series. All orders subject to approval. Credit or debit balances in a customer's account(s) may be offset by any other outstanding balance owed by or to the customer. Please allow 4 to 6 weeks for delivery. Offer available while quantities last.

Your Privacy—Your information is being collected by Harlequin Enterprises ULC, operating as Harlequin Reader Service. For a complete summary of the information we collect, how we use this information and to whom it is disclosed, please visit our privacy notice located at corporate.harlequin.com/privacy-notice. From time to time we may also exchange your personal information with reputable third parties. If you wish to opt out of this sharing of your personal information, please visit readerservice.com/consumerschoice or call 1-800-873-8635. **Notice to California Residents**—Under California law, you have specific rights to control and access your data. For more information on these rights and how to exercise them, visit corporate.harlequin.com/california-privacy.

HHHRLP22R3

Get 4 FREE REWARDS!

We'll send you 2 FREE Books <u>plus</u> 2 FREE Mystery Gifts.

FREE Value Over **$20**

Both the **Harlequin® Desire** and **Harlequin Presents®** series feature compelling novels filled with passion, sensuality and intriguing scandals.

HARLEQUIN
PLUS

Try the best multimedia subscription service for romance readers like you!

Read, Watch and Play.

Experience the easiest way to get the romance content you crave.

Start your **FREE TRIAL** at
<u>www.harlequinplus.com/freetrial</u>.